For A & O. You introduced unconditiona... ...e into my... ...
journey together has been more than I ... ... expected. And, I
promise, I am doing my best. I will ... ... this...

For my Dad. Thank you for everything.

Once again, thank you to the amazing people that helped and
supported me in getting this book from rough draft to publication.
You know who you are. I am eternally grateful.

Dark Angel Uprising

Russell Panter

Psalm 68:6

God makes a home for the lonely and leads the poor to prosperity.
Only the rebellious dwell in a parched land.

Prologue

The lightning flashed like a strobe and the ancient church flickered before them. The rain was relentless and swirled around them as the violent wind gusted from all directions.

They were drenched. And the uneven, rocky and sodden ground made for a difficult ascent to the track that led to the church. Each step up the hill sapped their energy and every few steps one of them slipped and had to be helped up by one of the others. When the wind blew against them they could barely hold their ground. But Tom was determined. He was sure they would make it.

Another flash lit up the whole sky, followed by a fork of lightning downwards to the earth, like a dart, somewhere off across the hills beyond. Not close enough to harm them but too close for comfort. The electric charge was so close it was almost tangible and the bitter, acid like odour filled the air. A clatter of thunder followed, sudden and powerful, crashing above their heads, forcing them to cower. The priest even threw himself to the ground, covering his head in fear. The thunder filled Tom with anxiety. It had a vicious presence, and a deep, long rumble slowly rolled across the sky and off into the distance.

Tom, rain battering his face, saw that they were now close to the church, higher up at the brow of the hill. Odin, just ahead of him and the priest, turned and beckoned them on.
"Come on! Keep going!" he shouted, his face being lashed by rain and his own hair, some of which stuck to his face.

Tom glanced at the priest who was now struggling. The journey to this point had been gruelling, but Tom knew that they had to make it. They had come so far and were now so close. Tom grabbed the priest's arm and put his other hand around his waist, pushing him on. Odin held out his hand which Tom grabbed and between them they surged up the wet, rocky hill onto the gravel path leading to the huge, wooden doors.

The church scared Tom. It was dark and oppressive, and a primal fear arose from deep within him. But he knew what he had to do, so he fought his fears and trudged wearily onto the final stretch and soon the doors were near. They all stopped and looked at each other. The wind howled and they were soaked to the skin, cold and tired. But one final push and they were in. Then, finally, Tom could end this.

The priest put his hand inside his jacket and pulled out a large black key. The key to the large wooden doors. And, with key in hand, he looked at Tom, who looked at Odin. Odin nodded and, in unison, they started to walk the final stretch of path to the huge wooden doors.

Then it happened. The dark figure approached fast from behind and the sudden, unwanted presence was felt by all three of them simultaneously. Tom spun as the figure burst up the hill towards them. The figure that, somehow, he felt he knew, but scared him to his core. Odin reacted and stepped down the hill. He shouted to Tom and the priest, his eyes focussing on the approaching nemesis. "Go! You know what to do!"

The priest immediately responded and ran towards the church doors. Tom went to move but hesitated, feeling he should stay and help. He moved behind Odin, offering support, but Odin turned and roared.
"I said go! You have to get inside!"

Tom noticed the dark figure now almost on them. Its face blurred and unrecognisable but known to Tom. The woman. He had felt her presence before. But he followed Odin's orders and ran. Up ahead the priest opened the church doors and, as they swung open, fear overwhelmed Tom. But he knew he had to fight it and not be afraid. He ran towards the doors and the horror that await him inside. He ran as hard and as fast as he could. Odin roared a battle cry from behind, but Tom never looked back. He ran with all his energy through the doors, stumbling, losing his footing and sliding onto the cold, stone floor. He heard the doors close behind him with a deep thud that echoed throughout the chamber. He gazed up into the darkness.

He was now inside the chilling lair, with only the priest and his instinct to help him.

Chapter 1

The cell was cold, dark and damp. The air was dense, and it was difficult to inhale a full lung of breath. The smell of urine was also now very apparent, and Rutherford knew it was his own as, since the interrogation started, he had not been allowed to relieve himself. During the last flurry of punches to his head he couldn't hold it in anymore. But maintaining his dignity was now the least of his concerns.

Rutherford looked across at Nokota. He just made him out in the darkness and realised that it was unlikely he would ever recover. From time to time the big man grunted and took a gulp of air, but for the most part it was clear he was almost gone. The Japanese giant had been beaten and tortured to the brink of death. His broken body slumped in the chair, head drooping and clothes covered in blood.

Rutherford was surprised Nokota was even still alive. The early part of the interrogation was beatings. He had taken fists, elbows and boots which progressed to baseball bats and iron bars, beatings that would probably have killed a buffalo. They had started intense, but short in length, before the men would leave them alone for a while. Then the beatings evolved into less intense but longer, more drawn-out sessions gradually becoming torture using cattle prods, knives and rope.

Rutherford had realised early on that his own beatings were not as hard or intense as the ones being given to Nokota. He also realised that he was more important to the woman, and that they were using Nokota's torture as a tool of fear to scare him into telling her who he was working with. He saw that no matter what they did to Nokota he wouldn't talk. He was drilled in the ways of the Yakuza and embraced pain. Taking the punishment was part of the service he had sworn to give. It had, at times, been so brutal that it was hard to watch, and Rutherford had closed his eyes. But the screams and groans had been loud and intense, so it was impossible not to allow it to have an effect. They needed Rutherford alive to tell her who he was working with and so the beating and torture he received had been more measured. He knew that this was the only reason he was still alive.

Although, even with that in mind, he was in serious pain and knew that he couldn't withstand much more. His face hurt to the point of him wanting to cry and his arms and ribs burnt with every slight movement of his body. They had worked their way downwards and eventually smashed his shins with an iron bar, making him feel physically sick. He had, at that point, wanted to plead with the woman to call her associates off, but he had just about held his nerve and not shown weakness. But he knew she wouldn't have listened anyway. She was cold and ruthless.

He had wondered who she was and who she worked for. His intuition told him that she worked for The Order and they had found out about his dealings with the Yakuza. It was the most logical explanation, although it wasn't definite. If she was working for The Order then surely he would've known. She acted with such efficient ruthlessness and commanded such respect from her associates that Rutherford believed she would certainly be high ranking and so felt sure he would've been informed of her existence before now. But he knew nothing of her.

He had even imagined them working together; they would've made a very efficient and successful partnership.

He had recalled seeing her at the hotel in San Francisco. At the time, as she glided across the foyer floor, she emanated cool efficiency and demanded respect without doing a thing or saying a word. Dressed all in black, with red hair, she appeared to him then to be the type of woman you would want to be with but, all the time, afraid of.

Little did he know that, as she walked across that hotel foyer, she was obviously checking it was him, confirming her target and setting the trap. For soon after leaving the hotel, Rutherford and Nokota were ambushed, tasered, bundled into the back of a van and blindfolded. So, when she had appeared in the cell, it had taken him by complete surprise. Even more so when she had joined in the beatings and torture. Quite small in stature but very athletic and wiry, like steel. When she hit Rutherford, he knew about it more than when the other men hit him. Her attacks were hard, sharp and on point, inflicting maximum pain with minimum effort.

She never appeared to get frustrated or angry and did everything in a calm, methodical manner. Her stare was stark and unrelenting, with the cold dark eyes of a great white shark. Showing no emotion or empathy. She had asked him several times during the beatings to tell her who he was working for. Her strong Russian accent added to her ruthless and intimidating manner. She was robotic and frightened him to the core.

At one point he had managed to summon up the effort and courage to ask her, through split swollen lips and broken, bloodied teeth, who she worked for. She had merely continued as if he had not spoken. His comment had not even registered or altered her emotion or response. It was like he didn't exist.

During one of the periods of respite, Rutherford had got around to thinking. He knew this was all Nokota's fault. On that night back in Misaki Port, when Okamoto, the Yakuza Oyabun, had decided that the big enforcer would be sent over to help Rutherford find the portal, he knew immediately it was a mistake.

Nokota had arrived with strict orders to find the portal 'no matter what it takes' so he hit America like a tornado and then spent the next two months bulldozing his way across different cities, throwing his weight and size 13 boots into everyone and everything to try and find the portal.

Rutherford had contacted the Oyabun and pleaded with him to order Nokota back to Japan, but he had not listened. As usual, he wanted results and wanted them fast. Rutherford told him that Nokota was making too many waves and too much noise. Information about his actions was almost certainly getting back to The Order. Information that Nokota was working with Rutherford. Information which would result in questions being asked. Questions that Rutherford believed had ultimately led to this point.

Eventually, The Order's high echelons contacted him and asked about the 'new Japanese agent' and there were concerns about his methods. Rutherford had no choice but to defend him and told them he would quieten him down and get him working in the correct way. He had done this as a favour to Nokota. For it had been him that had negotiated an extension of the deadline to bring the portal in. Rutherford had been genuinely thankful for that. It had given him some breathing space. But, by then, the heat was on and the people from within The Order, that Rutherford had aligned to his cause, were suddenly distancing themselves. It was then he knew that his time was up.

But there had been no way out. If he had turned his back on the Yakuza and retracted on their deal, then they would have had a price on his head. If he continued with them, he knew The Order would eventually find out and close it down. He assumed this was what the woman was now doing on their behalf. He had taken the gamble knowing the consequences. He had been greedy and fell for the promise of wealth beyond his wildest dreams if he helped the Yakuza bring down The Order.

But he had under-estimated The Order and he was angry with himself for doing so. An organisation that he had worked with for so long and knew so much about. He knew the methods they used to maintain their power. The brutal efficiency of the organisation was something that he promoted and even developed.

During the hours in the cell he had wondered how he had been so blind. He assumed he had got too comfortable and believed his own stature and power within the organisation had made him bullet-proof.

He had also recalled many times of the night when he nearly ended it all. As Nokota slept in the hotel room, Rutherford had stood over him with the gun pointing at him. His finger on the trigger. He had come so close to pulling it and walking away. He could've integrated back into The Order and forgotten about his arrangement. The Yakuza would never find him. But something had stopped him. The fact that they had been so close at that point. They had known where the portal was and were ready to strike.

He now knew he should've pulled the trigger. He wished he had never created his partnership with the Yakuza in the first place. He knew that, even for someone like him, he had got out of his depth. It had muddled and confused everything and allowed himself to lose control of matters. It left him believing that this cell would now be the last place he ever saw.

Nokota grunted again and Rutherford glanced over at him. He sighed in frustration and pain and wished he was anywhere but this place. Then suddenly he heard the clang of the lock and the metal door swung open. He prepared himself for another beating. The woman strolled in.
"I have spoken to my superiors and they wish to waste no more time. Who are you working for?"

Rutherford realised that even if he came clean and told her he was in partnership with the Yakuza, she would kill him anyway. He knew this was the end either way and was suddenly filled with courage.
"Go fuck yourself."

She stared at him in the usual non-responsive way then headed for the door. As she walked out, she calmly ordered,

"Take their heads off."

With that, several men came in, two of them holding huge hunting knives and they immediately surged towards Rutherford. He screamed, aware of what was happening and urinated himself again. The last sound he heard was the metal door banging as it closed.

The woman walked away from the cell along the dark corridor, the sound of muffled screams, desperate and fearful, coming from behind her. She had already got her phone out and was making a call. The ring tone on the other end sounded a few times before it clicked.

"Yes," came a quiet voice.

"I am sorry, Kane. They would not talk. I will send you their heads in the next few days for your confirmation. How would you like me to proceed?"

A deep breath came from the other end as Kane considered the information.

"Well, at least the betrayer Rutherford is now out of the way. So, your orders are now to find portal 294574 and eliminate him immediately"

"Thank you. It will be done."

There was a pause and Agent 7 heard breathing at the other end. She waited, not daring to speak. After a few more seconds he whispered.

"He is powerful."

Agent 7 wasn't sure how to respond. She knew it was a warning, but it was unusual, and not something she was used to. She had never been warned to be wary of anyone she had been assigned to terminate.

"It will be done," she repeated confidently.

"Just remember the prophecy. Be wary." Kane repeated, then she heard the phone click off.

Chapter 2

2 months later

The rainstorm arrived that morning and now, in the early afternoon, still showed no sign of relenting. The rain was heavy and as Tom stood, motionless, it penetrated his jacket and clothes underneath. Running down his cap, it dripped from the peak onto the sodden grass below. He was drenched and the cold was seeping into his bones and made him shiver. A tear rolled down his face and amalgamated with the rain already on his skin, forming streams that were running in various directions.

He had been standing for roughly fifteen minutes at his mother's grave. The first time he had been this close to her since she had died, and he had been integrated into The Network. Time had healed and allowed him the space and opportunity to grieve. However, in the last six months the urge to be close to her had been too strong. It was the final part of the grieving process he needed.

Soon the urge had become a burden. He had asked the Internal Department twice in the last four months if he had authorisation to go to the cemetery in New Jersey. Both requests had been denied due to reports of The Order having an active presence in the city and surrounding areas.

However, this time around, Tom's third assignment in Boston had brought him to the north-east and so ID had not been able to refuse his request. They had told him he can attend; but only stay for a maximum of fifteen minutes and then leave immediately. They couldn't provide support so, if The Order made a move, he would be on his own.

ID had previously identified two locations of high risk for him. One was the cemetery and the other, his sister's house. Both these locations were potentially where The Order could observe and then pick him up or terminate him. Depending on what their intentions were, which was still at this stage, not known to Tom and The Network.

Therefore, Tom knew that coming to the cemetery was a risk and so did The Network. They also knew, however, that by sending him on an assignment so close to New Jersey it would be unreasonable to not allow him to go. He had a few days before contact for his new assignment was to be made and so had taken this opportunity to go. He knew that he was putting himself at additional risk, but he believed it was a risk worth taking.

As he stood, he had transcended through different emotions and thoughts. At first, he felt angry and upset that he hadn't been able to go through this process at her funeral. Nor had he been there for Claire, to support her through it. She had been left to cope with it on her own. After all this time, he still felt bitter about the way it ended. He had processed his anger time and time again since he became part of The Network, always coming to the same conclusion. It had been hard, but not going to the funeral and also not visiting the cemetery until now had kept him alive. He knew there was a good chance The Order would be observing, waiting to pounce.

He had then remembered the good times, paid his respects, managing a brief smile through the tears and rain. Hoping that this time at her headstone would put some demons to bed and allow him to move on. He had then laid a small wreath and felt closer to her than he ever did since she had died.

While in New Jersey, he had also taken the opportunity to secretly check in with his sister, Claire, and her family. He had not informed The Network he had planned to do this as he knew they would not authorise it. The Network protected and guided portals but, as had always been advised, they did not control them. There had to be an element of flexibility and so if members chose to go off grid or refuse their help, then there was nothing they could do.

Tom had felt like he had followed their guidance strictly and to the letter up to now and so, on this one occasion, had gone against their advice.

Again, he knew it was a risk, but he had learnt much from his training and his time living undercover, always on the move. He had become a master of secrecy and covert behaviour. Moving quietly, out of plain sight amongst the underworld. Finding dark corners of society to lay low and live invisibly.

So, for a few nights, he had cruised past his sister's house and picked up some patterns of movement until one night he had taken the gamble and parked close to her house in the dead of night. A few times, he had gone for a short drive around the streets of her house to try and pick up any tail or any unusual movement from potential Order agents. Once he was satisfied that he was safe, he had sat and waited. Then in the morning, around 8am, the front door opened and out came Claire, Paul and the boys. The first thing he noticed was that the boys had grown. He also noticed that Paul Jnr's face had changed, and he got a split-second glimpse of the boy as a young adult.

Claire's husband, Paul, had dressed smart as usual, and was hurrying the boys along whilst holding an umbrella, a satchel and one of the boy's rucksacks. As always Tom felt a sense of pride in Paul as he was everything that Tom had hoped to be. Strong, caring and smart. He had a good job as an architect and amply provided for Claire and the boys. He was so happy that Claire had him.

Claire appeared a little flustered but appeared to be in control. She was talking as she walked and, like Paul, held various items - Her own bag, a rucksack, a coffee flask and an umbrella. She spun around twice as they walked to their car and she spoke, providing direction, school pick-up's, sport clubs and whatever else she needed to say so that her family functioned efficiently. Tom had felt a sense of pride engulf him and he realised how much he loved and missed her.

He had been concerned that they were in danger and realised how easy it would be for The Order to use them to get to him. It had been something that he had struggled with for a long time. Worried that by being off grid, if The Order did get to them nobody had any way of contacting him. Therefore, to see them alive and well was a huge comfort.

One night, he had confided in the parent he was with at that time. He told him that the issue was burning inside him, and he was finding it hard to cope with how vulnerable his sister and her family were. But the parent, a man named William, had re-assured him and had told him it was unlikely The Order would make a move on his sister and her family as there would not be any point unless they had a way to let Tom know. Tom had accepted this. What would be the point of putting bait in a lake if you didn't know the fish you wanted to catch was even there? William had also put the stark and brutal reality of the situation into perspective. "You just have to have hope."

It wasn't the answer that Tom had wanted. But he knew William was right. Protocols and systems were in place to reduce collateral damage, but The Network couldn't prevent The Order from doing anything. As William had said, you just had to hope.

No sooner had Claire and her family come outside they had got into their car and driven away. Oblivious to Tom's presence. Tom had then left the street and had gone back to his accommodation, putting them out of his mind for the time being.

Tom then realised that he had been at the graveside for longer than fifteen minutes. It was time to go. He gathered himself and took a deep breath. He kissed his fingers and leant forward and touched the headstone. He didn't know if he would ever get an opportunity to come here again. He was unsure if he needed to. Over the next few months, he would learn if this visit had allowed him to move on.

Tom looked around. The cemetery was empty, apart from an elderly couple standing under an umbrella on the far side, who had been there when he arrived. Initially they had made him nervous and he had second thoughts about the visit. But he knew that this was the perfect time and that he may not find the cemetery so empty again. So, he had gone in anyway, but using his learnt instinct, had kept them under surveillance for any unusual behaviour. During the time he was there, they had just stood motionless at a headstone, the man with his arm around the lady. They were no threat.

It was still raining but it had eased and the clouds above Tom's head had changed from dark grey to bright white. Their outline shone as the sun behind them fought to get through. A chill ran through his body as he walked back to his car, all the while keeping an eye on his surroundings.

He wanted to get back to his accommodation just outside the city, have a coffee and relax. He would then meditate and leave the real world behind for a while

Chapter 3

The New Orleans night was hot and uncomfortable. The warm, sticky humidity hung in the air and even at just after 10pm it was still unbearable. It was busy in the French Quarter and the sound of upbeat jazz music, laughter, chatter and the general humdrum sounded throughout the busy streets as the night people enjoyed themselves in the restaurants, bars and clubs.

In the hotel room, Agent 7 sat astride the young man. He gripped her hips, assisting her to thrust up and down. Sweat dripped from his brow and his panting and grunting was heard by other hotel guests through the wide-open window. A few times he had reached up to grope her breasts, but she had quickly swatted his hands down. Not allowing him any control.

She hoped she would soon finish. They had been engaged in this position for too long and her thoughts were drifting. She needed to get back to her assignment and wanted to feel something more pleasurable. Then he could leave, allowing her to re-focus on important matters.

Her breasts jolted as she slid up and down and she eventually felt the orgasm. She closed her eyes and moved faster, and the man groaned louder. The orgasm that came to her soon after was deep and strong and, as it surged through her, she lifted herself up to release him from inside of her. She always liked to orgasm on her own.

Her body trembled and she let out a small moan which she tried to keep to herself. She breathed hard as the pleasure faded, her body tingling as she relaxed, motionless, on her knees. Eventually turning to sit in the side of the bed.
"What the fuck?" the young man exclaimed, "Can I finish?"
"Of course. You have a hand," she replied condescendingly, walking over to the dressing table.
The man tutted, "Can you finish me off at least?" he asked.

"Are you paying me?" she asked. The man never answered. "No, you're not," continued Agent 7, "and I got what I paid for. So please leave," she concluded rudely.

She lit a cigarette, took a huge puff and sat at the stall next to the dressing table, staring into the mirror at the man on the bed behind her. He shook his head, got up off the bed and walked to the corner to pick up his clothes. He stood, removed the condom and threw it in the bin.

Agent 7 got up and walked to the window and sat on the ledge, watching the hustle and bustle three floors below her. A slight breeze brushed her body and offered temporary relief from the enveloping heat. She took another huge drag on her cigarette and wiped the sweat from her breasts.
"Your money is on the dressing table."

The man, now in jeans and holding his white T-shirt, walked over towards the dressing table. He picked up the money and walked towards the door. As she watched the people below, he spoke. "There's $200 here. It's only $150."
Without turning to face him she replied, "Call it a tip. And a deposit for tomorrow."
"Tomorrow?" the man enquired. "What's happening tomorrow?"
"Be here at 9.30pm. Sharp."

There was no reply from the man and, soon after, she heard the hotel door open and then close with a click. She finished her cigarette and had a cold shower. She dried herself but remained naked to try and get some more relief from the dense air in the room. The air-con was on and whirring loudly but with little effect.

She lay down on the bed and felt underneath for a leather document slipcase. She pulled the case up and unzipped it. Inside were several documents. She flicked through them and pulled out a photograph. It was a close-up of a man in a suit walking with a crowd of other people in a city, unaware that the photo had been taken. Written in black pen on the top corner of the photograph were the words – 'Portal 294574'.

She thought he was quite handsome and appeared unassuming. But that was of no consequence. He was to be terminated.

Meanwhile, 500 miles away at Fort Worth International airport, the wheels of the Boeing, that had left Tokyo twelve hours before, screeched with a burst of smoke as they hit the tarmac. The plane slowed down and taxied around to the main terminal as the passengers sat patiently waiting for it to park.

However, one of the passengers was not so patient. He was anxious to fulfil his secret assignment that he had been honoured with. He had clear and strict orders from his boss to locate Nokota, a fellow Yakuza associate, who had not made contact for some time. If, during this process, he also made contact with the man known as 'Rutherford' he was to kill him for failing to stick to an agreement. He was to also locate a person known as 'portal 294574', subdue him and hold him at the designated location until plans to get him back to Tokyo were organised.

The man was ready. He had been trained ever since he was a young boy for a task such as this. He had worked his way through the Yakuza levels. Rising from street soldier to trusted captain and onto becoming one of the most feared hitmen within the organisation. He had given up everything and committed his life to the Yakuza. This was what he had worked so hard for and he had no intention of failing.

The man. No longer known by his birth name, which had long since been forgotten. This was a man now known in the Japanese underworld as 'Ano Tora'. Or as anyone unfortunate enough to meet him from the western underworld knew him, 'The Tiger'. As the plane stopped, the passenger's heads lurched forward and people got up, desperate to be the first to get their hand luggage down.

But Ano Tora just sat, focussed, ready to move. He had no luggage, travelling light with only his passport, mobile phone, sunglasses and the suit on his back. Everything else he needed will be available to him from his contact who was picking him up to take him to the base from where he would organise his first moves.

Eventually, he walked out into the warm Dallas night and made his way to the designated pick up point. Ano Tora would rather die than fail. And he did not feel like dying anytime soon.

Chapter 4

The sweet smell of fragrance filled Tom's apartment and created a comforting and heady atmosphere. The gentle smoke looped and bounced from the incense sticks and then amalgamated into one mass, hanging and floating in the air. Tom sat, legs crossed and back upright in the centre of the lounge. His body in the present in that moment and place, but his mind miles away in a different place. A place that he had created. A place of love and sanctuary.

Tom flew high alongside the mountain-tops that pierced the bright white clouds that rolled underneath him. He aimed his body downwards and descended, swooping towards the clouds, his stomach rolling in excitement. He hit the clouds at speed and for a few seconds his vision was blurred by a white and grey blanket.

The brightness increased and then, in a flash, the world appeared from the soft white and the colours exploded in front of him. All around him. A mountainous and bright green landscape, the sun making the colours appear so vivid. He soared effortlessly above the green, rolling pine trees with mountains to his left that cascaded all the way down to a large, shimmering lake. At the far side of the lake was a small, pebble beach and a cabin. In front of the cabin, he made out three people. Warmth emanated from them and he suddenly felt an intense urge to be with them.

He aimed his body towards the lake, dazzling in the sun, as though it had millions of tiny lights flickering across it. Just above the lake, he levelled off and increased his speed, careering towards the spot he wanted to be, just metres above the clear water. Flying like a jet, his speed lifted the water in his wake like a speedboat careering full speed across the lake. His speed increased and very soon the people and the cabin were in full view and approaching fast and so he eased down, gradually reaching them in a calm and gentle floating motion. There, they sat, in front of the cabin, on a blanket on the beach. His mum, dad and sister. Huddled together, waiting, waving at him as he approached them from above.

Then Tom was with them. On the blanket in their arms. Intense love and contentment flowed through him. Their smiles and laughter lifting him. The four of them, together, surrounded by green mountains and rugged beauty, all showered in the warm, golden sun.

They spoke but Tom never quite worked out exact words or topics of conversation. Although every word meant so much to him and made complete sense. He felt involved and part of the conversations, agreeing, laughing, replying to what was being discussed, but never knowing the detail of it.

His senses high, the wonderful sight of his family and the landscape surrounding them. The smell of the fresh pine and the lake, the cool air drifting down from the mountains, across the lake and onto the beach. The sounds, birdsong and a waterfall off in the distance. The laughter of his dad filled the air as he grabbed Claire and tickled her as she tried to roll away giggling. Feeling the loving hands and the embrace of the only people that truly loved him.

He turned to his mum. The graceful, beautiful woman that she was. He moved closer and did not speak. Nor did she. She just held out her arms and he eased into her body and held her. Her arms surrounding him with such love and warmth, he felt it penetrating his soul. The love of a mother to a son.

Then they all just sat in silence, huddled together, and watched as the sun dipped below the peaks, creating a yellow and orange glow across the trees. He never wanted this moment to end. Whenever he reached this point it was then that he wanted it to stop in time.

He had first read about meditation when he was in Louisiana. His parent at the time, a man called Joe, had brought him a book, amongst many others, about yoga and meditation. There was a note on one of the books, 'Meditation is useful. Give it a try.'

At first Tom had been sceptical, but after a lot of reading about the techniques, he gave it a go but with little success. However, he persisted and soon grasped the concept and had some more positive sessions.

Like a lot of what he read, the information stayed inside his mind. He had known for a while that he was like a sponge and had an insatiable appetite for information. Every book he read, on whatever subject, he did so quickly and efficiently, finding that the knowledge he gathered was stored away, never forgotten and always available in his mind instantly.

 He never forgot or had to remember information or knowledge, it was always there, like a computer, instantly flashing information to the forefront of his mind when he needed it. It was this ability which he believed allowed him to meditate so well. And so, over the last year or so, Tom had trained himself to be able to go into a trance like state and transport his mind to wherever he wanted it to go. At first it was more difficult, and he found that the places he went to were not exactly where he wanted to go. But soon, he created a few places that were perfect, and he had the ability to control which place he went to and what would happen when he went there.

He had full control of his body when he visited these places and even controlled other people and events, to some degree. Over time, he developed and built the places with thought process and mapping, and each time he went back they were more vivid and realistic. Tom had created havens in his mind, and they provided him with the balance he needed to cope with the reality of the life that had been thrust upon him.

As he sat with his loved ones, he wondered if this vision would be extended. It had already gone on a little longer than usual and he was keen for it to continue.

But then it happened again, as the sun went down beyond the lake, the image appeared in front of him. The old, dark building, high on the hill, with the wind driving across the land battering the grass and foliage to the ground. Then the lightning strike which lit the building up and highlighted the hard rain lashing down. The building, dark and ominous, which gave him a sudden cold fear.

Then it disappeared and Tom found himself back on the beach within the serene landscape of before. But his family were gone. He turned and they stood at the cabin and waved, then slowly went inside and closed the door. This was the part he struggled to control. The end of his time with them. He knew he had to train further to be able to extend his time. He had learnt to create the landscape and go to them. But he couldn't control the time he was there. He hoped that would soon change.

But, worryingly, the image of the dark building on the hill had now played a part in his last three meditations. And each time it had ended abruptly, with his family leaving immediately after its image had flashed before him.

Soon after, Tom left the landscape, floated back up into the clouds and back to reality. He opened his eyes and was back in his apartment. He was pleased with this session. The love and warm feeling would last for a few days and sustain him until he felt the need to go in again, this time maybe to one of his other locations.

But the dark vision nagged at him. What was it? Where was it? Why could he not control it and hold it at bay? He would need to read more and train harder. He needed to create a higher threshold to block out unwanted images whilst in full meditation. Then a thought crossed his mind. Should he dismiss the image? Or was it something he needed to investigate? Something told him that its dark environment was more prevalent than just a random image. Something inside him told him it was linked to him in some way.

He glanced at the clock. The time was almost 7.30pm and this prompted him to refocus. He needed to prepare. His second assignment was looming, and he had arranged to meet his driver at 11pm for the drive to Boston.

He needed to get his mind and body focussed, ensure his contacts within The Network were ready, and go through the plan in his own head. He also had to get his weapons ready, all the while hoping that he would not need to use them.

Chapter 5

Ano Tora waited in the hotel room. He sat upright on the chair, focussed and ready for the meeting.

The previous night everything had gone to plan. His contact had been in touch, met him and had taken him to the meeting place. A safe house above a bar in the Cedars district. There he had been provided with money and credit cards, plus weapons, transport and a bed for the night.

This morning, he had been taken downtown to the Dallas Marriot where he would work out his strategy. And he had learned of the news he had been hoping for; his contact had come through with the promise of getting someone to meet him with information. An agent from The Order who, for a price, had intelligence on Nokota, Rutherford and possibly where portal 294574 could possibly be.

He had been informed, before now, that The Order were a 'religious organisation' but knew no more about them. However, he believed this lack of information gave him no disadvantage. He figured that if The Order worked with the mafia then they were no different to any other organisation he had worked with.

He felt good. All had gone smoothly and by the way things were going, he would have this assignment wrapped up and be on a flight back to Tokyo within a week, maybe two. He had handled similar assignments back in Japan with no problems. And even when he did run into problems, he knew he had the ability and focus to resolve them.

His contact from the Dallas mob, Alex, appeared nervous and was pacing up and down the hotel room. Ano Tora hadn't noticed it before, but now it distracted him.
"Sit down," he ordered calmly.

"Shit, sorry man, I just...Well y'know, I just don't want him to let us down. I have been setting this up for a while. I want it to go well..."

"Sit down," Ano Tora repeated, sending a chill through Alex, who never trusted the Japanese man anyway, and had been nervous of him right from the start when he had picked him up at the airport the night before.

"Sure, man," replied Alex, taking a seat on the end of the bed.

Ano Tora stared back at the door.

"Do you want a whisky?" asked Alex, who got up and walked to the minibar.

"No, I am working," replied Ano Tora, irritated by the tiresome American.

Ano Tora was tolerating him as he was his contact. Organised through the Yakuza and the Dallas mob. And so, whilst he accepted him from a professional perspective, he did not respect him. The American was too young and naïve to understand the intricate ways of how things really worked. The sacrifices he had made to be in this position. The honour that he and his fellow Yakuza associates had for each other. To Ano Tora, Alex was just low-level muscle that wasn't worthy of his respect.

But he needed Alex to get him his man from The Order. As soon as the meeting was over, he would have no need for him anymore. Alex was careless and brash, and it had crossed his mind to snuff the young man out when he no longer needed him, but that may damage relations between their organisations.

Alex poured himself a large whisky and sat back down the bed. He took a sip from the tumbler.

"Oh, that is good. You sure you don't want one?"

Ano Tora looked at him, "I said no. I am working"

"Well...OK, but you don't know what you are missing. This is good stuff."

Ano Tora then diverted his attention back at the door. Alex took another sip from the tumbler and as he did, his phone rang and startled him. He quickly stood, put the whisky down on the coffee table and patted his suit jacket to locate his phone. Ano Tora stared at him in annoyance. Alex found the phone and answered it. "Yo!" he exclaimed and paused as he listened, "OK man, that's cool. I will come down, stay put…Oh, do you like whisky?" he suddenly asked, walking to the door. There was another pause. "You do! Oh man! We have a fine bottle up here…"

Alex turned to Ano Tora, pointed to the floor and mouthed the words - 'He's here' - without speaking. Ano Tora stared at him and made no gesture that he had understood or acknowledged this. Alex continued towards and out the door and his voice faded away as he left the room and the door closed. Ano Tora rolled his eyes and shook his head in disgust. He hated the unprofessional American.

He diverted his attention back to the meeting. What information would this agent provide? He hoped it would be in the form of some places or locations he could start searching. This would set him off on the right track and get phase one of his assignment underway. In his mind he planned to call his boss tomorrow to inform him that he was locked onto the targets and was now putting phase 2 in place. His boss would be happy, and it would allow him to gain further honour and respect.

Ano Tora wanted this assignment to be the springboard he needed to elevate himself up to the higher echelons in the Yakuza organisation. He had big plans for the future but needed to get higher up to put them in place. He had sacrificed so much and worked so hard. From lowly Tekiya, running the streets on his patch to now working as an enforcer for his current So-Hunbucho. He felt his time had now come to make a move upwards through the ranks and he wanted to do it soon.

He waited some more. Then heard voices behind the door and a click. The door swung open and Alex entered, followed by a tall, dark haired man. He was dressed in a black leather jacket and trousers with smart shoes. His face was edgy and almost skeletal. Ano Tora immediately felt that he was not to be trusted, although he also felt an element of respect and that he would need to be on his guard.

Alex showed the man to a seat and he calmly approached Ano Tora and held his hand out. Ano Tora stood, bowed his head and shook the man's hand, realising then how tall he was. Ano Tora wasn't tall, around 5' 7", but the man stood at least another seven to eight inches above him. This did not bother Ano Tora though, he had taken down men much taller and larger in his past and he knew he could easily do the same to this man if required.

They both sat and the man smiled. Ano Tora found it hard to judge him. Normally he was on point and analysed people immediately. But there was something about this man that he couldn't quite work out.

"Leave us." Ano Tora ordered, glimpsing at Alex and then back at the man.

"Oh…Er…My boss told me to stay at all times. Just to…Well y'know, just to make sure things go smoothly," the young man replied.

Ano Tora stared back at Alex, "I am quite capable of managing my affairs. Now leave us."

"Look, man, I am not sure…I am under strict…"

Ano Tora stood, "Leave us! Now!"

Alex stared back, offended.

"Woah, man. Stay cool. But I will have to report this back to my boss."

"Report what you like," Ano Tora replied assertively.

Alex shook his head and walked towards the door.

"Jesus, so tetchy…"

He reached the door, opened it and then turned.

"Oh, do you want that whisky?" he asked the man excitedly.

The man did not turn and just stayed looking directly at Ano Tora. "No, thank you."

Alex looked disappointed and turned and closed the door behind him.

"Suit yourself," he whispered as he left.

"I apologise for his lack of respect," Ano Tora assured the man.

"It's fine. Don't worry," he replied, rolling his eyes in acknowledgement of Ano Tora's own annoyance.

Ano Tora liked the fact that the man had declined the whisky. He felt it showed that the man was not too relaxed and that he had judged Ano Tora as a threat. Ano Tora walked to the bed, reached under and pulled out a small briefcase, put it up onto the bed and clicked the metal locks open. He then opened it up to reveal a layer of money. He spun the case to show the man.

"$20,000. As we agreed"

The man nodded with approval, "Looks good."

Ano Tora left the briefcase open on the bed, walked back to his seat and sat down. He liked the man's demeanour. He emanated a cool professionalism and seemed to be the type of person he liked to work with. However, he didn't trust him. But in this business working with people you didn't trust was normal.

"So, what do you know of my associate Nokota? Where is he now?" asked Ano Tora without any hesitation or leading question.

The man smiled wryly at Ano Tora's direct approach, knowing he meant business.

"All I know is that he was brought in as an agent for The Order and started working with my boss."

"And, I assume by your boss you mean, Rutherford?" added Ano Tora.

"Yeah, that's right," confirmed the man.

"This man?" asked Ano Tora handing a photo of Rutherford to him.

The man studied it, nodded and then handed the photo back.

"Where are they now?" asked Ano Tora.

"Nobody knows. All I can say is your associate was a little heavy handed and used methods that gained attention from powerful people way above Rutherford in The Order. Real high up guys, way out of our league."

Ano Tora assessed the information.

"But why would that be an issue for the people at the top?"

The man took a deep breath.

"Rutherford was playing games with your organisation. I don't know the details. All I know is Rutherford paid me and some others to help him do what he wanted."

"Which was?"

"Like I said, I don't know the details. He paid three of us to be in a team to help him. All he told us was that we had to help him and Nokota find some guy. But it was a secret job and we were not to tell nobody else."

The man remained calm and Ano Tora liked that but, although he never trusted him, he felt a sincerity to his answers.

"So, where was their last known whereabouts?"

"San Francisco. We received intelligence that the guy we wanted was there and so Rutherford and Nokota went on ahead. He called me to tell me they had arrived. I was to get the team there in two days and await further instructions."

"And?" asked Ano Tora.

"We got there and never heard from either of them."

"And?"

"We left."

Ano Tora paused, "You just left?" he asked with a puzzled look.

The man shook his head, "Look, things had gotten out of control. Your man had been too clumsy, and we got intel that the masters had found out. Rutherford had also been edgy for a couple of months before they went missing too. We realised it wasn't safe being involved, so we cut contact with them…"

Ano Tora felt a surge of anger and interrupted him.

"So, you took your boss's money and then left him and my associate to carry on alone?"

The man was a little surprised by Ano Tora's allegation and felt a little angered.

"No, not exactly. We had heard a rumour that a new agent had been deployed to bring Rutherford in. A woman."

Ano Tora laughed out loud, much to the man's embarrassment.

"A woman? You hung your boss and my associate out to dry for a woman…"

"Hey, this is no ordinary woman. She is…"

"Silence!" Ordered Ano Tora but the man continued.

"We went to San Francisco but…"

"But you went reluctantly?" interrupted Ano Tora, probing and verbally jabbing the man.

There was a silence and Ano Tora waited until the man spoke.

"Yes. Reluctantly. But you don't know The Order. Any hint of treason or betrayal and they…"

"I work for Yakuza!" interrupted Ano Tora forcefully, "I know all about how organisations avenge dishonour and betrayal from its own members. It is part of my job description."

The man gulped in genuine fear and felt how dry his mouth was. Ano Tora noticed for the first time the man's cool exterior break a little and he knew he had found a weakness. He was going to offer the man a drink but then thought he would not give him any comfort.

"So, go on, what happened?"

The man composed himself, "Things had just got too hot from above and so we left San Francisco and carried on our usual business. I was expecting a call from Rutherford, but it never came. He has since been replaced and we are under a new boss."

Ano Tora assessed the information and, for confirmation, asked one more question about Rutherford and Nokota.

"And you're sure they were in San Francisco?"

"He told me that was where they were, so I assume so"

"How long ago?"

The man pondered for a few seconds, "It was around November time. So, I would say roughly six months ago."

Ano Tora felt frustrated. This was a setback. He was hoping this man's information would pinpoint them right now. A place they might have been that long ago was not what he had been hoping for.

"Do you think they are still there?" he asked.

The man stared at him and did not speak but he knew Ano Tora would not let him leave the question unanswered. He took a deep breath.

"For what it's worth, and it's just my opinion, I think they're dead. The Order found out about his little affair with your people and had them bumped off."

"No thanks to you," replied Ano Tora provocatively, waiting for the man to react.

The man was aware he was being taunted, but he wasn't going to take the bait and give the Japanese gangster the satisfaction.

"Look," the man stood, "if that's all then I have to be going…"

"Sit down!" snapped Ano Tora.

The man slowly sat down. He tried not to show it, but he was getting a little tired of the Japanese man's abrupt manner. He sat, but before he got comfortable Ano Tora fired another question.

"This man you were after. Portal 294574. Why were you after him?"

"I don't know. As far as I know he is a dark angel, but apparently there is something else special about him. I don't know what it is?"

"A dark angel?" Ano Tora asked, confused by the comment.

The man realised he might have finally got one up on his Japanese suitor and smirked.

"You do know what The Order do, don't you?" confident that Ano Tora did not know the answer. Ano Tora stared at him. He didn't know but knew he had to retrieve the upper ground.

"Of course. But that's not important. Where is he?"

The man replied still smiling, "Well, I do have some extra information which I gathered today. Hot off the press…But…It will cost you."

Ano Tora felt the anger surge upwards but he held back his emotions and tried not to show that the man's insolence had distracted him as much as it had. He stood and walked to the bed, knelt down, felt underneath and pulled out another small clutch case. He opened it and showed the man its contents.
"Another $5000?"

The man nodded and Ano Tora threw the case onto the bed next to the briefcase. He returned to his seat and as he did, the man put his hand inside his jacket. Ano Tora quickly stood and pulled a revolver from the back of his trousers and pointed it at the man. "Woah! Steady. Stay calm. It's just a photo," which he slid from his jacket and handed to Ano Tora who took the photo and instantly recognised it from a photo he had previously been given by the Yakuza.
"This was taken yesterday by one of our connections. It was taken in New Jersey. Intel informs he is on his way to Boston."

He took the photograph and put it on the table next to him. He felt content that he had retrieved enough information for now. Although he was slightly disappointed that he may not be able to locate Nokota and that The Order may have got to Rutherford first. He wanted to have been the one to dispose of him. But, during his time in the Yakuza, he had realised that you shouldn't let what you can't control annoy you.

If he had to report Nokota and Rutherford as missing, presumed dead, then this wasn't the end of the world. He had a lead on the portal, so he would get moving to Boston immediately. This was the most important part of the assignment. The part that he simply couldn't fail.
"That will be all. Take you money and leave."

The man wasn't offended by the rudeness as he realised this was just the way the Japanese man was. He got up and walked to the bed and took out a few individual bundles of cash.

"Do I need to count it?" he asked Ano Tora with a mischievous grin. A grin that deceived and hid the man's intention. Was this a genuine question or a joke?

Either way Ano Tora felt offended. In Japan people did not ask questions like this and, even if it was a joke, the same. You did not joke about the integrity of another associate. These constant offences were annoying him. The biggest one was asking for more cash. Ano Tora was surprised he had not taken the man out then and there but, at that point, he needed the extra information. Now, he had what he wanted.

The man had obviously meant it as a joke as he had put the money back and locked the briefcase with a smile. He had also put the smaller clutch bag into his jacket and was now walking towards the door. But, Ano Tora hated personal jokes against his professionalism and integrity and, for him, were the most insolent and disrespectful.

He also hated the man's obvious ability to betray for money without hesitating. First, he had betrayed his masters in The Order by working with Rutherford against them. Then he had betrayed Rutherford and Nokota by leaving San Francisco when his masters got wind of their plan. And finally, he had betrayed his masters again by speaking to Ano Tora now. The final insult was asking for more money. The more Ano Tora thought the more he despised the man. He was a mercenary. Devoid of loyalty. Rage ignited within him and he felt his fists clench.

The Tiger had been woken.

The man had got close to the door and reached up to open it. But Ano Tora ran and leapt, pulling the cord from his trousers as he attacked with intense speed. He wrapped the cord around the man's neck, put one knee into his back, thrusting his mid-rift forward. Ano Tora kicked the man's legs forward with his other foot, causing him to lose balance and topple backwards.

The man, with barely any time to realise what was happening, tried to stay upright and dropped the case to reach for the cord, fear and panic now overtaking him. But Ano Tora used his weight and then tied his legs tightly around the man's body and they both toppled back onto the floor with a huge thud. Now that Ano Tora had him down in this position he knew the man's height and weight offered no advantage.

He pulled on the cord with his wiry arms and the cord tightened. The man, desperate, tried to get his fingers underneath it, unable to manoeuvre it away from his neck. His eyes were now bulging. He was shocked at the power of the cord. He tried to roll to the left but Ano Tora had such a tight grip with his legs and was pulling the cord so tight the man felt as though he was glued to him. And the speed of the attack was such that the man had not had time to set himself or even take a breath.

The man gasped for air and the light in the room flickered as his consciousness started to fail. He tried one last time to get Ano Tora off his back, but his body, with such little oxygen, had no strength. He felt the life draining out of him with each passing second.

Ano Tora growled with the intensity that he was pulling on the cord and holding the man still with his legs and body. He knew it would be seconds more, and as predicted, with one last gurgle the man shuddered and spat saliva out and onto the wall, which was the last thing he ever did. He went rigid.

Ano Tora waited, maintaining the powerful grip on the cord. Then after another ten seconds, he released it. The man's huge body slumped to the left and he pulled himself out from under him. Sweat poured off his head and body soaking his shirt. He stood over the man, noticing the eyes bulbous and staring, tongue piercing angrily from his mouth. The cord had left an indent around his neck which was bleeding, and the man's face had turned a greyish colour with purple around the lips.

Ano Tora busied himself and stored the money back underneath the bed. He tidied the furniture and some items which had hit the floor during the struggle. He would take a shower and then get Alex's people to dispose of the body and he would clean up. He would notify them the man had attempted to kill him and it was self-defence. No big deal.

It had been a productive meeting. He had got some good information and a lead on portal 294574. He would soon be heading to Boston.

Chapter 6

Agent 7 sat at the window smoking while the young man took his money from the dressing table. This time it was just $150 as she was now bored with him and had told him she did not want him to return the next night. After he left, she showered and got ready for her night's work. With just a towel around her she got her clothes, boots and equipment prepared. Gun, mobile phone, rucksack, contact details and cigarettes.

She dropped her towel and sat on the window ledge with a cigarette, allowing the warm air to dry her body. As she smoked, she watched people and cars pass below. It was Friday night and the streets were busier than she had noticed the night before. The music, chatter and shouts, the sound of traffic was louder. Everything was busy and louder. The home of jazz and good times was opening up for the weekend.

She enjoyed her perch on the window ledge just watching. She always had. Wherever she had been, she had always been happy if her place of accommodation allowed her to do this. She had never been part of anything like it and so it interested her. Not in a tempting way but just out of curiosity. She had always loved to people watch just to get an idea about the people and what their lives entailed. How they reached that point? What was their story?

Her own story was unusual and, in some ways, sad. As a young child, at her home in the central Russian village of Bayanovka, on the gateway to Siberia, she had been visited by those strange men and remembered the suitcase that that they had handed her parents. Her mother sobbing in the kitchen and the guilty look on her father's face as the men led her away. She had never seen her parents again.

She had been driven for two days and taken to the fortress in the vast, dense Siberian forests, where she lived, was educated and trained. It was a regimented, hard and dismal life but, even then, she had focus and determination. She knew that being taken to that place was her calling. It was her destiny.

Twelve years later, at the age of sixteen, she was already an expert in mixed martial arts, weaponry and survival. She had endured physical training designed for special forces soldiers and had passed such rigorous mental torture training that the strange men in white suits had to create a newer, more advanced training regime with more extreme standards.

The other children that were there when she arrived gradually disappeared and she noticed that over time only a few remained until, on that day, she was told she was the last one. Then, after another six years in that place, being subjected to the harsh and ever-increasing training regime; what those strange men had wanted to create stood before them. Ready. A human being, but almost robotic in physical and mental state. Able to endure the harshest of conditions and environments and ready to kill in an instant with supreme efficiency and ability. With any weapon or by hand, able to take on any enemy. The Order's new assassin had been created.

In the few years after, working with a secret cell within the Russian secret service, she went to many places around the world. But she never saw much of it. Dropped in by private jet or military transport. Then driven to a hotel or base close to the assignment location to hole up and prepare. Waiting for the green light. Once given, she'd go to the location and wait for the mark; either make the snatch or the kill and get out. Singapore, Beijing, Rome, Sydney, Mumbai, London, Miami and Tehran. Eight cities, thirty kills and five kidnaps. All performed with a slick efficiency and in a calm, methodical manner.

But it was when she started working alone, while waiting for the green light in these random cities, that she liked to sit and watch. Undercover, silent and invisible within the crowds. Sitting in a small café with a coffee and cigarettes for company. Waiting for the green light. It was a life outside of her life. One that, from time to time, she imagined. The normal, everyday life.

She never told her superiors. They would not have allowed her to indulge in such fantasies. They would've worried it was a weakness and that she had not been trained to the robotic state that they thought she was. It was her secret. And so were the men. The men that she was addicted to. The feeling of men inside her that she craved. And that eventual orgasm erupting inside her that she needed so often. It was even more important that she kept this a secret from her superiors. They could never know. They trained her to be devoid of emotion, especially thoughts of lust or sexual emotion. But, it was her release. Her secret release from the life of a killer. A hard, cold blooded killer.

There was a music bar opposite her hotel. She watched a man working on the door. He was a large, tanned, blonde haired young man with a well-built, muscular body. She had noticed him the night before but, as tonight was warmer, he was wearing a polo shirt and shorts and she admired his thick arms and muscular legs. She wanted him inside her. But knew it was impossible. She could never have a relationship with anyone and never had. She had to pay for her men.

Her phone bleeped, snapping her mind from her sexual fantasy. She walked over to the bedside table and picked up her phone to see a text:

'Car will be at rear in 10 minutes'

She noted that the time was just after 10pm. The meet with the witch was at 11.30pm. Agent 7 had questioned whether this would have any purpose, but Kane had insisted, and so his insistence was enough for her. She followed orders. Always.

However, she still questioned why they had to leave so early for an 11.30p.m. meet, but her contact had told her that the witch lived 'very deep' into the swamps and was only accessible by boat and foot.

She dressed in a black vest, black combat trousers and boots. Knowing that these would suit the environment she was visiting soon. She pulled her damp, red hair back away from her face and into a ponytail. She grabbed the folder from underneath the bed, pulled out a small photo of Tom and put it inside her trouser pocket. A wave of scepticism hit her again, concerned that this night-time trek through the hot, sticky swamps would be a complete waste of time. If it was, then she would have to resort to plan B.

She felt under her pillow and pulled out a Glock 43X, her gun of choice, checked it was loaded and slipped it into a holster positioned on her lower back via a strap. She then slipped on her rucksack to conceal the gun whilst making her way downstairs. She closed the window but left it ajar, switched the small lamp on and switched the main light off. She had already worked out a quiet way out of the hotel, down a fire escape which led to the back and already given the hotel owner a large tip to 'look the other way'. She had been happy with the nod he had given as he slipped the money from the counter into his pocket the night before, realising it was not the first time he had been offered bribes.

As she descended the fire escape, the music got louder, and the humdrum gained momentum. But, instead of taking a right to the main reception area she went left, out the fire access door and out into a rear courtyard. The black SUV was waiting with the engine running. She strode across and got inside. The air-con was a welcome relief. Inside felt clean, sanitised and cool. Everything that her hotel room wasn't.

She glanced across at her contact and partner for this assignment and nodded. She liked him. A Mexican called Enrico. That was all she knew about him and all she needed to know. He was no nonsense and had a tough streak, but with a good attitude and professional manner. Plus, in the last few days since she arrived in New Orleans, they had met at various times and he had, at least, not done the two things that almost all the male contacts she work with did. Talk too much and come on to her. She respected him for that.

She removed the rucksack and gun holster and felt the sweat on her back where the rucksack had been for that short time. She enjoyed the feel of the car and instantly relaxed.
"Enjoy the cool air." said Enrico, "We are heading to Delacroix. It's a forty-minute drive."

She sat back and felt her body sink into the seat. Feeling focussed and comfortable, knowing that she would not have to endure constant small talk with Enrico who, she knew, spoke only when necessary.
"Do you have the photo?" Enrico asked.
Agent 7 nodded.

The car made its way south-east out of the city through the Lower Ninth Ward on the 46. After thirty minutes Agent 7 noticed a change in their surroundings. The joyful brashness, colour and the noise of the city now replaced with a dark, ominous and wild environment.
They headed through Wood Lake and into Delacroix, soon coming off the main road and onto a dirt track between an old disused motel and a bar that was no more than a shack. As they passed the buildings the dirt track slid into the forest and the car suddenly bumped and rocked. The driver then put the full beam on, and they headed deeper and deeper into the darkness.

After a mile or so the car stopped, and the driver switched off the full beam. Up ahead there were a few random lights and, as they got closer, a cabin appeared from which an old man emerged. The car stopped and Enrico turned to Agent 7.
"If you are ready?" he asked.

Agent 7 opened the car door. As she got out, the heat and the sound hit her. It was like being enveloped in a warm blanket and there was no air movement at all. The trees, mangroves and swamps held everything still and she felt uncomfortable. And then the noise. The sound of crickets was very intense, almost drill like. The odd sound of a warble from a frog or the sound of a roosting bird was heard from time to time, but the crickets dominated. It got into her head.

The car engine and the lights switched off and she was surprised by the darkness. It was thick. Everywhere was dense, heavy darkness. The light from the cabin provided her senses with its only point of reference. If the light went out, they would be completely blind. She heard Enrico shout, "Hey, spotlight!" and a moment later the area was suddenly lit. She noted a large light on top of the cabin had been switched on and it engulfed the area around her allowing her to gain a better sense of position. She noticed they were close to the water and a small jetty. In the water sat an airboat with a huge propeller at the rear.

Enrico walked around to the front of the cabin and the old man approached him and they shook hands.
"Enrico, where y'at?"
"I am very well, thank you. Good to see you." Enrico replied sincerely.

Enrico handed him a roll of cash and the old man walked a few steps towards the cabin and threw the roll of cash under arm towards it. It was then that Agent 7 noticed another man sitting on a chair by the cabin door. He caught the cash and put it inside his shirt. He spotted Agent 7 looking at him and he lifted his old, battered cap off his head.
"Ma'am," he greeted politely.

Agent 7 ignored him and walked towards the jetty. She scanned the black water and felt anxious. She wanted to get out to the witch, get the information and get back to the hotel. She didn't much care for this place. She was already sweating, getting tired of struggling to see in the dark and the constant noise of the crickets was becoming a distraction.

"Enrico," she called, "We go. Now," still staring into the black abyss ahead of her.

Enrico told the old man to hurry up and they both walked towards the boat. As they did, a phone rang. Enrico approached her and took a phone out from inside his cream linen suit jacket. She noticed he too was sweating.

"Yes?" he answered abruptly.

He listened for ten seconds and, again, Agent 7 grew impatient. Enrico then spoke into the phone.

"Good. Bring him to the cage in an hour."

He ended the call and glanced at Agent 7.

"I have a surprise for you later," he smiled, raising his eyebrows. She wasn't impressed nor had any anticipation for what the surprise was.

"Can we go?"

Enrico, a little embarrassed, turned to the old man.

"Come on, move it."

The old man walked with a limp as fast as he could to the jetty. He made his way to the boat and boarded.

"That's Herbert, by the way," informed Enrico to Agent 7 as he passed her and walked onto the jetty.

"Good to meet you Ma'am," shouted Herbert as he moved some boxes around on the boat to make room for the passengers.

Enrico stood on the jetty at the side of the boat and gestured with his hand for Agent 7 to board before him. She boarded and also took a seat in the middle. Enrico removed his suit jacket and boarded, the boat rocked with the additional weight and movement.

Agent 7 heard a loud whistle. It was Herbert and the other old man from the cabin had reacted to it and approached the jetty and removed the mooring rope. He then threw the looped end to

Herbert who caught it and tucked it into the boat. She stared into the vast blackness ahead of them, surprised that Herbert knew where he was going. It was as if Herbert had read her mind as a spotlight flashed on and the water ahead of them took some form. She noticed green reeds dotted around and mangroves to the right of them. It was more closed in than she had realised.

She felt a nudge and Enrico handed her a pair of ear defenders which she took and put on. As she did, she glanced at Enrico who was putting on his seat belt across his lap. She did the same. Then, without warning, from underneath her she felt a deep vibration and the noise of the engine surprised her. She turned and Herbert had taken his seat, higher up, perched in front of the huge spinning propeller.

She clicked her seat belt on as the vibrating became uncomfortable and jarred her body. But then, as the boat moved off, the vibration relaxed, and the ride became smoother. Herbert edged out away from the jetty. They dissected the mangroves and she noticed the light from the cabin disappear as they entered the main body of water.

She felt another nudge. Enrico politely held his arm out and intimated to her to sit back so she shifted her body and nuzzled her back into the seat. It was then she felt and heard the boat increase speed as a surge of power pushed them forward in an instant. Her body shifted hard back into the seat and the sensation of flying came across her. Water flashed and danced at the side of the boat as they skimmed their way into the darkness at a rate of knots, made to feel all the faster due to the darkness around them.

The wind in her face was a comfort from the heat although even with the huge spotlight pointing their way, very little was seen. She hoped Herbert knew these waters but was confident that, in view of the speed he was going, this was not a problem.

They roared along into the night, deeper and deeper into the swamps. At certain points the engine dropped, and the boat slowed to a gentle pace as they floated through smaller tributaries connecting different bayous. In some places the mangroves and large reeds were close enough to touch either side of them. Then, as they negotiated through them and made it out to a fresh, larger bayou, the sound and vibration would increase, and they would once again, be speeding along into the night.

After twenty minutes, the novelty of the boat ride had worn off and Agent 7 was getting impatient. She nudged Enrico who looked at her and she tapped her watch. He held up two fingers and mouthed the words 'two minutes'. Soon the engine dropped, and the boat slowed to a gentle forward drift. The forest and mangroves around them were dense, and large willow trees loomed over them like ghosts enveloping their victims. The boat entered a tunnel made of thick mangrove, foliage and willow branches that caused a sense of claustrophobia. Agent 7 noticed that Enrico was calm which reassured her.

As they emerged, the spotlight indicated the riverbank ahead of them. The engine increased just for a short burst which was enough to push them towards it. Their surroundings were eerie and unwelcoming, and Agent 7 noticed a fog drifting menacingly above the water.

Enrico released his seat belt and stood up and adjusted his trousers and shirt, tucking himself in. Agent 7 then felt a nudge behind her. Herbert was leaning towards her and pointed ahead and to their left. She faced the direction he had pointed and spotted a round red light in the water. As they got closer the light submerged into the black water. Agent 7 knew what it was and thought no more of it. She was not interested in alligators. Like her, they were efficient killers but were slow, cumbersome and prehistoric. Everything her training had taught her not to be.

The airboat bumped to a stop and Enrico lurched forward but held the side of the boat to stop himself from toppling. He then made his way to the front and got out onto a small jetty. Herbert threw him the rope and he tied it around an old tree stump on the shore. "If you are ready?" he asked her politely.

She moved to the front of the boat and Enrico offered her his hand to help her up onto the jetty. She ignored it, got up onto the jetty and walked to the end, then onto the shore, noticing fireflies circling above the water off to her left. She also noticed that the red eyes had emerged again as if the creature was watching them. They sat bright and motionless, watching, then slowly submerged again.

To her right she made out a small, ramshackle cabin. A gentle light emanated from one of its windows and smoke bellowed from its chimney. There was a strange smell in the air that was unrecognisable. Then the noise hit her again. The crickets. The constant, high pitched drilling sound of the crickets.

Suddenly she was engulfed in darkness and she realised that the spotlight from the boat had been switched off. She held her position awaiting advice or guidance from Enrico. A few seconds later, another light appeared which bobbed and circled in front of her. She realised it was Enrico walking off the jetty with a torch. He approached her.
"Clarissa doesn't like the spotlight," he informed her as he walked towards the cabin. Agent 7 followed.

As they approached, she felt a vulnerability that she had not felt before. She didn't like this place. It had a presence that unsettled her, but she didn't know why. They reached the entrance to the cabin which was a small raised wooden walkway across a swampy, muddy patch.

The cabin was ghostly and unforgiving. The walkway creaked under their weight as they crossed. The smell got stronger and caught in the back of Agent 7's throat. It was a mixture of cooking fat, sweet fragrance and methylated spirits. It repulsed her and the desire to get away from this place grew within her.

Agent 7 had found herself in all manner of dangerous places before. Most of her past work was being sent to do things that nobody else was able, or wanted, to do. Almost always in places that nobody wanted to go. But she had never felt as anxious and wanting to leave a place so much as this. Its presence enveloped her, and she felt restricted and edgy. Her training had taught her to push emotion down and hide it away. To be a robot in a human body. This is what allowed her to be what she was. These feelings were new to her and she didn't like them.

Enrico opened the rickety door and a warm, dark sensation flowed out from the cabin. Warily she entered and Enrico followed closely behind.

Chapter 7

Tom's car had picked him up at the meeting point at the arranged time. The driver gave the correct code word and they set off. He introduced himself as Leo and, although it was Network protocol not to divulge too much information between members, he had informed Tom he had been a member for three years and had undertaken countless driving jobs.

The payments were good, always on time and supplemented the salary from his day job. A lot of work had been coming his way as of late and he had done lots of miles to all different cities and states across the country. Much of which was just drop-offs, pick-ups, collection and delivery of documents, that type of thing. Leo was one of the small cogs that kept the big cog grinding.

Tom had told him he had been a proper member for roughly two years, but this was only his third assignment. No more was discussed, as giving information on your back story and what assignment you were on was strictly forbidden. Everything that The Network did was on a 'need to know' basis and all members understood this and complied with it. These were the little details which prevented infiltration and compromise. The little details that kept people alive.

It was just after one o'clock in the morning and they had been driving for a couple of hours. For the first half an hour, Tom and Leo chatted and made small talk. Moving from music to sports to politics. But gradually the chat ebbed away, and Tom closed his eyes. Tom had grown to realise that members of The Network did silences very well which was a consequence of all the travelling they did.

Tom was dozing but still awake and aware of his surroundings. He checked the road and caught a sign for Hartford, indicating to him they were just over halfway. He took his phone from his holdall and checked his last message from The Network again:

'Tom. Your driver will be at the meeting point at 11am. He will give you the code word 'Mercury'. He will drive you directly to Boston and your accommodation. Your temporary parent will be Helen. She will give you the code word 'Zeppelin'. Once there await further instructions. Do not reply and delete this message. ID.'

Tom memorised the code words and deleted the message. Safe in the knowledge that if The Order did obtain his phone it contained no information for them to use.

He felt a pang of worry. He was nervous before his first assignments, almost to the point of it disabling him just before he was due to head to the contact point. However, both assignments went smoothly with no issues and, more importantly, no involvement from The Order.

In San Francisco his assignment was to make first contact with the portal and organise the meeting point. He did this and picked up a young girl called Debbie from a parking lot. From there he drove her out of the city to a huge retail park. There he linked up with another Network agent who took Debbie from him and onto the next part of her integration into The Network.

During the drive out of the city she kept asking lots of questions, but Tom was under advice not to go into the details of what she was and how she was involved. He figured that, at that point, he was not yet experienced enough to do this part of getting a portal out. Even though he had read and read so much on it and his mind stored every little detail.

Once safe he had assured her that she was going to be cared for. He never knew her story and so was not aware of what had happened to her to make her realise something wasn't right. But, being in that position himself, he knew how difficult it was for her. When he had passed her to the next agent, she was bewildered. He tried to re-assure her again but didn't get through to her and understood why. The young girl was scared and confused.

However, on his way back from the drop off he felt some pride that he had assisted her towards her new life.

His second assignment was in Omaha and more involved than the first. This time he had to make contact, pick up and drive out of the city but then lay low with them for two days until a driver could take them onto their first accommodation.

It was a middle-aged man called Chris. And this time, as they had a lot more time together, Tom had to explain to him what was going on. And, just like him and Odin, Chris almost walked away several times. As Tom spoke to him, he had re-lived all of his own conversations with Odin and the eventual ultimatum he had given him, "You are either with The Network or you are not."

Chris had struggled so much. He had split from his wife two years before and had eventually had a relationship with a lady who worked at his company. It had transpired that she worked for The Order. But, before Chris knew that, he had spiraled into a world of madness and paranoia and had, on two occasions, tried to take his own life. Luckily Chris' brother somehow knew of The Network who organized the intervention and got him out. The next thing Chris knew, he was being driven through the night to Garrison where they were to hole up and wait for the next driver. He had not seen his brother since. And had not seen his children for almost three months.

The next day Tom gave Chris his own back story and they compared what had happened to them. Unusual situations, strange coincidences, feelings of insanity. The similarities were obvious. It was therapeutic for them and Tom felt much better afterwards. Like Odin did to him, Tom gave Chris documents and information to help him on his way. Tom recalled how he sat in the room watching Chris read them with a confused look on his face and remembered him doing the same.

He assured Chris that things would be OK and to use himself as an example. Again, after Chris had thanked him and he left, Tom felt a huge sense of pride and achievement. It was then he realised that he might be a good agent for The Network after all. However, he wasn't naïve and knew that the real test would be when he has an assignment where The Order are involved. He put that thought to the back of his mind.

He heard a beep from his phone and reached into the holdall again. He recovered his phone and noticed he had a new message:

'Tom. Amber Alert. Intelligence indicates movement from The Order in Boston. Assignment safe to continue but support deployed. Agent will make contact upon arrival. Do not reply and delete this message. ID.'

Anxiety swept over him. An amber alert meant that agents within that specific area or city had to be on guard. Both The Order and The Network had eyes and ears everywhere. Either way it put Tom on edge. He told himself that just because there was activity or agents from The Order in a city it didn't mean they would be there to get him or to intervene in what he was doing. Boston was a big place and, as ID had advised, he was getting another agent sent in support.

It just meant he would have to be extra vigilant and keep himself under the radar. And he had learnt to do this very well.

Chapter 8

Agent 7 and Enrico lowered their heads as they walked through the initial section of the cabin. It was dark, but candlelight in various places created enough light to see your way.

Bones, dead chickens, animal furs and blood-stained cloths lined the walls and various items of junk filled the room. Snake skins hung down from hooks on the wooden beams. A table to the left of them had more candles and maps strewn across it in amongst a human skull, a small dead animal, bowls, trinkets and other odd bones. A fire in the corner smouldered and the white embers gave off a little heat which added to the close and dense atmosphere of the cabin.

Enrico prompted Agent 7 forward towards another opening and they both made their way over. Enrico then held Agent 7 back and moved forward to stand in the small doorway from which a low glow emanated from.
"Clarissa?"
"Who goes there?" came a low gruff voice from inside the room with a thick Cajun accent.
"It's Enrico. I have brought the lady. Our guest from The Order."
"Ah! It's good to hear your voice, Enrico. Enter, s 'il vous plait."

Enrico waved Agent 7 forward and into the room. In the middle of the hazy, smoke filled room sat a woman. She was filthy and her clothes no more than rags. She had dreadlocks that were as thick as rope, matted and hard. As they entered, she laughed a wheezy cackle, of which Agent 7 was unsure why. As they moved closer, she spoke.
"You sit, s 'il vous plait."

The old lady gestured for them to sit in front of her. Surrounding her were bones, furs, animal skulls and various implements. Next to her was a cage with a dark green snake curled into a huge mass. Just behind her, a large alligator skull and next to it, a pot sat on a fire which steamed and bubbled. Agent 7 realised that the stench she disliked, which had now got stronger, was coming from the pot. The bubbling fluid inside was a dark, grey colour.

They sat and it was then that Agent 7 realised that the lady was blind. One of her eyes was closed, with a chunk of skin growing across it. The other eye was open but pure white with a hint of blue. Black paint on her face had encrusted and wrinkled as she moved and spoke. Her hands were black with dirt and grime and her nails long and sharp.

Agent 7 looked at Enrico for some guidance, but he just sat staring at the witch.
"So, it's the power of voodoo you seek, ah?" Clarissa asked quietly.
"Oui, Clarissa," said Enrico, "We have the photo you require."
Agent 7 retrieved the photo from her trousers. She leant forward and held the photo in front of Clarissa's face, but the witch just sat motionless.
"Clarissa. In front of you," Enrico advised.

She reached up and touched Agent 7's hand who felt her hard fingers traverse her own as the witch gave a smile of black and yellow teeth. The fingers felt like bone and gave a cold deathly touch. She felt the photo and snatched it from Agent 7. The witch held the photo in one hand and caressed it with the other, murmuring inaudible words and phrases.

Her head raised up and she looked up at the ceiling of the cabin as her murmuring became louder and turned into ancient chanting. She swayed her head and her body circled as the smoke from the pot behind drifted up and entwined her. She cackled again, ending with her coughing and then spitting the contents of her mouth into a bowl at her side. The witch then reached to her side and picked up several bones, shark teeth and alligator teeth. She picked up the bowl she had spat into and dropped the bones in. She then moved them around coating them in the phlegm and saliva. As she did, her head continued to sway, and her body circled.

She took a huge deep breath and chanted loudly. Agent 7 glanced at Enrico and saw his face full of concentration. She realised that something was going to happen. Enrico turned to Agent 7 and nodded back towards the witch, urging Agent 7 to watch Clarissa and not him.

Suddenly the witch gasped and sat bolt upright. The gasp sent fear through Agent 7. The witch laughed, low and sinister. A laugh that indicated that she knew something that they didn't.

Agent 7 watched intently. The witch waved her hand, summoning Enrico, who leant forward, pulled his shirt sleeve up and turned his hand over to reveal the underside of his arm. The witch then picked up another bowl which had a dark fluid inside and a small, sharp bone protruding from the bowl. She stirred the contents of the bowl with the bone and then grabbed Enrico's arm. She then took the bone out and Agent 7 noticed it dripping in what she now recognised as blood. She put the bone to Enrico's arm and moved it in a scratching motion. Enrico held firm but grimaced.

Then the witch began chanting again but this time louder. Almost in a shout. Unknown, inaudible alien words and phrases, her head now shaking and twisting and her body convulsing. Making the scratching on Enrico's arm harder and more painful. He tried to hold his arm steady, but the movement made it shake and he, again, grimaced in pain. The chanting became louder than ever and the convulsing made her head and body shake relentlessly. Then, suddenly, the witch stopped and dropped the bone to the floor, breathing heavily and murmuring to herself.

Enrico lifted his arm and studied it. He smiled and his eyes widened. He shuffled across to Agent 7 and showed her. And there, written and scratched onto his wrist and lower arm were, what appeared to be letters. They were difficult to read and due to the shaking and convulsing were very untidy.
"Do you see it?" asked Enrico.
"No," replied Agent 7, frustrated.

Enrico shuffled over to his suit jacket which was on the floor where he had been sitting. He took a handkerchief from the jacket pocket that he had laid on the floor and dabbed his arm. He then spat on the handkerchief and wiped his arm, moving closer to Agent 7.

"Look closely."

Agent 7 took his arm and held it closer. Barely recognisable among the red smudges and scratches. Six letters that were exactly what she had hoped for:

b Ostο N

She felt a sudden wave of relief. She knew now she had the information she craved and could get on with the next part of her assignment. Plus, she could now leave this hot, backward place. Back to her hotel and away from New Orleans. She had no desire to stay here longer than she needed. She got up. Enrico gathered his jacket and then approached the witch and bent down. He mumbled something to her, and the witch held his hands. He smiled and nodded as she spoke.

Enrico then stood and gestured towards the way out. Agent 7 needed no persuading to leave and left the small room without turning back. She moved into the larger room of the cabin and turned to Enrico when they heard the witch.

"Enrico, s 'il vous plait?

He stopped in the doorway and turned to face the witch. She laughed that sinister laugh again and then spoke.

"A warning to the lady. He is strong. Much power in him."

Enrico looked around at Agent 7. They both knew what had been said but he wasn't sure if or how it had affected her. Agent 7 spun and walked towards the door, leaving the cabin. Enrico rushed after her. He switched on his torch and walked to the end of the raised walkway where Agent 7 had made her way already in total darkness. As they walked back to the boat, they heard screams of laughter from the cabin and the witch shouting.

"He is strong! Much power!"

Agent 7 ignored it and walked faster. Enrico shouted to Herbert and suddenly the spotlight engulfed them, and the environment they were in became visible. They got onto the boat and it roared into life. They slowly made their way out and Agent 7 turned and glanced back at the cabin. How dare that hag make her feel that way. Nobody had ever done that. Agent 7 felt angry and ashamed that the witch had forced her to experience those unwanted emotions. Agent 7 had a vision of standing on her neck and pushing down until it cracks.

As they skimmed across the water, Enrico noticed the look on Agent 7's face but knew it best not to ask. It wasn't his problem. Plus, he didn't want to upset her. He had been informed that she was to be treated with the upmost respect and, by all accounts, was deadly. Enrico was too wily and had been in this business too long to upset the wrong people.

They made their way back to Herbert's cabin. As they disembarked, Agent 7 spotted the other old man still sitting in the chair outside the cabin. Herbert kept the spotlight on so they could see what they were doing, and Enrico immediately took his phone out and made a call.

"Are you here?" he asked, and after a few seconds continued,

"Good, we will be there shortly."

He turned to Agent 7.

"That surprise I told you about. It's ready."

"What is it?" she asked, not in the mood to do anything else except get back to her room and take a shower.

"Get in," he said, gesturing to her to get into the car that was still waiting.

The car slowly traversed the thin, bumpy track it had come down from the main road. Their heads bumped from side to side as Enrico explained that one of his agents had been tracking an agent from The Network. His agent had, earlier that night, found him close to Agent 7's hotel and had taken the opportunity to subdue him. He had been taken to a location close by.

"Do you want to attend or go back to the hotel?" Enrico asked.

Agent 7 pondered. The thought of going back to the hotel was inviting. But she was intrigued, so she advised that she would like to see the prisoner, despite her desire to get back. Enrico barked an order to the driver in French. A short time later, the driver turned off the dirt track they were on and took a left leading to another track.

It was even tighter and bumpier, and the branches and bushes scraped the side of the car and the windows like creatures trying to get at them. Eventually, after a bumpy ride, they came to a small clearing, close to the water. There was another cabin with spotlights which made vision much easier. They pulled up and there were two men standing smoking by the water, one tall and slim, the other short and overweight. Both wearing suits. They looked around as the car approached, the shorter guy immediately darted off into the cabin.

The car stopped and Agent 7 and Enrico got out. They walked over and the taller man politely nodded at Enrico who acknowledged him with a nod back.

"This is Agent 7," Enrico notified the man.

The man nodded and held out his hand.

"My pleasure. I'm Baxter."

Agent 7 ignored his hand, "Where is the prisoner?" she asked assertively, noticing his cheap suit.

"Oh…Just bringing him out," Baxter confirmed, embarrassed, as he retracted his hand.

Suddenly a door banged open and the short guy appeared with another man who he shoved forward. Agent 7 noticed that the man had been beaten badly. His face swollen and bloodied, his shirt stained red and ripped, his wrists tied. The short man brought him over by the arm, stood him in front of Enrico and Agent 7 and pushed prisoner to his knees.

The man grunted in pain. He gazed up at Enrico and Agent 7 and then looked down in a demonstration of either fear or insolence. "He hasn't confessed yet," confirmed the short fat man in a strong Louisiana accent, "but we have all we need to prove he is from The Network. We searched the car he was using and found these."

The man handed Enrico some documents. He studied them quickly, noting that much of it was code and jargon. Nothing too incriminating. But the last document was a photo of Agent 7. Enrico glanced at it and handed it to Agent 7, "The Network obviously know of you."

She studied it and then crouched down so her face was close to the prisoner. She spoke calmly.
"Why do you have a photo of me?"
The prisoner's eyes peered up at her and then down again.
"Why do you have a photo of me?" she asked again but like before, he responded with silence.
"Do you understand English?" she asked
"Of course he understands Goddam English!" shouted the short man. Enrico glared at him.
"Who the fuck do think you're talking to!?" he shouted. "Apologise to Agent 7 immediately."
"But…Enrico…I was just saying…" pleaded the man, sweat patches covering the whole of his suit jacket. Agent 7 waved her arm as if to confirm to Enrico she was not bothered and required no apology. She lent in closer to the prisoner and whispered.
"Why do you have a photo of me?"
The prisoner glanced up, one eye swollen shut, dried blood on his face and neck.

"I promise. This is a mistake. The photo was planted on me."
"You're a fucking God-damn liar!" shouted Baxter and kicked the prisoner, making him fall forward onto the sand and mud.
"Enrico! Control these men!" shouted Agent 7.

Enrico walked around to the man and swung a slap which connected to his head.
"If you two fucking morons don't shut the fuck up you will end up in the cage too!" he shouted.

Visibly upset by their lack of professionalism, he glared at them both and the two men knew they should say and do no more.
"What is the cage?" asked Agent 7.
Enrico picked the prisoner up by the arm and looked at her.
"Please, come."

He dragged the prisoner towards the water and then knelt him down at the water's edge. Agent 7 followed, it was then that she noticed a large cage roughly two metres into the water, the bottom submerged, but the majority of it above the water. It was roughly five feet high and twenty feet long. The metal was tightly bound with two-inch squares and so, once inside, not very much could escape.
"The stick!" shouted Enrico.

And with that, the larger man went to the cabin and returned with a large metal rod. He walked into the water alongside the cage and inserted the rod in through one of the small holes. He then jabbed the rod hard and the beast thrashed and showed itself with water splashing and spraying the man at the side of the cage. He jumped back with excitement and laughter. The alligator's tail thrashed so hard it rocked the cage.
"Whoa there!" Baxter shouted holding the cage to stop it rocking.

The prisoner panicked and tried to get up, but Enrico cuffed him hard around the back of the neck knocking him down to the mud. Agent 7 was surprised by the size of the beast but did not show it.

The alligator then settled back down into the water and half submerged itself again. It let out a slow, growl that came from deep within its primal body. It was a sound that sent a wave of fear through all five of the humans close by. The prisoner, now close to hysterical, was physically shaking.

"No, no, no no…" he kept repeating.

Enrico pulled him up to his knees, moved round to the front of him and crouched down.

"Start talking you pig! Why do you have a photo of the lady!? Are there any more Network agents close by!?"

He punched the man's face and sent him sprawling. In the background Baxter laughed. Enrico grabbed the man by the hair and pulled him up to his knees. Pulling his arm back to hit the man again, Agent 7 intervened and put her hand up to stop him. Enrico lowered his arm and walked round the back of the man and held him upright. Agent 7 crouched down to the prisoner's level, who was now shaking and close to crying. She grabbed his face roughly.

"OK. I will ask you two questions. Why do you have a photo of me? What do you know of portal 294574? Now, tell me the answers or you go in the cage."

The prisoner again tried to state it was all a mistake, that he knew nothing, and that the photo was planted on him. During his plea he started to cry. Agent 7 shook her head and continued.

"You are being very loyal or very stupid. One last chance. Why do you have a photo of me? What do you know of portal 294574?"

There was a pause. The prisoner looked down at the sand, stopped crying and composed himself. He took a deep breath and then glared at her.

"See you in hell, you cunt," and he spat blood and saliva into her face.

Agent 7 never flinched. Enrico moved in but she held her arm up to stop him. She stood and then reached forward and took the handkerchief from his jacket pocket, wiped her face and gave it back to him.

"I wish to go back to the hotel now."

Enrico stared at her as she ambled past him towards the waiting car. He glanced towards Baxter who shrugged his shoulders.

"Agent 7?" Enrico shouted. "The prisoner?"

She stopped and paused.

"Put him in," she ordered and continued walking.

Enrico turned back to the men.

"OK, open the cage!"

With that, the short man quickly got into the water splashing as he went. He reached up and took out a bolt at the top of one side of the cage. Then walked across and did the other side. Baxter then walked into the water to the opposite side and in unison they bent down and lifted the cage entrance up.

The prisoner screamed and tried to get up, but Enrico slapped him and dragged him by his hair towards the water. He screamed louder and it filled the dense night air with the sound of horror. Enrico got behind him and grabbed him by the waist and the arm and bundled him unceremoniously into the cage. The prisoner attempted to get up again, but this time Enrico shoved his body with his foot and, with his arms tied behind him, he fell into the cage with a splash. The two men at the side then closed down the door quickly and bolted it.

Agent 7 got to the car. She opened the door to get inside but stopped as her curiosity got the better of her. She looked back, seeing the prisoner scramble backwards away from the far end of the cage. And for a few seconds all was quiet and still. Then the beast moved. The prisoner screamed again, but the beast stopped and submerged itself. For a few seconds the only sound filling the air was crickets.

Then it struck. The huge, dark green body lunged, cumbersome at first, but then with speed and ferocity. Its jaws wide open, its light green underbelly flashed as it surged forward, grabbing the prisoner by the head and body as he screamed. Agent 7 was surprised at the power in which it took him, making the grown adult look like a rag doll.

It dragged backwards with a surge of power. Primal and vicious. The man's body pulled further into its mouth. It opened its wide jaw and snapped powerfully down, gaining more grip with each bite. The man's legs and body now dangling from the deadly mouth. The beast submerged, then flipped and rolled, breaking bones and tendons like twigs, ripping muscle like paper. Agent 7 heard one last frantic, desperate wail from the prisoner as she got into the car and closed the door.

She relaxed. The air conditioning was like a cleanser from the stifling night air. She took a deep breath and relaxed into the seat. It had been a good night's work and she was content. She had the lead on portal 294574 and so would book a flight to Boston tomorrow. She would call Kane and update him and ensure a new contact from The Order was deployed to meet her there.

But that was tomorrow. Tonight, she would go back to the hotel and clean herself. To erase this hot, dirty, pitiful place off of her body and out of her mind.

Chapter 9

As the sun dipped beyond the horizon, its glow created a peach-coloured sky of orange and red. The sound of the sea flowing back and forth, caressing the beach, filled the air. A hundred metres from the shore, a flock of flamingo's, in perfect arrow shaped formation, glided effortlessly, a metre or so above the aqua-blue, crystal clear ocean. The beach was surrounded by high cliffs, covered in green palms and tropical ferns, and a waterfall cascaded down one side into the frothing lagoon below.

It was a place of such natural beauty, with a warm, vibrant and exotic atmosphere.

It was Tom's favourite place. He loved it here. It had taken him a few meditation sessions to create it, but it was now perfect. His family loved it too. They all sat on the beach, content and happy. Each of them giving off their own love and affection, whilst also feeding off each other's. It was a scene of tranquillity and bliss.

As usual Tom never wanted it to end but he sensed his time with them was almost over for now. It was a strange feeling and he had learnt to push it aside and extend his visits with them, but he knew, for now, this visit was over.

His family slowly stood and stared at him lovingly. And as they walked away it happened. A flash of darkness. The dark building on the hill appeared. A flash of lightning pierced the sky, a gust of wind blew violently as the rain came lashing down. Another lightning strike lit the building again, but this time Tom saw it clearly. Was it a church? An old, foreboding place that hid dark secrets and a presence that made him uneasy.

He saw a figure. All in black, floating up the hill towards him, angry and in attack mode, then it suddenly stopped, and Tom was back on the beach staring out to sea. He turned and his family were leaving the beach and entering the thick jungle behind them. His mum stepped into the trees but then looked back and smiled lovingly. Then she was gone.

Tom pulled himself from the trance-like state, opened his eyes and was in his small room. He felt invigorated and content. It had been his longest session yet and it had felt like he had spent hours with them. Although, after checking the clock, in reality he had been meditating for roughly half an hour.

However, his contentment was again marred by the vision of the building. Tom knew now it was an old castle or a church, but he didn't know why it spooked him. He also wondered who or what the figure was that was coming towards him up the hill. He felt frustrated. Just as he had opened his mind to this new ability and learnt to hone it and control it, this vision started appearing. Was it relevant? And, if so, how?

Tom stretched and cricked his neck. He took a deep breath and walked to the window. It was an ordinary house in a quiet neighbourhood with very little going on. A small single storey, wood cladded property, tucked between two larger properties. It was not very noticeable and unassuming. The room was decorated very basically and hadn't appeared to have been updated since the 1980's. Cheap wooden furniture, non-descript hanging pictures and mustard curtains gave it an old-fashioned feel.

But, it had a roof, a bed, running water and was dry and warm. And Tom had grown accustomed to a basic life. He had learnt to live and thrive in whatever accommodation The Network provided him with. He had adapted and matured, and so luxury and mod-cons were no longer a necessity for him.

The night before, Leo had driven quickly into the early hours, so they had made it to the outskirts of Boston by 2.30am. He then informed Tom that he was under instructions to skirt around the city, so left the Massachusetts Turnpike just before Auburndale and picked up the 95. They drove clockwise around the city and then further on towards the coast, eventually heading into Beverly. Tom had eventually got into his room and settled by around 3.30am. He fell asleep immediately and had slept well.

His instructions were simple. Hole up and sit tight. The support agent was set to arrive later that afternoon. Further instructions would then be sent, and once received, they can devise their strategy to get the portal recovered and out to the scheduled hand over point.

He had time to kill. And he enjoyed that time. He was currently reading a book on Ancient Egypt and also dipping in and out of the Bible. Analysing various psalms and quotes that he found of relevance to him. He was also studying several theory papers on the existence of angels that had recently intrigued him. Therefore, he had set aside some time in the afternoon to read and study. Gaining knowledge and understanding what he was, where he came from and how he came to be was a major part of acceptance and moving forward.

He had learnt to read and process almost robot like, scanning pages, absorbing the information with it staying prominent in his mind. Often, he found himself reading five or six books at a time and as soon as he had finished, storing that information and not forgetting a detail. It was an ability that he had not always had and so, he knew at some point, this had developed naturally. The room had also contained puzzle books and jigsaw puzzles to do. Again, The Network helping their members kill time by staying occupied and focussed. Tom decided that he would train, have some lunch and settle down in the afternoon with his books and documents.

After a half an hour of high intensity training, Tom sat on the end of his bed, sweating and trying to catch his breath. His parent, a lady called Michaela, had brought him some bottled water and fruit that morning and so he gulped down the water. As he did, he heard his phone bleep and noticed that he got a text message:

'Tom. Your support agent will arrive at 4pm. Your parent will do security check. Amber warning still in place. Recovery of portal still scheduled for tomorrow night. Transport and weapons to be provided soon. Further instructions to follow. Do not reply and delete this message. ID'

Tom scanned the information and deleted the text.

At the same time, thirty miles away in the city, Ano Tora stood next to Park Street Church. It was a busy junction and there were lots of pedestrians moving in all directions, so he had tucked himself back into one of the crevasses, leaning on a plinth which held one of the huge columns. He was meeting his contact from The Order on Boston Common, just across the road from the church. He was early. Things had run smoothly. Although the incident in the hotel room had delayed his progress. Alex had come back to the room and was shocked at the dead body of the agent. He had panicked and berated Ano Tora for, "causing problems between his people and The Order."

Ano Tora had calmed Alex down by telling him that if he did not relax then he would be lying next to the man with the same outcome. He had managed to get him to see sense and organise a cleaner to get to the room to dispose of the body and any evidence of the incident. He knew Alex was right. Even though he despised the young mobster, he realised that he had a point. From this moment on Ano Tora would need Alex and his crime family to provide contacts for him from within The Order.

He and the Yakuza were paying well and so this helped. He needed the mafia and The Order for information; but also needed them to be on good terms. It was this that made him think that perhaps his actions had been rash. But he had always had a temperament which did not tolerate insolence and disrespect. It made him who he was.

Things has been smoothed over and the next day he and Alex had boarded a flight to Boston for a meeting that had been set up with another agent from The Order who was on the mob's payroll.

Ano Tora checked his watch and realised it was time. He joined the throng of people, made his way to the crossing, crossed Tremont Street and made his way into the park. He followed the pathway into the centre and spotted the bench that had been designated as the meeting point.

A man in a shirt and Chino's sat at the bench, reading a book. He looked unassuming and not what Ano Tora had expected. But he was at the exact place at the exact time doing exactly what he said he would be doing. Reading a book. Ano Tora approached and sat on the bench. He then removed the pouch full of cash he was wearing from his shoulder and put it on the bench next to him.

He noticed what a nice place it was. There was a play park just across the grass section and he could hear the sound of children shouting and laughing. Close by, a stall sold Italian ice cream and two young girls were happily choosing their flavours. It was a nice day, and the sun penetrated the trees, engulfing the bench in warm light.

The man reading the book sat motionless and had not acknowledged his arrival.
"What book are you reading?" asked Ano Tora, staring straight ahead, confirming he was the man's contact.
"It's my favourite book," replied the man, confirming the same to Ano Tora.
Aware that the coded greeting had checked out Ano Tora got down to business.
"What is the status?" he asked, moving shiftily and seeking to get more comfortable.
"Our intelligence informs us that the portal is close. As of yet we have not located him within the city, but we have intel. He will arrive in Boston soon."
"How soon?"
"In a day or two."

The man spoke but did not divert his gaze from the book. An elderly couple walked past and stared at them for a few moments. Ano Tora smiled politely and they did the same and walked on. Then Ano Tora continued.

"How will you locate him?"

"Our intelligence tells us he is here for an assignment in the city. We already have agents watching the portal he has come for. Once he makes his move, we will pick up his position." replied the man confidently.

"And then I can then step in and remove him?" enquired Ano Tora.

The man looked away from the book pretending to survey his surroundings.

"I can help as much as I can. But I warn you that The Order's masters have requested termination. If it comes to it that's what will happen. I can't be seen doing anything else. Nobody else is involved in our arrangement. So, you will need to be ready. And be quick."

The man went back to his book. Ano Tora made one final enquiry.

"But you will keep me informed and make sure I am positioned correctly? As agreed?"

The man shifted, suddenly uncomfortable.

"As I said, I will do what I can but within reason. If my associates get an opportunity first, they will take him out...I can't guarant...

"Just make sure you follow the plan," Ano Tora interrupted, "The Yakuza don't like being let down."

The man shifted again and Ano Tora sensed weakness in him. He didn't want to upset or offend the man at this stage as he was too important.

"There is plenty more where this came from," Ano Tora confirmed and nudged the pouch closer to the man.

With that Ano Tora stood, looked around and then headed off the way he had come. A minute or so later, the man also got up, picked up the pouch and set off in the opposite direction.

Chapter 10

Tom sat at the desk studying the assignment details. He was studying a city map and marking points of reference and potential important locations. There was a knock at the door.

"Tom? It's Michaela. Your associate has arrived. Shall I show them in?

"Yes please," replied Tom, still scanning documents.

He heard the door open, stood up and turned. The person that entered wasn't who he was expecting. For some reason he had an image of a man in his head but the person who walked through the door was a small, athletic, young woman that he immediately recognised.

It was Laura. The young woman that he had completed his training with all that time ago up in the northern wilderness. A time that seemed like an eternity ago, but now after seeing her again, became so fresh and vivid in his memory. A warm, happy feeling washed over him, and he knew he was still attracted to her. He had known at the time that he had feelings for her but the situation they were in at that time had not been right for them to develop a relationship. It was just a group of people thrown together in the most unusual of circumstance, undertaking harsh, brutal training in an environment to match.

Tom had been a little sad for a few days after he had departed from the training. And since then, he had thought of her from time to time. He believed she felt the same about him and always wondered if he would ever get a chance to find out.

"Wow, Laura, I…I…Hi," Tom was taken aback and was almost lost for words.

She stepped forward and embraced him, "Hi Tom, I hope you are well."

At first, he was too surprised to hold her but then, after a brief moment, he put his arms around her and pulled her in towards him. It felt good to hold someone again. When they released themselves she just stood and smiled.

"You look well. Healthy," she commented.

"Thanks. So do you…You look great,"

Tom noticed her light brown hair was pushed back and framed her pretty face. Tom continued.

"I don't know what to say…Did you know? I mean, did you know it would be me?"

"I guessed. Once Michaela had cleared security, she said I would be working with a 'nice man named Tom'. I don't know any other nice men called Tom."

Tom laughed. He loved her face and wanted to stare at her all day, then realised it may be too obvious what he was thinking, so he looked away.

"Er…Look…Sorry, make yourself comfortable."

He then proceeded to tidy up and cleared the table, kicking his clothes under the bed. Laura noticed and laughed.

"Tom, there's no need…"

Tom realised how stupid he must've looked and took a deep breath and relaxed. He sat down on the bay window behind him, smiled and shook his head.

"I just can't believe it. I have been alone for so long, just moving around and doing my own thing and then…Well…you appear…"

Laura put her backpack in the corner and removed her jacket.

"I know. When I realised it was you, I felt the same. I suppose we have just got used to living alone and so it feels weird to be with someone you know."

Tom nodded in agreement. He stood and offered his hand to direct her to the bed, "Here, sit down."

Laura sat, appearing a little uncomfortable, running her hands up and down her jeans, smiling awkwardly. Tom noticed this and interjected to break the silence.

"So, how long has it been?"

Laura screwed her face to demonstrate she was thinking.

"Couple of years?" she suggested.

"Must be. So, how have you been? What's happened since. Tell me," said Tom.

Laura took a deep breath and told him everything that had happened to her since she had departed from the training. She had been taken to Seattle where she stayed overnight and was then moved on to Denver and had stayed there for a month before taking part in her first of two assignments. She had then been contacted to come to Boston to assist on this assignment.

For her first assignment in Denver, she had just been a driver and recalled how she had to be at an organised location at a certain time, which she did. Suddenly a man got in with a young boy who appeared frightened and confused. She was told by the man to drive to a location about ten miles away which she had done, got told to stop and the man and the boy got out. That was all her involvement was and she never heard more about it.

But in her second assignment, although she did not make first contact with the portal, she was told to meet them, inform them what was happening, then deliver them to a hotel room where another agent would take over.

She explained that the portal, a 27-year-old man called Ryan, was in a bad way. She had been sure he was high on drugs when he arrived, and he didn't want to be there. She had told him that she can help him, and he was to go with her. But it wasn't a good situation and she felt from the start that she had never been able to get through to him. Somehow, she managed to get him to the hotel room and the other agent tried to explain and calm him but to no avail. He just got up and left. She tried to go after him, but the other agent advised against it. They never saw nor heard from Ryan or his family again. It was almost certain that he was now dead.

Tom listened intently, showing the genuine interest that he had. It was so refreshing to be able to discuss all of this with someone who had the same experiences. They discussed how difficult it was to earn people's trust and explain what was happening. In some cases, like Ryan's, it was impossible and they both knew that there will be times when they aren't successful in integrating portals.

Michaela had brought them coffee and they soon relaxed, spending the afternoon catching up and reminiscing. They both had so much to share and talk about. Both now comfortable after the awkwardness of earlier.

As Laura spoke, there was an excitement and anticipation in her voice. She was also finding the conversation of value too. Laura told Tom about her constant yearning for family and friends and how difficult she was finding not being able to see anyone. How difficult she had found it to settle and what she had done to help herself adapt. She spoke for an hour or so and Tom listened to every word, enjoying her voice and her face. Smiling from time to time at the animation in her voice and nodding sincerely at any negative or sadder parts of her story.

Tom soon took over and told her about San Francisco and the assignments he had been involved with, what part he played and what happened. He told her how it had come around to this point and his visit to New Jersey recently, seeing his sister and going to the cemetery. She informed him that she had family in San Antonio and so, if she was ever near there, it would be something she would consider. Tom urged her to do it as he found it so comforting. Laura listened to every word and detail.

They spoke into the early evening about their lives, how they had adapted, the positives and the negatives. They shared their thoughts on The Network and how it operated, the different parents they had had along the way, accommodation, all of the different places they had been to and the things they had seen and done. Tom found it fascinating to hear someone else's experiences and, even though they were similar to his, he found it exciting and interesting.

They agreed that they had both, in their own individual ways, dealt with it very well. And Tom then recalled and explained to her how he had also struggled to cope at first and felt depressed and lonely, but things had got better.

As they spoke, they both realised that they had huge pride. They were proud of themselves, proud of each other and were proud to be part of The Network. It was an inclusive feeling. They were very special beings. And found it special being in The Network, part of the resistance helping other angels and their families rid themselves of The Order.

Eventually the conversation came to a close. They had spoken for hours. They both gazed at each other. A connection created by similar circumstances now bound and strengthened. Laura got up from the bed and moved towards Tom. Tom stood and they embraced. Neither of them had family or friends for comfort or help and so had stood in as replacement. They were each other's shoulder to lean on.

Tom looked at the clock on the wall which told him it was almost 7.30pm. It was then it occurred to him how dark it was in the room.
"Look at the time."
Laura raised her eyebrows in surprise.
"It's been nice to see you, Tom," she replied, "And good to talk."
Tom moved to a desk in the corner of the room and switched the lamp on. It softened the room in a gentle glow.
"You hungry?" he asked.
"Famished."

Tom left the room and spoke to Michaela. He had come back with a menu for Chinese food from a takeaway, not too far away, that delivered. Michaela had offered to order it for them and after Tom had told her what they had chosen, he returned with a bottle of red wine and two glasses. He poured them both a glass and, whilst waiting for their food, they went over the assignment documents and set about devising their plan of action for the next day.

Chapter 11

It was almost 10pm and the church was quiet. The only sound was the ghostly moans from a fresh wind that had blown in from the Atlantic onto the west coast of Ireland in the last half an hour.

Father O'Dowd walked around the church putting the candles out as he went. As he extinguished each candle, the church got gradually darker, until the only light came from the pulpit at the far end. He approached the pulpit, extinguishing a candle at a marble font on route, and climbed the three steps to stand at the lectern where he had given too many sermons to remember. Staring out across the dark wooden pews of the nave.

He had loved his time here. The people from the local villages had been so kind to him and had offered him all the friendship and support he had needed. Since his move from Kilkenny to Westport, four years ago, he had been adopted as one of their own. However, he had known this day would come. But he had always hoped it wouldn't.

He sighed, stepped down from the pulpit and made his way to the door at the rear of the church, stopping to make a sign of the cross in front of a large bronze statue of the Virgin Mary that stood proudly below the stain glass window. He took out a key, unlocked the door and went through, closing it behind him. It accessed his office and living quarters. He went through to his office, closed the door and sat at his desk. He looked at the clock on the wall in front of him and sighed again. He was nervous and the anxiety in his stomach weighed heavy upon him.

He checked his calendar. Monday May 5 circled in black. Today's date. A date that had carried worry and dread for him for a long time. He pondered. He had hoped that he would have had more information by now. But from experience he knew that it was always just a matter of waiting for instructions. Information filtered through eventually, but it frustrated him that he always found out snippets at different times. For so long, he had wanted to sit with Father Reilly and just talk about it. Discuss it in detail and at length. But Father Reilly had told him why this was not possible.

He heard a noise and sat up, alert. Eyes wide, awaiting another sound. Then he heard a knock at his door.
"Father?" came a gentle Irish voice. It was Maggie, the church assistant. He was relieved.
"Maggie, come in," he replied.

The door opened, and Maggie popped her head around the door. Her young innocent face still alert and happy even though it was so late.
"Are you still here? At this hour?" he asked her.
"Aye, I told you. I've been preparing all the raffle tickets for the fete on Sunday."
Father O'Dowd smiled, "Of course."
"Don't you worry. This week I will be making sure everyone in Ireland has a ticket!" she said enthusiastically.
Father O'Dowd laughed.
"Bless you, Maggie. I don't know what this church would do without you, my dear."
"Oh, it's nothing. I enjoy it."
"I know. But I am very grateful for your hard work."
"Thanks. I appreciate that. Anyway, I will be off now."
"OK, Maggie. There's a fresh wind blowing in so drive carefully. Text me when you get back to the village…Just let me know you got home OK."
Maggie rolled her eyes, "OK. If you insist. I'll be fine though."
She paused and looked at him concerned.
"Are you OK, Father?"
"I am fine…Just tired."

She nodded and closed the door. The anxiety that had dissipated from Father O'Dowd's stomach returned after its brief disappearance when he had spoken to Maggie. Suddenly the door opened, and her head appeared again.

"Oh, Father. Mother said she is doing a stew on Friday and she'd welcome your company."

Father O'Dowd felt a warm glow inside him. Most Friday's Maggie's mother made a stew and they invited him to their home. They were a warm and charming family. He loved Friday's there for dinner, which usually ended up with a few bitters in the Cross Key's across the village square from their house. Being invited into people's lives and families was a perk of the job he loved more than anything.
"As always, it would be my pleasure. Thank your mother, won't you?"
"Great, I will. See you tomorrow."

The door closed again, and he pondered. He clasped his hands together on the desk. He smiled and shook his head in disbelief at how lucky he had been to have served this area for so long.

He took a deep breath and checked the clock. He had another ten minutes until the phone call. He had hoped to have timed it better as he didn't want to think about it. He stood and went to the window. He opened the blinds and noticed that the trees swaying harder, and drizzle was spotting the window.

The trees were used to it. They had stood for hundreds of years and had taken many more battering's from the weather along this wild and rugged coastline. Father O'Dowd hoped that he would be able to be as strong. He closed the blinds and went across to his kettle. He put some coffee in his mug but then stopped. He didn't want coffee. He couldn't face it. The knot in his stomach was too tight. He sat back down, relaxed back in his chair and closed his eyes.

He waited. Then, after several minutes, he noted it was 10.29pm and the second hand was looming towards 10.30pm. As the hand passed the 12 his phone rang which made him jump. He had known it was coming at that exact point, but it still scared him. He shook his head, took a deep breath and picked up the phone.

"Father O'Dowd?" came a quiet but very gruff Irish voice at the other end.

"Hello, Father Reilly," he replied.

"It is time."

There was a pause.

"Are you sure?" asked Father O'Dowd.

"Yes. You have to make the call."

O'Dowd paused, but this time longer. He felt uncomfortable doing it but had told himself he would raise the question.

"Father Reilly, without being rude, these people…The Network, are you sure they are…"

"Father O'Dowd," came the interruption, "We have discussed this on many occasions."

"I am sorry. But you must understand, it's so unusual and…Well, can they really help? Are they what they say are they are?"

"Father O'Dowd. Please. This is not the time!"

O'Dowd hated questioning Father Reilly. He was a genuine and decent man and had been good to him. Plus, he was right, this had been discussed before and all was in place. Father Reilly continued. "Every 44 years for the last 1000 years this happens. You are now in place and so you must do your duty."

Father Reilly paused and then continued again but this time spoke more quietly, almost in a whisper.

"But this time they have the angel. The Archangel. This time we can defeat The Order for good."

O'Dowd trusted Father Reilly implicitly and knew what he had to do. It had been discussed many times, planned to the smallest detail and, as fate had played its part, Father O'Dowd was the person that this had fallen to. He knew there was no arguing. Father Reilly sensed the anxiety from his friend and spoke, to compose and reassure him.

"We have prepared you, my son. For the last four years you have learnt so much. The honour and duty that falls to you must be fulfilled. Now call them. They are waiting. They can help. It's all been arranged."

Father O'Dowd then heard a click from the other end, so he put the phone down. He leant over to a drawer and opened it. He pulled out a mobile phone and a wallet, then from inside the wallet a piece of paper. He switched the mobile phone on and entered the number from the paper into the phone. Reluctantly he pressed the call button.

The ring tone sounded several times, then he heard a click. No voice came from the other end. At first Father O'Dowd hesitated but then spoke the words he had been told to speak, clearly and quietly.
"If anyone does not abide in me, he is thrown away like a branch and withers; and the branches are gathered, thrown unto the fire, and burned."

There was silence at the other end. Father O'Dowd grew even more anxious. His words had triggered the 'happening' and there was now no going back. He heard a click, and the call was terminated. He was now to wait for further instruction which, he was told, would be immediate.

He had entered a world he didn't understand and neither did he want to. From his first conversation about it with Father Reilly all those years ago up to now he had dreaded the thought of it. The chances of him being here when this happened were slim. He always knew that. But it had happened. And there was nothing he could do now. Nothing he had learnt could've prepared him for it. Much of it, he didn't even believe. He had hoped for so long it would all be fantasy and myth. But he knew deep down it wasn't. And now he was playing a central part to it.

The day he got the phone call from Father Reilly to tell him, "The Archangel has been found," was a day that would live with him for the rest of his days. Up until then, despite Father Reilly's numerous talks and warnings he still hoped it wouldn't happen. Why had it been this place? And why when he was here? Why him? He had asked himself the same questions so many times.

He stood, stretched his back and yawned. He had not slept well for a few weeks and last night was no exception. It had been a long tiring day, but he knew nervous anxiety would not allow him to sleep again tonight. He would lay thinking, worrying about how this was going to play out.

The phone beeped and dragged him from his thoughts. A small envelope symbol had appeared, so he opened it:

'Father O'Dowd. I will be arriving within a week. I will be with the Archangel. Exact meeting details to be confirmed. Do not reply and delete this message. Odin.'

Chapter 12

It was late. Tom had switched all but one of the lamps off. A soft gentle glow lit one half of the room. They had sifted through the documents and devised an extraction plan for the portal, a teenage boy called Mikey.

The documents had advised them on a strategy which was to use the Boston Red Sox game as cover. The streets around Fenway Park would be busy with crowds attending the game and so it could be used as a distraction, allowing them to melt into the crowd and hide in plain sight. They had selected a bar called Tony's near the stadium, which was frequented by Red Sox fans, so it would be busy. This would be where the contact was made. It was Tom's job to explain to the portal what the situation was and what was going to happen. They had decided that Laura would be close by to gauge the situation and, if Tom got the portal on their side, he would give her a sign to go and warn the driver they were on their way.

She would also be Tom's eyes and ears outside of the conversation he would be having. The amber alert was still on and so if she spotted anything unusual, or anyone which she believed to be from The Order, she was to alert Tom, break up the conversation and all of them were to get out.

The Network gave one specific order. If you have to choose between yourself and the portal, then choose yourself. Do not sacrifice yourself. The purpose of this was that The Network found it more useful to have experienced, trained agents as members. If there was no hope of getting the portal out, then leave. Every agent hoped they would never be in that situation. It was harsh but was the brutal reality of the situation.

The extraction time would be about half an hour before the game starts so Tom and the portal could move within the crowds outside going into the stadium. They would then divert to the meeting point where Laura and another agent would drive them out of the city to the safe house.

However, these things could never be planned exactly. Tom and Laura discussed their first meetings with Odin and how they felt at the time. They recalled all the questions they had asked him and the things he had said and done to assure them. Tom also recalled how his own reaction and questions had eventually forced Odin to give him an ultimatum; come with me now or go on your own.

They knew that this was not an exact science and they couldn't account for how the portal may react. This was the most difficult part of the plan. Trying to judge how long this meeting would take was almost impossible.

Then they discussed the final part of the plan. A safe house had been selected and this would be where they would hole up for the night, then at 10am the next day the portal was to be taken by a Network contact to his first accommodation. Once the plan had been set and they had gone over it a few times the conversation had reverted back to them and their situations.

They had laughed out loud at times at the absurdity of it all. And it had felt good to be able to see the funny side of it. But Laura had also cried at missing her parents and Tom had comforted her. As they talked, they connected even more and strengthened the bond that had been created between them.

The table in the corner of the room was littered with empty boxes of Chinese food and two empty bottles of wine. Tom lay on one side of the bed while Laura sat up with her back against the headboard. He had been telling her about his mediation in more detail and how much comfort it had brought him. She listened to every word, noting the genuine emotion from him as he spoke. There was a moment of silence and then Tom spoke again. "I could teach you."

"You said it had taken you months and months to learn and develop. We don't have that time."

Tom knew he had got carried away and that she was right. When they had devised their extraction plan there had been an awkward moment when they had reached the part where the portal was then taken from the safe house. They had both realised that the next step would be to go their separate ways, wherever The Network sent them. Tom knew they didn't have time and their circumstances did not allow for them to be together and develop their relationship the way he wanted.
"I missed you when we finished the training."
Tom informed her, not really knowing why he had said it other than just stating a fact.
"Me too," she replied with genuine affection.

Tom shifted his body around and took her hand. She gazed into his eyes knowing what her body wanted but she couldn't allow herself to follow her instinct and emotions. She had thought this moment would come at some point and, in some way, had been hoping it would happen. But, deep down, she knew it would cause more harm to her than good. She stood up and put her wine glass on the bedside table.
"I need to freshen up. Is there a shower? Towels?"
She realised that her sudden change in attitude had confused Tom, but she needed to protect herself and knew it was for the best.
Tom quickly stood, embarrassed but trying to hide it.
"Yeah…Of course…Just down the hall on the right. Shower, bath…There are towels in there."

She smiled awkwardly and went to her backpack and retrieved a small wash bag from inside then left the room.
Tom sat down. He was angry with himself for inadvertently pushing her into a difficult situation. Although he was surprised by what she had done, he couldn't be too hard on himself. He thought he had read the signs correctly.

He got up and cleared the table. Clearing the empty food boxes into the brown bags they all came in. He then put the bags and wine bottles by the door to be taken out the next morning.

It had got stuffy in the room, and so he opened the window. The fresh air blew in and felt good. He scanned up and down the street. It was very dark with odd lights on from different houses. There was a very quiet, gentle hum of traffic coming from a distance away and the odd sound of a car passing by every now and then. A dog barked from the yard of a nearby house and then it was quiet again.

All the talk with Laura had got him thinking. It was times like this that cemented how delicate his position was. This mild, calm night would be thrown into chaos instantly if The Order located him. His life, despite how he had adapted, was always on a knife edge. He was always in danger, never able to fully relax. How Laura and even the homeowner, Michaela, as members of The Network in their own ways, with their own duties, were in danger every day. Michaela, their parent at this time, constantly at risk by helping The Network and shielding people in her home.

In a split second the peace of the night could be broken by violence and death. Tom had a vision of the door being kicked in and armed men entering with their brutal mission to exterminate all three of them. He erased the images from his mind. The dog barked again. It was a warm night, and he would want to leave the window open.

He then thought about sleeping arrangements. He moved over to the sofa bed that Michaela had shown him when he first arrived. He opened it and pulled out the blankets then started to make the bed up. He would let Laura sleep in the main bed, and he would sleep on the sofa bed. It was comfortable enough. He sat and finished his wine, enjoying the peace.

Soon he heard a click and the door opened. To his surprise Laura came in with just a towel around her. Her hair was still a little wet but had been combed back. It reinforced to him how pretty she was. No make-up and her hair just swept back. She looked beautiful. She noticed that he had made up the sofa bed.

"Oh, thanks, you didn't need to…"

"No, this is where I am sleeping. You can have the bed…"

"No way!" she argued.

"Don't be silly. It's fine."

She smiled, confirming that she had agreed. She was tired. She sat down on the bed while Tom continued making the sofa bed up.

"I'm sorry," she said.

Tom stopped and turned to her, looking confused.

"For what?" he asked.

She took a deep breath and looked up at him.

"I do have feelings for you, Tom. It's just that…Well…I just don't want to get hurt anymore."

Tom screwed his face up, confused, and went across to her and sat down.

"I don't understand. What did I…"

"You haven't done anything," she confirmed.

She took his hand and held it in hers.

"Tom, before all this happened, I was so happy. My family were all happy. My parents were comfortable. My sister just married. And I was so in love. Engaged to be married to my teenage sweetheart. Up to then, we had lived a perfect life and our marriage was set to be a new chapter. Then it all went wrong. The nightmares, the strange coincidences and the deaths. Then it was just a blur. Next thing I know I am sitting in a seedy apartment in some shit hole of a town wondering what the fuck happened."

Tom nodded in acknowledgement, understanding her perspective, allowing her to continue.

"And then the hurt. The hurt that comes smashing into you like a freight train. That takes all the love you had for people and rips it out of your heart. The guilt and the pain. Knowing I am all alone, that I will never see them again. And the hurt of missing someone that you have fallen so deeply in love with. Knowing that because of you they are dead. Killed by some maniac for what? For some religious game…"

Her voice cracked and tailed off. She looked down at her lap and started to cry. Tom put his arm around her.
"You can't blame yourself. None of this is your fault…"

Laura sobbed, and he pulled her in closer to him. She put her arm around him and her head into his chest. She sat and cried for a few minutes and Tom just held her. She stopped crying and wiped her eyes then turned to face him.
"So…I can't go there again, Tom. I know once this assignment is over, I may never ever see you again and…I can't go through that, not again."

Tom understood. He recalled how depressed he had been. He had never known why but now he knew. Perhaps it was all the pain, the grief, the loneliness and the guilt. As Laura had said, all hitting you at once, like a freight train.
"But you don't need to apologise for anything. Not to me especially. I understand."

Tom gazed into her eyes and, despite all she had just said to him, it was a look that was contrary. It was a look of vulnerability and of someone that needed comfort. She leaned into him and kissed his lips gently. She had obviously been trying to talk herself out of it, fearing that what she had experienced in her past would happen again. But because of what she had just said Tom hesitated, not sure what to do. She kissed him again but more intimately. Tom lifted his hand and caressed her cheek then moved his head back.
"Are you sure?" he whispered.

She sat up and undid the loose knot at the top of her towel allowing it to slip to her waist. Tom touched her shoulder and moved his hand down her arm, then slowly across to caress one of her breasts. He felt her body shiver as they kissed and lay down on the bed.

As they made love, each touch was electric. The situation, and the danger they were in, heightening their senses and pleasure. Eventually, as she arched her back with Tom deep inside her, they orgasmed in unison and the only thing on their minds was the present and the lust that overwhelmed them both.

Chapter 13

Tom woke. It was still dark. He leant over and picked up his phone and noted it was 3.36am. He was thirsty and needed to pee. He sat up and made out Laura's slender back on the other side of the bed as she slept. He left the room to go to the toilet and have a drink. He felt a little groggy, so he splashed water across his face. As he got back into bed, he noticed Laura move and her hand pat the bed behind her, feeling for him.

He moved his body close into hers, shifting his left arm under her head and his right arm around her body. She took his hand and held it into her bosom. It was peaceful and they lay motionless for several minutes. Then she turned her body and arched her head to face him.

"Did you ever find out if you were special?" she whispered, surprising him with her line of questioning.

"Special?" he replied, confused.

"Yes, special. You were the last to arrive at the training camp and before you got there Odin told us that you were different...Special."

Tom pondered for a moment.

"Well, my Mom always told me I was special...But who's Mom doesn't say that to their kid? And Rutherford, who I spoke about, he also said similar things...But...Well, I just put it down to me being an angel. But you are an angel too. So, aren't we both special?"

"I suppose so," Laura replied and then paused, "but...there was another thing...Odin told us that you done something that he had not seen any other angel do."

"Like what?" Tom asked, although he had an inkling that he may already know.

"Oh, he just mentioned he had seen the power you had."

Tom recalled the night at the warehouse in Pittsburgh. The light and the heat, the electricity and rising up above Rutherford and the fire transmitting from his body. He also recalled that he omitted that part on the first night of the training camp when they all sat around and told their stories. He was not sure why he had omitted it. Although he recalled how at the time, he didn't want to appear superior to the others and had already spoken for an hour, so he felt that he didn't want to take up most of the time with just his story.

He then told Laura, in detail, about that moment in the warehouse. He explained the sensation, how the heat suddenly rose from within him and, at first, scared him but then how he felt powerful and in control of it until he struck Rutherford down. Then falling to the floor. He told her about what Odin had told him afterwards. That it was 'beautiful' and how he had been 'mesmerised'.

"Has it ever happened again," Laura asked.

"No. I just felt it was a moment in my life where I sensed it was the end. Rutherford was seconds from killing me when it happened. I was almost gone. He had been screaming at me to 'show him' but I never knew what that meant."

"It sounds like he knew. That he was forcing it out of you."

"Maybe," replied Tom, "who knows?"

"Rutherford knows," Laura replied confidently.

"Yeah, wherever he is. And I hope I never find out."

There was a silence.

"There is another thing." Laura whispered as she leant up and caressed his face, "Something Odin said, again before you arrived."

"Oh?"

She took a deep breath, "He told us to watch you. And be guided by you."

"What?" Tom quizzed, lifting himself up onto his elbows. Laura did the same.

"He said…Let him lead you. If you feel like quitting, then use Tom as your strength. Use the strength that flows from him."

Tom was stunned. He had no idea. He hadn't known any of this and had no clue what this meant.

"Let Tom lead you - were his words. One day he will be your leader – was what he said."

Tom shook his head and lay back down, staring at the ceiling.

Why had Odin not told him any of this?

"I had no idea."

"I realise that now. At the time, I thought you knew. I had wondered, but then it had dawned on me that you didn't know. You never overtly acted like a leader or a guide to us. But...Well...I can tell you first-hand that you pulled me through at times."

"How?" asked Tom, surprised at what he was hearing.

"Just... At times when it got to tough, I would just watch you. Your focus and determination had such an influence on me. And, at other times, when I got too tired and was unable to go on, I would just get close to you. And you would give off a strength, a power...I can't explain it, but it felt like I was being energised. Almost like a mobile phone being plugged into its charger. You gave off a warmth...A flow of positivity."

Tom was stunned. His mind racing. Laura then sat up, appearing excited by what she was saying.

"Others felt it too. Everyone who completed the training felt it. We all noticed the change in you. And as the days and weeks went by and you got stronger and learnt more, so did we. We fed off you. Without you we would not have completed it...I am certain of that."

There was another silence. Laura lay back down on her back also staring up at the ceiling.

"I felt it last night too."

She leant across and kissed his lips. Tom felt immediately aroused and moved in closer. He kissed her lovingly and pushed her head back down to the pillow with his. He then pulled his head back and they stared at each other.

"When you were inside me. I felt it more than ever," she whispered.

She turned her back to him and shifted her body into his, offering herself to his arousal. Tom felt a surge of lust and positioned himself close enough then slowly eased himself inside her. For several minutes they were connected, not just by love and a moment of lust, but something more important. As she felt the sexual feeling inside her, she also felt a higher, more spiritual sensation. A surge of emotional power that transported her to a place beyond earth.

Shortly after, they climaxed and their deliberately subdued groans of pleasure came together, then they settled. And as their breathing calmed, they lay in unison and fell back to sleep.

Chapter 14

The sound was so loud it immersed everything. A chorus of tweets and chirps from hundreds, if not thousands, of birds, roosting in the pine forest behind them. Ahead of them an open stretch of grass that swayed in the summer breeze. Beyond that, rock formations covered in moss and ivy sat close to the edge. An edge that sat on a drop of roughly a hundred feet down to the forest below. Through the rocks meandered a stream that flowed to a waterfall cascading into the pool below.

The air was filled with the smell of pine and, although it was warm, there was also a fresh, cleanliness to the air carried by the mountain breeze.

Tom lay on the blanket with his head in his mum's lap. They laughed as they watched Claire and his dad larking around on the grass, playing tag and wrestling. His dad then lay on his back with his legs and arms upright and Claire attempted to lay flat on his feet and hands, wobbling as they fought to get her balanced. It ended up with them toppling and falling to the grass in a heap.

Tom's mum got up and stood over him, beckoning him to stand. He stood and took her hand. They walked over to where Claire and Tom's dad lay on the grass and she beckoned them also. They both stood and joined them, holding hands, they all walked to the rocks and the edge beyond. As they approached, the bird song got quieter as it began to be drowned out by the pool below which churned and frothed as water from the stream above continuously pounded into it after its long fall.

As they got close to the edge, they sat on a large rock. The sound coming up from below was like a thunderous roar that became the only noise they heard. They gazed ahead, to the far side of the green, pine covered mountain. A rainbow shimmered as the sun reflected into the wet air and drizzle that drifted above the water.

They stared out for several minutes. All holding hands, their love connecting and flowing through them from one to the other.

Eventually, Tom's mum let his hand go and he knew it was time. It was disappointing as always, but he felt confident that he was extending his time with them at each session. This time he felt as though he had been with them for hours. His mum smiled and walked away. He turned the other way, and his sister and dad were walking away and looked back affectionately.

As they got further away, they came together and all three held hands and walked towards the pine trees. He always felt an urge to go with them when they left but something, deep down, held him back. He knew it was not right to follow them as he felt it would lead to something upsetting. So, he always did the right thing and held his ground, waiting for them to disappear.

They reached the pines and waved. Tom waved back. He felt love flowing through him and, suddenly, as they went into the trees a flash of lightning splintered the sky above him and, instantly, all around him was dark and cold. The rain battered into him and a shiver buzzed through his body. Then ahead of him on the hill, was the dark building, much clearer now, and so, this time, Tom was able to confirm it was a church. Old, decrepit and sinister. A place of deep, dark secrets of which Tom felt its ominous presence.

The wind lashed across the hill pushing him back and making him lose his footing. He regained his balance and, instinctively, set off up the hill towards the church. But this time, he felt the presence of others, either side of him, two men of whom he was unable to make out their features. But he felt a warmness to them, a connection. He felt that they all had the same goal.

They all made their way further up the hill as the rain and wind did its best to prevent them but then, from behind, came an evil presence. Tom spun, a figure approached, dark, focussed and with its intent on preventing them from going any further. A woman.

Tom studied her face and her features were blurred. But he noted her red hair. She filled him with dread and then, in an instant, the vision changed back, and he was standing, staring at the lush pine forest which his family had just disappeared into. He looked back out across the vast valley in front of him and sat down. Gradually the image faded and, soon after, he opened his eyes and was in the room with Laura who was sitting on the bed staring at him, smiling.

"Hello stranger," she quipped.

Tom took a deep breath. He blinked and arched his back to stretch. Laura moved from her position to the edge of the bed and sat upright.

"How was it?" she asked.

"Good," Tom replied.

"Good? Just good?"

"Well, OK, it was amazing."

Tom then proceeded to tell her about the vision. The landscape that surrounded him and his family, what they did together and his feelings and emotions. Tom also told her that he felt like he was with them for hours, but she confirmed that he had been in deep mediation for about half an hour or so.

"It's an amazing ability. It must give you so much comfort,"

"It does…And I am sure I can teach you. You can get the same comfort. You just need to learn and then develop it from there."

Laura smiled politely, but she knew deep down they would never have enough time together.

"Maybe, one day."

She got up, crossed to the window and opened it wider. It had been a warm day and the late afternoon humidity had created a musty atmosphere in the room. She looked at Tom and noticed he appeared to be deep in thought.

"You OK?" she asked, leaning back on the bay window.

"Huh? Oh…Well…There is something. It's the visions. As good as they are, the last three or four have been interrupted. I see another place, always the same place, but it's not a place I want to go to or that I direct myself to. I have no control. It just appears in a flash."

Laura showed concern in acknowledgement of Tom's comments as he continued.

"It's weird. Each time it gets progressively more detailed. At first it was just a building in a storm, at the top of a hill. Then I realised it was an old church. And now I am with two men. We are heading up the hill towards it. In a storm and we are being battered by the wind. I…Well…I don't know where it is or why I am there. It seems to come towards the end of my time with my family. It flashes into view and I am at that place, then suddenly back where I was."

"And you do not recognise the place or the church?"

"No. But I feel like I might have been there before. Or seen it before. But it's not a nice place. I am anxious and afraid when I'm there."

Laura shook her head. Then spoke again.

"It could just be from a film or a place that you have read about in a book and it's in your mind, just somehow finding its way into the vision?"

"But it has only started happening recently. I had plenty of visions prior to that which weren't interrupted."

"But the human mind is complex. You are delving into a realm that even now we know so little about."

"Yeah, you are right," Tom concluded as he stood up.

He walked over to where she sat on the bed and kissed her head. He sat down next to her and held her hand.

"There is one other thing though. There is someone else at that place."

Laura turned to him as he continued, "It's a person that approaches at the end. I can't make them out. But…I know this sounds strange; I think it's a woman. It's just a feeling I get from her presence. But she's dangerous, and totally focussed on me. All I can make out is her hair. It's red. Almost blood red."

Laura noticed Tom appear unsettled.

"Well, don't worry too much. It's just a vision. It could be anything. As I said, something in your mind that is finding its way in. You read a lot, is she a character from a book?"

"I don't know."

"Someone you have met before?"

Tom shrugged, "No. Not that I am aware of," he replied, "but whoever she is, I don't like her. She scares me."

Chapter 15

Agent 7 was relaxed. She lay naked on the bed in the hotel room which over-looked Copley Square and the imposing grandeur of Trinity Church.

Everything appeared to be in order. She had made all the preparations that she could and so now it was just a waiting game. Waiting until tonight when she would venture out to end this assignment and get back to Moscow. The place she loved.

She had just finished a phone call with Kane. At the start of the assignment, he had ordered her to check in every three days. It was not normal protocol for someone like him to speak directly to agents. There was an intricate system for communication flow within The Order and having a direct line to someone of that status was unusual. Kane was Lord Ganlar's personal advisor. All information and direction from the Council went through Ganlar to Kane and then to 'Statesmen' who were in place to move agents around like chess pieces. But she had direct contact to Kane and so, technically, direct contact to Ganlar.

She knew there were people even above Ganlar, but the upper echelons of The Order were shrouded in secrecy. She was the first agent to ever have personal contact that high up. But she was no ordinary agent and Kane had emphasised the importance of this assignment during their brief calls. He had made it very clear to her, several times, that the death of the portal 294574 is essential to the continuance of The Order's work. Even to its long-term existence.

He had advised her that Ganlar and the Council had been happy with her progress. She had advised him that she had obtained the position of the portal and was due to make contact with the lead agent from The Order who had details of when and where, later that night, they were set to pounce.

Once she had this information it would only be a matter of time before she would ring him with news of the assignment's completion. As she had spoken to him, she had a vision of the portal's head being put into a box and delivered to Ganlar. She smirked. She always liked to please her superiors.

She had finished by informing that she would ring him around midnight local time to confirm. Although she had been a little offended by Kane's tone which intimated to her that he was not quite as confident as she was. It was just a hunch, he had not said anything particular that told her this, but it added fuel to her burning desire to get the job done. She would prove to him and Ganlar, once and for all, that she was the best and no assignment would be beyond her. No assignment up to this point ever had been.

She felt like lighting a cigarette but knew she had to go onto the balcony to avoid the smoke alarm. She had one last call to make. She picked up her mobile phone and dialled a number. The tone at the other end rang a few times and then clicked.
"Yes?" came the voice.
"Is everything ready?" she asked.
"Yes, we don't have eyes yet, but we know where we can pick the portal up. Once he is close to the city, we will tail him. Once he meets with the new portal, we will make a move on them both…"
"I am not interested in the new portal. I am only interested in portal 294574. Nothing else matters."
There was a pause.
"Do you understand?" she asked abruptly.
"Yes, Agent 7. I understand," the agent replied, hiding his frustration.

His job was to recover the new portal and he feared that Agent 7's own assignment would get in the way. However, if it did, then he had an excuse to give to his superiors within The Order. Although, they weren't particularly caring of excuses. He didn't like it. It made things a little complicated.

"Make sure the weapons I asked for are brought to my hotel room before tonight," she ordered.

"Yes, Agent 7, it's all prepared" he confirmed.

"A Glock 43X and hunting knife?"

"Yes, Agent 7."

"Good," she finally confirmed.

There was another pause and the agent at the other end felt a little intimidated, but Agent 7 then spoke, clearing the silence.

"One more thing…Portal 294574 is mine. Do you understand?"

"Yes, Agent 7, I underst…."

She had terminated the call before he finished. She took a deep breath and put the phone on the bedside table. Now she would wait. She was good at waiting. It was a big part of her job. Wait, wait and wait. Then move. Then kill.

But she had planned something to fill the wait and to fulfil her needs. She checked the time. He was late and she felt frustrated. She hated a lack of punctuality. She picked up her cigarettes and went out to the balcony. The fresh breeze washed over her. She sat and lit a cigarette. She was too high to watch people, but she enjoyed the view of the city. She smoked her cigarette and soon there was a knock. She stubbed out the cigarette and walked to the door to check through the peep hole. It was the man she had ordered. She opened the door and stood there naked.

"You are late," she notified him.

"Oh…Sorry…Traffic was heavy y'know…It's busy out and…"

"Come in," she ordered, oblivious to his explanation, "get undressed, clean yourself and get on the bed."

The young man was taken aback but did exactly as he was told. When he came from the bathroom, he looked over at her on the bed. She was already touching herself intimately with one hand and holding a condom packet in the other. She felt his presence, so she opened her eyes.

"Come. Join me," she ordered calmly.

Across the city, Ano Tora's phone rang. He put his book down and picked up his phone.

"Yes."

"I have just spoken to her. It's all set," confirmed the agent at the other end.

"That's good. Ring me half an hour before you move."

"OK."

There was a pause and after several seconds the agent continued.

"Look, it's important it appears you have acted alone. If there is anything that makes it look like I am involved…"

"Do not fear." Ano Toro assured him, "I am a professional. I will make my move when I am ready, and it will surprise everyone. Even you."

"I appreciate that. But, it's just that, you know the risk I am taking…"

"A risk that we have paid you handsomely for, yes?" Ano Tora interrupted.

"Well, yes, but…It's dangerous…"

"Life is dangerous my friend," replied Ano Tora calmly, "Just stay focussed and do what I have informed you to do. I will do the rest."

There was another pause. Ano Tora sensed the agent had more to say but waited and didn't prompt him. As he had assumed the agent spoke again.

"Another thing. I don't want this to sound like you can't handle it but…Well…You will need to move fast."

"Oh?" queried Ano Tora, "And why do you say this?"

"Well, the agent they have sent to kill the portal. She's…She's good. We are surprised they have sent her. She is very dangerous."

"Ah, my dear friend, I appreciate your concern. But I am 'The Tiger' and I did not gain this name through myth. But a reputation built over many, many years. Just be concerned with what you have to do. I will be fine."

And with that, he ended the call and resumed reading.

Alex started at him from across the room. His eyes wide open. But he saw nothing. Nor did he hear or feel anything. His mouth gaping and his body slumped in the chair.

Alex had asked questions about the person that Ano Tora was seeking and who he had been meeting. Ano Tora had ignored him at first but Alex had then stated that his bosses were starting to show an interest. He said they wanted to meet.

Ano Tora didn't like people interfering with his business. The Dallas mob had no reason to be interested in this. It was obvious that they were suddenly looking at how this situation suited their own interests. They had been employed by the Yakuza to act as a host and intermediary. No more than that.

The information had alarmed Ano Tora. And when Alex had made a comment about his bosses looking to secure more money for their services he had been unable to contain his anger further. He would not pay any more money. And he no longer needed Alex or the Dallas mob.

So, when Alex had turned to look out of the hotel window, Ano Tora had grabbed him from behind in a death hold. And in less than thirty seconds had put him to sleep by starving the oxygen to his brain. In his state of slumber and no ability to resist, it had been easy for Ano Tora to take Alex's head and, with one swift movement, snap his neck.

Ano Tora looked up from his book at the young man. He would need to dispose of the body at some point but he was enjoying his book. He would do it later. The hotel room was booked in Alex's name and they were seventeen floors up. Before he left he would drag the body out to the balcony and tip it over. Suicide. Good plan.

And with that, he returned to his book again.

Chapter 16

Tom and Laura had travelled quietly. They were on the coast road heading into Boston, approaching the road through Revere Beach. "I have made a decision and I want to know what you think."

Laura looked at him inquisitively. He didn't speak at first, eyes on the road, and she realised that he was choosing his words carefully. After a short time, he spoke.

"After this assignment I want to get away. Get away from The Network and all of this secret, underground life. It's too dangerous."

Laura was confused. It was a strange thing to say. It was not something she had ever considered. Although, like Tom, she didn't like her life on the move, creeping in the shadows, but she had adapted. She also felt she had no choice. But now Tom had sowed this seed in her mind, and she was unsure how to analyse it. As she pondered, Tom spoke again.

"I was hoping...Maybe with you."

"Look...Tom...I don't know..."

"Why?" Tom interrupted.

"It's...well...It's dangerous...I mean..." Laura stuttered.

"Yes, but I have learnt so much. I sense danger inside me and know when it's safe to move and when to hide. I have an idea of setting up way up in the north, being self-sustainable...Trapping and growing food..."

"Woah, Tom. You need to slow down..."

"Why? This is no life. We are nomads. Loners. Being told where to go, when to move and when to stay put. It's so unsettled. I have been thinking about it for a long time. And...Well...Last night with you made me realised *we* could have a life away from all this...Together."

Laura stared out the window at the passing houses and buildings. Thinking about their situation but unable to imagine what Tom was describing.

"Is it me? Do you not want to be with me?" asked Tom directly.

"No, of course that's not what it is. But you need to remember what The Network does for us. They keep us safe."

"Yes. But we don't *have* to do this. Odin told me we aren't prisoners. That the Network aren't a cult; they are a resistance. But they don't force us to be members…It's our choice."

Laura glanced at him and then back out at the window at nothing in particular. She knew what she wanted to say but didn't know how to say it. Instead, she tried another angle.

"But, recall how you were. How I was. Alone, confused. Scared. Without The Network we end up being pawns for The Order and then being killed at the end of it. This young man, Mikey, he will be feeling exactly the same. We have a responsibility…We have to help these people."

Tom nodded, "But The Network have other agents. It's growing all the time. Each angel it recovers has the potential to become another agent. Look at us. We did."

"Yes, I would agree with you, if you were talking about me or someone else but it's you."

Tom looked at her, "So? What does that matter?"

She shook her head, "Tom, seriously?"

He screwed his face up in confusion, Laura noticed, so she confirmed what she meant.

"The information that has been filtering out. That the angel has been located who can defeat The Order. An Archangel.".

Tom shook his head in frustration. It had started with Laura informing him that Odin had told the other angels before the training that he was their guide. Now he was being told this.

"I haven't heard this information!" he stated.

Laura laughed sarcastically and shook her head.

"Oh, I wonder why?"

Tom never replied.

"It's because it's you, Tom. You are the one. You are the Archangel, the leader, the one that will defeat The Order. It has to be."

Tom didn't know what to say. He knew he had changed. He was more focussed and intent. His ability to read books in such quick time. How fast he learnt. How confident he felt. His ability to meditate and use his visions. His acquired combat and survival skills. He didn't say anymore. The conversation hadn't gone as planned. He felt like he had been dropped further into this situation when his intention was to go the other way and get out.

Soon after, they stopped to get some drinks. Laura went inside and, whilst in the shop, Tom realised he had not yet sent the final confirmation text to the portal they were assigned to retrieve. He leant over and got his phone, opened a blank text and typed the following message:

'Mikey. Sorry for delay. I have selected a meeting place. Tony's Bar. Landsdowne Street. Be there at 7.45pm. Get a drink and wait. Do not reply and delete this message. Tom.'

He then pressed send to the number he had been given. As he was about to put his phone back, it bleeped. He cursed, hoping that Mikey had not replied. But when he checked, he had a text from another unknown number. He opened it:

'Tom. I need to meet you urgently – This is vital. After your assignment, go to Long Island tomorrow. Arrive at 2pm and wait for details of meeting point. Do not reply and delete this message. Odin.'

He suddenly felt anxious. He hadn't heard from Odin for a long time and then suddenly this text had come out of the blue. What on earth was 'vital'?

Laura got back into the car and handed Tom a drink. She noticed his face appeared disturbed.
"You OK?" she asked.

Tom just nodded. He never told her about Odin's message.

Chapter 17

The roads around Fenway Park were very busy. Tom had pre-empted this. Checking his watch, he was content they had left early enough to still be on time. Tom sat in the back and Laura in the front with their designated driver, who they had met at the pick-up point a short time before. They crawled through the traffic and eventually got close enough to Lansdowne Street where the bar was situated.

"This will be fine," Tom announced suddenly. The driver pulled over. Laura turned to face Tom.

"Good luck. See you in the bar soon."

Tom smiled. She looked good in her Red Sox cap. It suited her. He wanted to kiss her. He put his hand on her shoulder and squeezed gently and got out. The air was thick with noise. The smell of onions and sausages drifted through the streets. Horns were blaring, and the sounds of shouting and music, roars and clapping could be heard from the nearby stadium, that shadowed and overlooked all below and around it.

Tom slipped into the crowd and made his way up the street to the bar. He got inside and noticed, as predicted, that it was very crowded. Tom knew it would be on a game night. That was why it had been chosen. But as he walked in, it felt too busy. If, for any reason, they had to make a quick exit then it would be difficult and could get messy. But Tom quickly erased the issue from his mind. He couldn't change the plan now.

He politely eased through small groups of people, drinking and talking. It was loud with the heavy drone of chatter and laughter. There was an excitement and a jovial, party atmosphere in the place and Tom did his best to appear part of it when, in reality, he was focussed and on high alert.

He got closer to the bar and looked for Mikey. Tom had studied the photograph of him and knew he would recognise him, but he couldn't spot him.

The place had a large oval shaped bar with wide-screen TV's above it, so the bar was busy not just with people buying drinks but also standing watching sports. Tom found a small enough gap to manoeuvre into and eased himself in. He got $20 out and held it aloft to get a bar tender's attention.

As he waited, it gave him an opportunity to scan the perimeter of the bar. He checked left and right but was unable to spot him. Suddenly he saw a person move from the bar, but it wasn't him. He then noticed Laura also move into the bar and that she had also checked the same man out. They caught each other's eyes and then both quickly averted their gaze. Tom realised that he may appear too serious, so he smiled and glanced up at the TV above him. It was showing highlights of the Dodgers v Athletics. Tom pretended to be interested, but nothing was registering accept the frustration at not being able to see Mikey.

It was now 7.45pm. The time he had said he would arrive and meet Mikey at the bar. Tom realised he may just be late, so he settled and waited. A bar tender approached and pointed his finger at Tom. He ordered a Coors Light. As Tom was waiting for his drink another man with friends tried to ease into the bar. Tom acknowledged him and shuffled over. His drink arrived and he paid. He took a sip. It refreshed him. He barely drank these days but enjoyed the odd one now and then. He thought it best to try and fit in, so it was a good excuse.

He scanned the bar again, not trying to make it too obvious, and, like before, couldn't see Mikey. He thought ahead and went over the plan. He was hoping to, at the very least, have seen Mikey by now and that he would be weighing up his options on how to approach. He sipped his beer and checked the TV again then focussed back on the bar, this time he concentrated harder. But each face, either watching a TV, talking or laughing with another person or drinking a beer was not the one he wanted. He then noticed a man speak to Laura who politely said something back and shook her head. The man smiled, shrugged and walked away. He noticed Laura scan the bar again.

Mikey wasn't at the bar. What would Odin do? How long would he give? He remembered when he first met Odin, he had been later than him and Odin was just having a drink and waiting. He decided to relax and do that. Just stay calm, have a drink, and walk around without appearing suspicious. He moved away from the bar and to the outer area which, although busy, was a lot easier to navigate through. Their plan had been that Tom was the key person and so it wasn't his job to keep tabs on Laura. It was her job to keep tabs on him. So he knew that moving away would be fine.

He sipped his beer and checked his watch as if to intimate he was killing time before the game. Looking to the right he spotted the toilets, so he headed for them to search there. If he spotted Mikey inside, he would either leave and wait for him to come out or follow him out and then make contact. He went inside and the toilets weren't too busy. A few guys at the sinks talking about various Red Sox players. He checked the cubicles and one was closed and the other two were open. He shuffled into the end cubicle, leaving the door open and downed his drink. He put his bottle on the cistern and started to pee.

As he finished, the entrance door of the toilets slammed open, Tom grabbed his bottle by the neck and held it ready. Glancing behind he saw a large man, with a Red Sox cap on, shuffle past on his way to the urinals. Tom put the bottle back down. He wanted to see who came out of the cubicle next to him, so he waited, pretending to pee. And soon after, he heard the lock click, the door open and footsteps. He eased out of his cubicle to look. It was Mikey.

But to his surprise Mikey rushed to the door and left the toilets. He wanted to shout after him, but he needed to be careful. He didn't want to stand out or alert anyone to his presence. So he followed, but when he got back into the bar, he noticed Mikey making his way through the groups of people. He appeared afraid and anxious as he headed for the exit.

Tom rushed, easing his way around people as quickly, but as inconspicuously, as possible. He didn't want Mikey to leave the bar as he would have to make contact outside and that was not deemed as good protocol. It was dangerous. Tom remembered the amber alert on the city. The Order could be anywhere.

He had to be quick. Mikey glanced back as if to check for potential followers but didn't notice Tom approaching from behind. Just as he was about to make a move for the exit Tom noticed Laura move in and bump into Mikey. He tried to go around Laura, but she moved the same way and for several seconds they did the awkward dance. Laura laughed and apologised. But it gave Tom enough time to approach and he grabbed Mikey's arm. Mikey jumped and turned with concern on his face. Tom acted on instinct and said the first thing what came to mind.
"Where are you going, man? It's too early to leave."
As he spoke Laura evaporated back into the crowd, but he became aware of a security guy at the main door was staring at them. Tom made another attempt calming him and trying to tell him he should go with him. He showed him his watch.
"Game's not for another hour or so. Let's get a drink."
"I need to go," Mikey replied anxiously. Tom grabbed his arm tighter.
"No. Let's get a drink and talk."
The security guy made his way over.
"Is everything OK, guys?"
Tom weakened his grip on Mikey's arm, "Yeah man, he's from out of town, his first game. We just got separated."
The security guy glanced at Mikey to confirm this was correct. To Tom's relief Mikey nodded.

"Er…Yeah…Just got separated," he confirmed unconvincingly.
Tom turned and faced the bar.
"Let's get another drink!"

The security guy smiled and left them alone. Mikey followed Tom
who had slowed, allowing him to catch up.
"Follow me. And stay calm." he ordered.

Tom spotted a gap in the bar on the far side, so he made his way
through the people again, checking that Mikey was following. It
hadn't been the smoothest meet but at least he had now made
contact. They both shuffled and navigated their way around to the
far side and Tom headed to the gap in the bar. As he got there, he
looked up at one of the TV's and a bartender approached.
"Two Coors Light" Tom ordered.
"Oh…No…I don't drink," Mikey advised him.
"Shhh…You do now."
As their drinks were being collected Tom checked behind him and
noticed a pool table at the far end which had a seating area and
some spare seats. It was as good a place as any to speak.
"Where the fuck were you going?" he asked, under his breath.
Mikey looked at him, taken aback, "I…I didn't like it. It's too busy.
I just freaked out…"
"You must follow instructions. Do not deviate from them, OK?"

Mikey nodded, but Tom was still concerned that he was too
anxious and edgy. They got their drinks. Tom told Mikey to follow
him and they made their way over to the seats. Two young guys
were playing pool, but Tom ascertained the seats near the table
were far enough away to have their discussion without anyone
hearing. As they approached, Tom nodded to the young guys in
polite acknowledgement and they both returned a nod.

Tom shuffled past the pool table and took a seat up on a raised
platform beyond it. There were people seated and standing, talking
but Tom felt it was discreet enough for a short chat. He didn't
want to be too long. As he sat, he scanned the area. To the left of

where they sat, a short distance away, there was a back door with a fire exit sign. It wasn't obstructed. Tom now knew there was two ways out, although, the fire exit would now be their prime means of escape if necessary. He also noticed that Laura had taken up a perfect position next to a juke box a few steps from the fire exit. He could get a visual message to her. Things were now set, and he felt more comfortable.

"Just be calm. Everything is going to be fine," Tom assured.

Mikey was frantic, "Look…What the fuck is going on?"

"I know things are weird for you right now…"

"Weird? Why the fuck am I even here? With you…And baseball, I don't even like baseball. I don't like sports. Why I am here? I need to go…"

Mikey was jittery and Tom needed to act fast. He leant in closer to him.

"You just need to sit, shut the fuck up and listen."

Mikey glanced around the bar.

"Don't do that," ordered Tom.

Mikey looked back at him. Tom continued.

"OK, as you might have guessed, I am Tom. Your brother made contact with us and told us that you were struggling with some issues. But we can help."

"My brother? Struggling with some issues?" Mikey interrupted, "My life is a fucking freak show. I have lost my job, my boyfriend, I can't sleep, I think people are following me and watching me. I mean, what the fuck? I moved to Boston a year ago and four people I have met have fucking died…Including my boyfriend's dad!"

Tom cut in, "I know. It's strange. But this is not just bad luck. It's planned…"

"My boyfriend started acting weird a few weeks ago. My fucking boss got so weird; I just couldn't work…I couldn't even get out of bed…"

Tom tried to speak but Mikey continued, cutting him off.

"I had an interview two weeks ago. It went well. Then the next day I got a call to ask why I hadn't attended. I told them that a Mr.

John Allen interviewed me but, hey, guess what? He fucking died the night before…I mean what the fuck?"

"OK. Stop! Just stop."

Tom held his hand up to Mikey's face. Mikey stopped talking. Tom realised now that he was not properly prepared for this. He wondered why The Network had not done more to prepare him. He had been given some advice which included a script of what to say. With some guidance about not taking too long, not deviating from the script, making it look like a friendly conversation and, worse of all, when to abandon the assignment if the portal compromises you. How the hell do you coach this? Each portal you meet is so different. They will react in such diverse ways. There isn't a manual for this type of thing.

Tom snapped his mind back to the conversation and tried to steer it back to the script.

"I am from an organisation. The Network. It's an underground resistance that helps people like you. I know what you have been going through…"

"How the fuck is my brother involved in all of this?" Mikey interjected.

"It's a little complicated but, somehow, he would've got a contact and made some arrangements. You are part of something that you don't understand. And you are in danger…"

"Look, no disrespect. You seem like a nice guy, but can you just cut to the fucking chase so we get can the fuck outta' here."

Mikey nervously glanced around again both ways, scanning the bar.

"Don't do that!" Tom warned him again. Mikey stared at Tom and shook his head. Tom knew he had to wrap this up and get Mikey to listen and then get to the car.

Tom took a deep breath.

"OK. Look at me. I am going to speak to you. Try to look like it's a fun conversation."

Mikey stared at him nervously.

"What has been happening to you is unusual, but it can all be explained. But there is no time for that right now. You are in danger. An organisation called The Order is using you and when they are finished, they will kill you. I can help you. I can get you into The Network and you can be protected by them. But you have to…"

"Why the fuck do they want to kill me? What have I done?"

"None of this is your fault. OK? You have to believe me. Anything that has been unusual or weird recently is explainable. And it will all be explained in time. But right now, I have a car waiting a few blocks away ready to go…"

"Whoa…Hold on…" Mikey cut in, "How the fuck do I not know you are those Order people…I mean, this is fucked up, man."

Tom glanced at the men playing pool and one of them looked over at them and then back at the table when he spotted Tom's glance. Tom maintained his calm approach.

"I promise you can trust me. Why would I know about your brother? He wouldn't put you in danger, would he?"

It resonated with Mikey and Tom noticed him calm down a little.

"I know this is hard. But the easiest way around this is for you to just be calm. Come with me. There is a colleague of mine in this bar also and she is just waiting for my signal. It's all prepared. I can get you safe and then all will be explained to you. I just need you to confirm you are with me, OK?"

Tom noticed the fear and confusion in his eyes. And he hoped that he would not have to go into more detail now. Trying to explain to Mikey that he was an angel now seemed impossible to do. He recalled when Odin had told him and what his reaction was. This was not an easy task, he now appreciated this. He also realised he could've been more helpful when he first met Odin.

"I haven't seen my parents in ages," exclaimed Mikey, "I tried to call them, but they aren't answering. My brother doesn't know where they are…"

Mikey was unsettled. Tom knew The Order might have got to them. But if Mikey knew that it would be devastating. Mikey took a sip of his beer. His face creased and it was obvious he didn't drink.

"I just want to know what's wrong with me?" Mikey asked.

Tom had to make a decision. Did he tell him the whole story? It may help, but it will mean at least another maybe 10 or 15 minutes in the bar. Which wasn't ideal. But it may also send him the other way and freak him out more. If Tom tells him he is an angel, it may be the final straw. He wasn't ready for it just yet.
"You are in danger. We both are. The Order are dangerous. Come with me now. I am your only hope of you getting out of this city alive. Once we are safe it will all be explained to you. I promise."

After a pause Mikey nodded. Tom glanced over at Laura and they made eye contact. He winked and Laura put her drink down and headed towards the main door. She would make her way to the car and alert the driver to be ready. Tom would follow up with Mikey shortly after and they would drive away.

Tom downed his beer. He was ready. He scanned the bar and was content that all inside were acting normally. Nobody stood out as suspicious. He was nervous and that nagging feeling hit him again. He tried to contain it. This wasn't about him. Mikey needed him to focus and do what he had promised. He took a deep breath.
"OK, in a minute we will get up and head to the main exit. Be calm, happy, as though you are heading to the game."
"I have never been to any game in my life so…"
"Just look calm then. Just don't look like I am forcing you to leave with me, OK?"
Mikey nodded.
Tom smiled and prompted Mikey to get up.
"OK, let's go."

Tom led the way and Mikey followed as they made their way through the bar. Tom discreetly glanced back a few times to make sure Mikey was still with him. As they got to the main door Tom stopped and allowed Mikey to catch up. He put his arm round him and spoke in his ear.
"Look like you are having fun."

Mikey glanced at him and smiled. It was unconvincing. He wasn't a good actor. Everything he did was half-hearted, but Tom knew it was the best he was going to get. As they walked out, the security guy from earlier checked them out.

"You going to the game?"

"Yeah!" replied Tom excitedly.

The man nodded politely and stepped aside, "Enjoy."

Tom winked at him. As they stepped out into the early evening, the cool air hit them making Tom realise how stuffy it was in the bar. Tom took a right diverting Mikey in the same direction towards the stadium. The walkways and roads were busy, and Mikey burst into a trot to keep up with Tom. Every now and then, Tom glanced behind to check that Mikey was still there and keeping up. They passed the Lansdown Gate and flowed with the crowds up to the main junction with Brookline Avenue.

Most of the crowd filtered left to make its way to the gates on the Jersey Street side of the stadium. But, Tom stopped, waited for Mikey to catch up, grabbed his arm discreetly and they filtered right, out of the main crowds, and along towards Brookline Avenue Bridge. Tom had studied their route over and over again, so he knew exactly where to go and what roads to take.

They made their way to Commonwealth Avenue and Tom became aware that there were no longer crowds to envelope and hide them, but they weren't too far away. They headed towards the huge Citgo sign and crossed Beacon Street, then walked down the alleyway which led to the meeting point.

"Almost there," Tom assured him.

They walked through and came out to a service area at the rear of some industrial buildings and apartments. There were parked cars dotted about and areas that housed waste bins and rubbish. It was quiet and suddenly their footsteps and Mikey's heavy breathing were now too loud. Tom turned to him.

"Just relax. Slow down. It's just up here."

Tom realised how difficult this must be for him. He didn't know Tom and here he was leading him into a back-alley service area at night. Mikey was petrified and confused. But he was glad he was keeping up and just holding it together. They passed some trash on the left and Tom knew he was close, and the meeting point was just at the next corner on the right. They approached it and walked around the corner and Tom spotted the car on the left, but something was wrong.

The passenger door was open. Tom felt a wave of nervousness. Mikey stood behind him, panting after the quick walk, waiting for instructions. Tom peered into the darkness and noticed the driver in the car waiting but nobody else. He put his hand behind his back and pulled out his revolver.
"What the fuck's going on, man?" asked Mikey nervously.
"Shhh," replied Tom, "Wait here."

Mikey moved to the side using the building as a shield. Tom approached with caution. He held his gun up and aimed at the car. Why was the driver not moving? Where was Laura? Tom thought she might not have made it back yet.

Tom now felt isolated. He sped up expecting the driver to wave or acknowledge him, but he didn't. Tom reached the car and swung himself towards the open door, leading with his revolver.
"Where's Laura?" he asked the driver, but he just sat, motionless, staring straight ahead.
"Hey, you OK?" asked Tom urgently.

Tom moved closer and lent inside. Then he noticed to his horror that the man was staring ahead but he was obviously not seeing anything. The bullet hole in his forehead had killed him. And a single trickle of blood snaked its way down the man's face and was now staining his shirt.
"Fuck!" cursed Tom, now feeling vulnerable.

He turned to Mikey who was peering around the corner, clearly scared. Tom moved away from the vehicle into the shadows of some crates. He got his phone out and scrolled down his numbers. He selected the number for Laura. He pressed call, desperately hoping she would answer. The phone rang at the other end but as it did, Tom heard another noise, a louder ring, coming from close to the car.

He scanned the area and noticed a light appear on the floor next to the car. His gut wrenched. He jogged across and saw a phone on the floor. He picked it up as it buzzed and rang. Desperation and anger rose up within him. But he knew he had to fight and control it. He stopped the call worried about the noise of the phone, knowing that The Order could be close, waiting to pounce. It could be a trap.

He put the phone is his jacket pocket and ran around to the driver's side and opened the door. There were no keys in the barrel. Tom checked the back and, to his horror, laying on the back seat was Laura's Red Sox cap.
"No, no, no…" he uttered to himself.

A feeling of helplessness washed over him, knowing that without her phone it was almost impossible to find her. But his training kicked in and he knew that the main priority was Mikey, who was watching and wondering what the hell was going on. He grabbed the cap and stuffed it into his other pocket.

Luckily, Tom still had the keys from the car they had used to drive in from Beverly. It was parked back down the alley way they had walked from. Tom got his head focussed. He knew at any time he may hear the noise of footsteps or a car as The Order made their move. He ran back and, as he approached, Mikey spoke.
"What's happening? I thought we…"
Tom just grabbed his arm, spun him around and rushed past him.
"Just fucking move!" he ordered.

Mikey hurried after him and Tom spotted the car they had travelled in from Beverly. He got the key out and pressed the fob to unlock. The car bleeped and the lights came on. Then they heard another car engine start further down, roughly fifty metres away. The headlights flashed on and pierced their eyes.

"Quick!" Tom shouted.

Mikey was now struggling to keep up. They heard the other car rev its engine and it suddenly screeched from its parking place, accelerating hard. Tom ran around to the driver's side.

"Get in! Now!"

Tom jumped in and put the keys in the ignition. The car started just as Mikey got in. Tom noticed the utter fear and panic on his face. He put it in gear and burst out of the parking space just as the other car reached their position. Tom looked in the rear-view mirror and the headlights approached fast then blinded him.

There was a sickening crunch as the car rear ended them. Metal crashed together. Tom and Mikey's heads jolted forward viciously. The rear end slid out and Tom gathered control and put his foot down, heading out of the service road and onto the main road. He had no time to stop and check for oncoming vehicles and barrelled out with a screech, turning immediately left.

There were cones, temporary fencing and site toilets on the opposite side of the road for road works. The car sideswiped them and with a bang and clatter, sending them all flying and crashing across the street. The car bumped as it rode over the temporary fence posts and both their heads bounced and hit the car roof.

"Shit!" shouted Mikey.

Tom threw a right and the back end of the car slid but Tom gained control and he pushed the power up.

"Buckle up!" he shouted.

Mikey's head and body were pushed back into the seat as Tom forced as much power into the engine as possible. The engine roared and Mikey held on for dear life.

Chapter 18

Tom powered through another red light. Instantly a car appeared from the right and Tom took evasive action, swerving to avoid it. The car screeched to a halt and, as they passed by only a few inches, the horn blared and faded as they sped away.

He checked the mirror hoping the manoeuvre would cause their pursuer to crash or, at least slow them down enough to gain an advantage. But Tom noticed the chasing head lights also swerve to avoid and then, with a surge of power, creep up onto their rear again.

Tom's mind raced with too many thoughts to contend with. His first and most important priority was losing the car behind. He hadn't been able to shake them off. With each random junction he took he had hoped if he slid smoothly and got the power down quickly enough, the head lights would fade away. But the roads were quite busy and whenever Tom felt he had got away something slowed him down and they caught up. He was now taking major risks and the horns blaring at him were increasing.

He also no longer knew where he was in relation to where he needed to be. The safe house Mikey was being taken to was in Cranston and so the initial plan was to pick up the road west out of the city but in the heat of the chase he had lost his sense of direction.

Although, with this unwanted development now unfolding, was the existing plan still possible? It may be that he needed to lose the pursuers and then hole up somewhere completely different until it was safe to reconnect with The Network and evaluate the situation. That is if he ever got to that point and, given that the pursuer kept surging into his rear-view mirror, this couldn't be taken for granted.

He was also unable to work out what to do about Laura. Was there a way to locate her? Should he go back to look for her? Did he just have to accept she was gone? He needed to contact The Network and get them to run a check on her GPS locator. But he didn't have time do that now. It would have to wait.

Tom knew if he lost the tail, he could get back to the Fenway Park area and search for Laura himself. Her cap being in the car meant she made it back at some point. She might have taken the cap off before something spooked her. Or she may have evaded The Order and was now searching for him. Although he felt a niggling doubt that this was very unlikely. And all agents were advised never to return to where they had already come from, especially if there had been an incident.

He felt a knot in his stomach as it dawned on him that his chances of seeing her again were slim at best. It unnerved him and he felt emotion hit him, but he contained it. He knew his first priority right now was Mikey's safety.

Tom spotted a sign which indicated that he was leaving downtown. He increased the power, swerving in and out of two slower cars, then he hit the steering wheel hard left, pushing the car into a controlled slide. The back end drifted out and Tom fought the wheel for control while Mikey grimaced as his body was pummelled into the passenger door. As Tom battled the under-steer, he glanced in the mirror and to his relief the pursing vehicle drifted into the junction with too much speed and it smashed into the parked cars lined along the road. The headlights bounced upwards, down again and spun, then they disappeared.

This was his chance. But he then noticed that the fuel was almost at the bottom of the red bar. They had driven this car into the city from Beverly but, as the plan was always to abandon it and use the decoy car to drive out to Cranston, they had not bothered to refill it.

He needed to find somewhere to lay low so he could stop, compose himself and think. Mikey needed calming down and some time to relax. Tom could then contact the support number, update The Network and hope they could run a trace on Laura's GPS to then send someone in to search for her. He could then fuel up and get out of the city to the meeting point.

"Is this how it was supposed to be?" asked Mikey frantically, breaking Tom's train of thought.

"Don't worry," Tom replied, "It's OK. We'll be fine."

But just as he had finished speaking, he heard a screech of tyres and out of nowhere, to the right, a black SUV suddenly appeared into view heading straight for them. With just a few feet to spare Tom accelerated and swerved out of the collision line. Mikey screamed and put his hands up in defence, expecting the hit. The SUV barrelled across the junction at speed, did a handbrake turn and spun back around in the direction Tom was travelling.

Smoke bellowed from its tyres, then it surged forward, back in pursuit. Tom powered off, hoping that he had enough of a jump on them to take another junction and then lose them. But to his frustration no junctions appeared and gradually the headlights got larger and brighter as it careered close to their bumper. Powerful and intimidating. Tom knew that on the straight he had no chance of outrunning it. And worse of all he didn't have the fuel to drive at this speed for too long.

Suddenly Tom and Mikey's heads were barged forward as the SUV hit their rear. Mikey screamed again. Tom tried to get more power from the car, but it was almost at full throttle. He veered to the left and then back to the right to try and prevent their pursuer from being able to hit them from behind. They hit traffic again and Tom was able to weave in and out and use the cars as a way of blocking the SUV but as he dodged in and out it followed, hard on their tail, mimicking his every move.

Then, on the left, Tom spotted a junction, but he was unable to take it due to other traffic being in the way. As they passed it, he then noticed the oncoming lane clear. Instinctively he swung the car into the oncoming lane, braking hard and yanking the hand brake up. The car skidded and the back end snapped around. In the blink of an eye, the car was facing the other way.

The SUV careered past as Tom hit the power and aimed for the junction. Tom saw the SUV hit the brakes hard. Cars crossing the junction flashed their lights and horns sounded as Tom flashed across their paths and off in the new direction. Mikey glanced over at Tom for some assurance, but it never came. He spotted the focus in Tom's eyes, so he just held on. Hoping the chase would soon be over.

Tom continued driving at full speed; even though looking back in his rear-view mirror it didn't appear that the SUV had managed to catch up with them. He forced the car hard left into a junction and then soon after another right. Hoping that his random directions would throw off his pursuers. He slowed to the speed of the other traffic. Trying his best to fit in. They approached a red light and Tom stopped in the queue, several cars from the light.
"What now?" asked Mikey, shaken and a little upset.

Tom never answered. His mind racing. He knew now he had to get out of the city. Up ahead he saw a sign directing traffic to the 93 and then south. That would be the road he would take. Then to his left he noticed a black SUV cruising along with the oncoming traffic. It slowed as it passed the queue they were sitting in. It may not be them, but he couldn't take a chance.
"Just look straight ahead," he ordered.

Mikey stiffened and did as he was told. Tom turned away, hoping they wouldn't see his face. He felt their presence as they passed, and he couldn't help but glance. The SUV sped up and suddenly did a handbrake turn. It was them and they had been spotted. Tom put the gear into reverse, hit the power and slammed into the car behind them, forcing it back and giving him room to manoeuvre out of the traffic queue. He forced the gears into drive and hit the power, screeching away.

He crossed the junction, swerving to avoid crossing traffic. He checked the mirror and to his dismay the SUV had already made ground on them and soon it was on their tail. Again, Tom used traffic to dodge in and out. Up ahead he spotted a row of three cars in a line and went for the small gap, hoping to get through before they block the way for the SUV. He careered through, clipping the side of one of the cars with a spark. But, to his horror, suddenly one the cars exploded forward with glass and metal flying in all directions. The car spun to the side and the SUV pushed into its rear, spinning it, then powered forward on their tail again.

Tom knew he would now have to take drastic action. He was almost out of fuel and he couldn't keep fleeing all night. He swerved and veered into the lane of the oncoming traffic. "What the fuck are you doing!" shouted Mikey.

Tom didn't answer. Head lights shot at them from different angles and Tom fought the steering wheel to avoid them. Blaring horns and lights came at them, flashing past as the oncoming drivers also swerved. The noise of the passing cars loud and scary. Tom accelerated harder. The engine roared louder. Mikey scrunched himself into a ball, pre-empting the inevitable collision.

Tom checked the SUV to his right in the correct lane and waited for his opportunity. But he needed to stay ahead of it. Headlights ahead of them flashed as drivers tried to warn them. Tom then veered past one truck that sounded its deep horn as it passed. Smoke bellowing from its tyres as it broke hard. They heard a smash as the car behind rear ended it.

Then he spotted his chance. The SUV was now directly adjacent to them and so, without warning, Tom careered back across the lanes, out of the direction of the oncoming traffic and headed for the SUV. He noticed the driver spot him and realise what Tom was doing. He saw the man shout and put his arm up in protection as Tom smashed into them side on. Mikey screamed and their bodies jolted violently as the sound of metal and steel crashing filled the air. The SUV was sent rocketing across the road and up onto the footway smashing into a set of newspaper stands. Glass, metal, and newspapers exploded into the air.

Tom got the car back into a straight line and accelerated again. He looked in the mirror. The SUV had stopped, but then jumped to life and then headed off again.
"Fuck!" he shouted, hoping it would have ended their pursuit. However, it had given him some distance to lose them.

Up ahead he spotted a series of industrial buildings, so he powered towards them, then drifted the car skilfully around the corner into the industrial area. He took the next right and noticed the traffic was less busy, and so he sped up. Mikey held on again, not able to believe that the car had more power. As Tom sped around the next junction, he spotted a flash of headlights behind them.

He hoped it was not the SUV, but he wasn't waiting to find out. He took two more junctions. A left and right, and eventually found himself driving down into a service area at the back of a row of industrial buildings.

He noticed that the needle on the fuel gauge was now resting fully on the empty pin, unable to get any lower. He knew now that he wouldn't be able to go much further even if he wanted to. He checked the rear-view mirror and there were no head lights, so he slowed suddenly and pulled into a row of parking bays and stopped hard, Mikey propelled forward putting his hands on the dash to prevent himself from hitting it.
"What the fu...!?" he shouted.
"Get out! Now!" Tom shouted back at him.

Tom got out and ran around to the passenger door and opened it before Mikey had even got his seatbelt off. Tom noticed him trembling, his face ashen grey. Tom knew he had to resolve this soon for Mikey's sake. He needed to get him to the safe house and handed over to the next person in The Network. How he was going to do this with no transport, he had no idea. He hoped that when he phoned the support number, they would get his GPS location and send some help.

Tom scanned the buildings, trying to find an entrance. There was fencing all the way along and then, at the end of the row, he spotted a stair well. He grabbed Mikey's arm and urged him forward.
"Come on, get to those stairs!" he ordered.

Mikey tried to run but didn't have a lot of energy left. Sapped by the confusion and fear that he was experiencing. They made it to the stairs and at the top of the four levels was a door. As he pushed Mikey up the first set of stairs, he heard a screech. To his horror a set of headlights appeared at the far end of the road. It was the black SUV.
"Fuck!" he shouted, "Get up the stairs. Now!"
He bundled Mikey up the stair well and noticed him labouring and breathing heavy.
"I can't…" Mikey pleaded.
"Yes, you can!" Tom shouted and grabbed his arm, pulling him up one by one, almost dragging him. Mikey held the stair rail to prevent himself slumping to the floor.

They eventually got to the top level as the SUV stopped next to their car below with a screech. They got to the door and Tom felt a sudden dread. If it was locked, they were trapped, and it would only be a minute or so before their pursuers trap them. They got to the door. Tom reached out to the handle and took a deep breath. He held it and twisted it. To his relief it clicked, and the door swung open. They had been given another chance.

He pushed Mikey through into the darkness, then eased his way in, out of sight. He stopped and turned then inched his head past the door frame to look back down at the street below. He heard doors banging shut and inaudible shouting. A man ran over to the car they had been in and pointed a gun at the window. Another man was in the road looking around trying to spot them.

Then one of the rear doors of the SUV opened. Tom watched as someone got out. To his surprise it was a woman. She moved around to the front of the car almost in a gliding motion. She wore all back and her hair was pulled back into a ponytail. Red hair. "The stairs!" she shouted, and the two men ran towards the stair well as she followed.

Fear flashed through Tom's body. It was the woman from his visions. He gasped. Although he had always known that she would eventually find him, he had hoped it would not have been so soon.

The visions of her had penetrated into his primal fear and he wasn't sure if he was ready. Although he knew he was about to find out.

Chapter 19

Beyond the outer door was a dark hallway. At the end, Tom spotted a tiny green light and a sign above a door, 'Authorised staff only'. He grabbed Mikey's arm.

"Go! Through that door" and he shoved Mikey towards it.

They burst through the door and into the main building, finding themselves on a four-metre wide metal platform that continued around the whole perimeter of the level. It was dark inside and low red lighting emanated from various points which allowed for limited vision. But quickly their eyes adjusted. It looked to Tom like it was a steel or metal factory. Beyond the platform in the central area were large finishing machines and conveyer belts that continued all the way across.

Through the caged walkway below, Tom noticed pretty much the same set up on the level below and all the way down four levels to the ground floor. It gave Tom hope. He could mingle in with the machinery, belts and pipes and try to surprise his pursuers.

Mikey was breathing heavily after ascending the outer stairs and Tom knew he had thirty seconds or so before the woman and her associates entered the building to hunt them down. He needed to get Mikey hidden and settled, then get himself somewhere to lay low. From there, he could assess the situation and make his moves. It was pointless trying to hide from them. Tom knew he had to be offensive and it would take all his learnt skills to turn the odds in his favour. It was going to be difficult. Three against one was not good odds. But Tom had nowhere left to run. Now was the time to fight.

Tom urged Mikey on, and they ran all the way to the far end before stopping at the corner. Tom looked back and the main door remained closed. He tugged Mikey and they ducked down behind a huge machine with metal pipes and ducting protruding up to the ceiling. He then noticed a door and a set of windows roughly ten metres along from their hiding place.

"Quick, in there," he whispered and pushed Mikey's back to get him to move as quickly as possible.

Tom got there first and opened the door. Inside was a standard office with a desk covered with various documents, a PC, a monitor and various charts and graphs on the walls. It was then Tom heard the main door into the building crash open. The sound echoed throughout the building and Tom knew he had only a few seconds.

"Get under the desk and do not make a sound."

Mikey was now trembling with fear and close to tears. Tom didn't hold much hope of him being quiet enough if the office was searched. He just hoped that if they did look inside, they would just scan it and move on. Luckily, Mikey complied, despite almost being overwhelmed with fear. He rushed into the office and scrambled onto his knees, got under the desk, then pulled the chair back as far under as it would go. Tom closed the office door quietly.

Tom spun and took a walkway which headed into the labyrinth of machinery. He moved quickly, knowing he had to make it to a central position to get a good starting point. Every few metres, he looked along different access routes leading back to the main outer walkway. He stopped and peered around the corner of a large machine. He spotted one of the men slowly walking along the outer walkway. He waited for him to pass and then continued into the centre.

There were lots of hiding places and areas to get out of sight. This was good for him. But it also made it more difficult as his pursuers could do the same. Tom knew this was going to be like a lottery. Your life decided by split second decisions on what direction to take, or when to move or stay still. Each decision and move you make could be your last. Suddenly, to his left, he heard the clanging of the walkway and realised that the men had split up, and that one of them had taken one side of the outer walkway and the other man had gone to the other side. It made sense. Like hunting dogs in a rabbit warren, they were trying to push their prey into a dead-end.

Next to Tom was a set of shelves. On the shelves were some tools and some nuts, bolts and washers. Tom picked up a nut and made his way over to a caged stairwell which led to the level below, treading lightly so as not to give his position away. Upon reaching the stairs, he crouched down and glanced across. He spotted the other man, just making him out, lurking in the dark red light.

Tom tossed the nut over the side and after a few seconds the sound of clanging echoed through the building. The man stopped and looked to the floor below. He ran back the way he had come, feet banging on the metal as he went. He disappeared out of view, but Tom assumed he was going back to the stairwell at the corner they had entered to check the level below. Tom's plan had worked. He had reduced the enemy temporarily. Now he had to take out the other man. But in the back of his mind, he was nervous about the woman. He had not yet seen her, but it did not mean she wasn't there.

Tom checked his surroundings again and made his way to where he would get a visual on the other man. He ducked behind a set of huge, thick pipes. He peered along the walkway. The man wasn't there. Staying crouched he shuffled along to the next walkway. A cage filled with waste metal stood next to him and he put his back to it and eased himself up. He heard a shuffle and the sound of a footstep nearby. He froze and controlled his breathing. Then another footstep, this time closer, only a few feet away. He looked left and slowly the front of a gun came into view, then a hand, then an arm and then a body.

Tom spun and lunged forward, grabbing the arm holding the gun, pulling it into his body. He raised his elbow and smashed it into the man's face, feeling a crunch as it landed. He twisted and got the arm in perfect position out front of him. With a flat hand he then powered down onto the elbow with all his force and felt the arm snap. The man screamed and the gun dropped to the floor with a bang.

Before the man gained an advantage, Tom grabbed his jacket and pulled him in and delivered a powerful and sickening headbutt to the face. Still holding his jacket, he then swept his feet from under him, the man toppled and hit the floor with a thud. Tom then raised a foot and smashed it down onto the man's jaw, his face jarring with a dull thud and then a snap. He bent down and raised his fist to finish him off, but the man was dead. Tom lifted the man's sleeve and checked his wrist. He saw the tattoo. A crude T inside an O. It confirmed he was an agent for The Order.

He heard a clanging sound and realised that the other man that he had tempted to the level below had heard and was now running back up. But where was the woman? He knew she must be somewhere inside the building. She may even be watching him right now.

Tom focussed and got his breathing under control. He worked out where the man had ascended. But then there was silence. Just the gentle hum of the machines and extractor units in sleep mode. Tom knew he could be silently making his way into the machinery and could come out anywhere and surprise him. He slid his gun from the back of his jeans. He took the safety off and cocked the hammer back with a click, trying not to make too much noise. "There!" he heard the man shout.
"He's mine," came a female voice. The robotic Russian accent made Tom go cold.

He needed to get off the level but now with two against him he didn't know which way to move. He was hidden, but he knew they were getting closer. Looking behind, he spotted an access leading from the machinery section to the outer walkway. He got up and made a move. He came to a crossroads and knew he had to take a

chance. He crossed and the sound of a gunshot rang out. A bullet slammed into the metal next to his head with a deafening crash, sending sparks flying. Tom ducked and then sprinted away.
Now that he knew his position was compromised, he no longer needed to be silent. The cage floor banged with each step and as he got to the corner another shot sounded. He felt the wind brush his shoulder. Sparks showered him as the bullet ricocheted into the metal pipes on the wall.

He made it to the main stairwell and rushed around the corner onto the stairs which were protected by a cage. He was safe from the bullets for now. He sprinted down the stairs and onto the level below. He saw the man running towards the top of the stairs, but Tom stopped. He watched him intently. The man looked across to the other side and made a sign with his finger pointing downwards. Tom looked across, trying to catch a glimpse of the woman but, again, failed to spot her.

Tom moved back into the maze of machines and metal, fighting his fear. He found a nook behind some pipes where he shuffled in, getting out of sight. It gave him time to calm himself and get his heart rate down. He was trained to maintain a low heart rate and control his breathing in any situation. But even with his training, he was struggling. It was also hot inside the building and the sweat was trickling down onto his face. He moved his arm up and wiped his head and face with his sleeve.

He heard a shuffle and a footstep. He edged his head out from his hiding place. Nobody there. He ducked back in and held his breath. He heard another footstep and lifted his gun up, so it was close to his face. He knew his position was a good one and that if he waited long enough, he would get his chance.

Then another footstep, closer, and then he felt a presence. From his hidden position his view was minimal, but he knew when whoever it was passed, they would have their back to him and be vulnerable. He froze. Not making a sound. And waited. He hoped it would be the woman.

He caught a glimpse of the man pass. Tom knew if the man checked behind the pipes, he was dead, as he was restricted and unable to get his gun aimed in the direction the man would attack from. He was a sitting duck. But he knew that if he gave it a few seconds the man may pass. But he also knew he couldn't wait too long, or the man would be engulfed by the dark red and would be out of view. Tom waited for a few seconds and silently shuffled out from behind the pipes.

He had to be decisive. When he stepped out it was all or nothing. He stepped out, raised his gun and aimed at the back of the man's head. The man sensed him and spun but the shot rang out and a thud sent blood and brain matter exploding up and the man fell to his knees and collapsed onto the floor.

Tom shuffled back into the section of pipe. The odds were much better now. However, Tom was concerned that there could be more agents on the way. His mind raced back to Mikey. The gunshots must've frightened him half to death. Tom needed to get him out. He knew he had to move. The woman may have figured out a location from his gunshot, and he wondered, if he could draw her to this point and then get to Mikey, get him out of the office and get out of the building, they had a chance of escape. If he could do it quietly then they could leave the woman inside searching for them. It was a slim chance, but it was the only chance he had. Plus, he knew it was better than facing her.

Tom stepped out and glanced left and right. He decided to make his way to the other side of the level as he had hoped she would be making her way across and they would pass on different aisles. If he could avoid her, he could get up to Mikey. Tom crept along to the edge of a machine. The walkway was clear. He made his move and slowly edged his way along. The silence was deafening. He got closer to the outer walkway. He peered out and it was clear. The

134

caged spiral stairway upwards was roughly twenty metres away. He didn't hesitate. He made his move, knowing he was now isolated and in danger. He got to the stairs and crept up them. His heart beating faster than he wanted. His breathing becoming frantic. He peered around the cage and the office he had put Mikey in was at the far end. He knew it was risky. The door they had come through that led outside was a few steps away. But the thought of leaving and escaping without Mikey never crossed his mind. He quickly made his way to the office.

With each step he expected a gunshot to ring out, but it never came. He got to the office and opened the door. It was dark inside. "Mikey," he whispered, "It's me, Tom."
The chair budged and Mikey's eyes appeared over the desk.
"Come on, quick," Tom urged.
Mikey got up and barged into the chair and it moved with a clunk.
"Be quiet!" Tom snapped at him in a hiss like whisper.

Tom peered out. They had a fifty-metre stretch of walkway to navigate and they were out. They edged along, and Tom knew that, if they did make it to the door, they needed to be quiet leaving. If they crashed out and it alerted the woman, they would get caught on the stairs like fish in a barrel.

They edged slowly along. With every few metres the door loomed nearer. At each junction that led into the machinery from the walkway, Tom's heart stopped as he hoped that it would be clear. They got closer and Tom wondered if his risky plan was actually going to work. Before he knew it, the door was a few metres away. He grabbed Mikey's sleeve.

Suddenly, there she was. Her eyes, sharp as razors, with a stare of death. Tom's stomach turned and his heart sank.

She delivered a blow to Tom's face and he had a sensation of flying. Then he felt and heard the clatter and crunch of the metal caged floor banging and scraping his head and back. Tom shook

135

his head and looked up, slightly dazed. He noticed that both he and
Mikey had been knocked to the floor. She then took one step
forward and aimed her gun between his eyes. The red laser dot
hovering ominously on his forehead.

Tom held his breath waiting for the end.

Chapter 20

The door behind them burst open with a crash and to Tom's surprise a man rushed in. Agent 7 spun, but before she reacted, he had surged towards her and delivered a lightning quick round-house kick to her head. The impact was hard, and she dropped her gun and stumbled back towards where Tom was laying.

Tom noticed that the man was Japanese. He was small, agile, but appeared to be very powerful. He retrieved a gun from the rear of his belt and took aim at the woman. In the blink of an eye she had propelled herself into a shoulder roll and was on him. He fired a shot which missed her and hit the cage floor, it ricocheted around sending up sparks and banging that clattered around their ears.

She grabbed Ano Tora's arm that was holding the gun, twisted her body and took control, aiming the gun at Tom. He rolled to the right and a shot, followed by a loud ricochet and sparks exploded where he was laying a split second before. Mikey screamed and scurried on his hands and knees towards the exit door, crying.

She thrust her elbow back into Ano Tora's face and tried to get the gun from his grip. He punched her hard in the face, but she wouldn't let go. Then, in the scrap, the gun flew from their grasp, slid across the grated platform and dropped off the level, clanging loudly as it hit the floor below.

In an instant, Ano Tora spun behind her and levered her into a head lock. She grabbed his arms and threw him over her head, and he smashed into the hard, grated floor. But, within a split second, he was up and on guard in a traditional karate pose.

They stared at each other. Now circling. Slowly Agent 7 came around to where Tom was laying. He scrambled back away from her but, to his horror, she refocussed on him. She made a move towards him but Ano Tora again came at her, grabbed her body, twisted her and head-butted her with force.

Tom then noticed through the melee that Mikey had made it to the door and had stumbled out, with it banging shut behind him.

Ano Tora slammed Agent 7 back into the wall and went at her again. He sent a sickening kick to her stomach and she doubled over due to the impact. He then countered with an uppercut that connected cleanly and thrust her head back against the wall with a thud. She ignored the blows and grabbed his neck, twisted him and sent a high knee crashing into his ribs.

He arched in pain and moved away. She then moved backwards and almost trod on Tom's leg so, again, he scrambled back trying to get clear of her, expecting her to attack him again. But she never did. Now fully focussed on her attacker. She stood up straight and wiped the blood from her nose and mouth. She faced the man down and circled to the left and he reacted by circling in the same direction. Ano Tora then realised she was getting closer to her gun on the floor that she had dropped when he first attacked her. He glared at her. There was a moment of silence.

But Tom had also spotted this and pre-empted it. He jumped up and moved fast towards the gun. She reacted and darted towards it. Tom dived reaching it a split-second before her and swiped it as hard as he could. The gun slid off the level banging and clattering as it hit a stair well, coming to rest below them.

As she had crouched down to grab it, her face was now close to Tom's. She glared at him and lashed out. The blow was vicious, and Tom felt like he had been hit by a rock. It knocked his head back and for an instant affected his vision. He panicked and scrambled to get away from her, blood now dripping from his nose.

She stood, now staring at Ano Tora. Both of them circled slowly around the platform waiting for their opponent to make a move. Agent 7 wondered who he was. He was strong and fast. And she knew he was dangerous. But she now knew she had the upper hand. The element of surprise was gone, and she was confident she could finish him and then deal with Tom.

Ano Tora stared into her eyes. He knew this was the woman that he had been warned of. Deep down he had hoped to complete his assignment without having to face her. But fate had brought them together. In some ways he was glad that the guns had been removed. Now he could fight with honour.

Agent 7 surged at him. They exchanged a flurry of blows from fists, arms and elbows. The blocking and attacks almost too fast for Tom to see. Their bodies entwined in a whirl of motion and movements as they attacked, defended, parried, evaded and ducked. The noise and power of the blows shocked Tom.

Ano Tora then evaded a chop aimed at his temple, moved aside, grabbed her and twisted her into the wall with a crunch. He came at her with a punch and she ducked and delivered a sickening blow to his stomach. The man flinched and stepped back. The woman glared at Tom, and then back at her attacker. Tom realised that she knew she would have to leave Tom until she had dealt with her new opponent.

Ano Tora stared her down. She had hurt him. But he never showed it. He never showed pain. It was weakness.
"He is mine. I am taking him," he said with calm authority.
Agent 7 smiled and shook her head.
"We will see."

Tom froze but he knew he now had a chance to escape. However, the ensuing battle blocked his route to the door. He could go all the way around the perimeter, but it would be obvious what he was doing and one of them, if not both of them, would stop him.

He wondered who the Japanese man was. It was obvious he wasn't from The Order. But, more important than that, Tom was lucky to be alive. Why had the man stopped the woman from killing him?

Despite their obvious differences, if they did have the same goal of killing Tom, he would surely now be dead. There was a chance the man wanted him alive. Either way, Tom had to escape but knew it would be reliant on when their battle would end and the outcome.

The two fighters then attacked each other again. Punches, elbows and kicks rained onto each of them with alarming speed and power. They blocked and attacked, ferociously and brutally, almost robotic in manner. Each time a blow connected it was shrugged off and the battle continued. Ano Tora felt he was getting the upper hand when a succession of punches connected to Agent 7's body and head. She stumbled back and he moved in to finish her. He lunged forward but she read the counter. She grabbed his body and pulled him in and delivered a deft blow to his kidneys to which he responded with a loud grunt.

She pushed him towards the platform rail and attacked, delivering a spinning back-hand punch. Ano Tora grabbed her fist but the momentum took them both towards the rail which they hit and then toppled over, their legs going upright and then disappearing. Tom heard a sickening thud as their bodies hit the metal machinery fifteen feet below.

Tom's eyes widened. This was his chance. He jumped up. He thought about checking the platform below, but he darted towards the door, not looking back. He burst through and ran along the thin, dark hallway, clattering through the next door into the cool night air that hit him with relief. He stood at the top of the outer stair-well looking down at the cars. The car he had used, and the SUV were still there but now, there was also a black sports car, obviously used by the Japanese man.

He ran down the stair-well, three or four steps at a time. Halfway down he stopped and checked up and down the road below him. To his left he spotted Mikey, 100 metres away, running for dear life.

"Mikey!" he shouted and then continued to descend the rest of the stairs.

Inside, Ano Tora felt dazed. His shoulder hurt and there was a sharp pain in his head, an obvious consequence of the impact of the fall onto the solid steel. He lifted his head and focussed. Nearby, the woman lay on the floor. His first instinct was to finish her off, but he knew the portal was more important. He looked past her and spotted a stair-well back up to the level from which they had fallen.

He moved in its direction and winced in pain. He looked down, there was blood on his trousers. He felt his leg and a sharp, jagged bone stuck out and stung him. He held the scream in, breathing heavily. He shuffled along, but as he passed Agent 7's motionless body he suddenly felt a tight grip clamp onto on his ankle. She was alive. She forced his leg back and punched the other leg. He stumbled forward in pain and turned.

She clambered to her feet. Blood pulsing from a cut on her head and dripping from her nose. Her eyes thinned and she stared straight through him. He knew he had to finish her before getting back to his assignment. The open fracture would compromise him, but he took a deep breath and prepared himself for another assault.

Outside, Tom was now in the road. Mikey had stopped and looked back, then continued running away.

"Fuck!" Tom shouted to himself.

He had to get Mikey under control and then get away. He could use his car, but he knew it was out of fuel, so he instinctively ran to the SUV and tried to open it, but it was locked. He darted towards the other car noticing it was a Mazda. He tried the handle, the door opened and to his utter relief the keys were there, hanging in the ignition barrel. Another chance.

"Mikey! Wait!" he shouted.

He then jumped in and turned the key, the engine roared to life. Tom powered away in the direction that Mikey was running.

Inside, the blows were taking their toll. Agent 7 was trying to block out of her mind how tired she was. She was also in pain and kept telling herself to carry on and not be overwhelmed by the situation. Ano Tora felt weak. The pain from his leg pulsed and seared with pain. How much more punishment could the woman take? How much could he take? He had been told she was dangerous, but he had not figured she would be this dangerous.

As the fight went on, less focus was being given to defence and blocking, and more blows connected. But, with the tiredness, the blows became less powerful. The two of them were cancelling each other out. Both had too much to lose. They dug deep. Circling and breathing heavily, clearing blood and sweat from their eyes and face. Knowing they had only one last flurry of attack left in them. They knew that the next minute would determine if they would live or die.

Agent 7's eyes darted to her right. A hammer lay on a work surface. She edged closer, trying not to make it obvious what her plan was. She took a deep breath. Then made her move. In a flash she grabbed the hammer with her right hand pulled it back past her head and threw it at Ano Tora. The hammer spun with precision. He put his hands up, but it connected with his shoulder and he grunted in pain. He stumbled backwards. And following up closely behind the hammer was Agent 7.

She converged onto him with surprising speed. As she moved, she flicked her wrist back and the concealed blade slid ominously from her sleeve, ready to meet its target. She grabbed him around his waist with one hand and, with the other, plunged the blade into his stomach. She rested her head on his shoulder and heard a whimper. She held the blade in place waiting for him to die.

He gently pushed her back, staring. Knowing now that she was the victor. He had failed. He smiled; teeth stained red with blood. He was disappointed that he had let his masters down, but happy that he had died with honour. Killed by someone who he now respected as a warrior.

Agent 7 pulled the blade from his stomach and blood splattered onto the floor. He cowered and gasped in pain. He held his stomach, which was now shredded and bleeding profusely. He inspected the deadly wound. Then he looked up again, stood up straight, wanting one last glimpse at his slayer.

Then, in a final flash, she moved in and sent a vicious uppercut to his jaw and the blade rammed through his chin and up into his mouth. She held the blade in position and his eyes, wide and staring, suddenly lost all focus and rolled back into his head. She pulled the blade out and he fell to the floor, in a defeated slump.

She breathed hard. She may still have one final chance to get the portal. And even though she was exhausted and in severe pain, she made her way to the exit door. Her tired and battered body, dragging her injured leg behind her.

Tom sped up, getting closer to Mikey and it dawned on him that they may just make it. The intervention of the Japanese man had saved him. A sense of relief washed over him, but he knew he still needed to focus. Mikey glanced back as the car approached, the fear in his face visible. Tom drove past him and screeched to a halt and got out.
"Get in!"
Mikey stopped running. His hands on his knees, breathing hard and crying.
"I don't want any part of this. Just let me go…Please!"
Tom approached, grabbed him and slapped his face with all the force he could muster.
"Shut the fuck up and get in the Goddamn car! Now!"

And with that, he dragged Mikey by his jacket lapels around to the passenger side, opened the door and bundled him in. Tom stood next to him as he sat awkwardly in the car.

"Put your belt on!" Tom ordered talking through gritted teeth.

Mikey's eyes were wide with shock. He put his belt on as Tom slammed the door and ran around to the driver's side. He got in and put his foot on the accelerator harder than had ever done before. The wheels spun and smoked. The rear end drifted and gradually found traction and the car sped away. Mikey's body and head shot back into the seat and he held on as the power kicked in.

Agent 7 stood at the top of the stairs and watched the Mazda reach the end of the road. It skidded and the red lights disappeared around the corner and away.

There would be consequences. She took a deep breath and quelled the anger rumbling up inside her. She needed to re-focus and assess the situation. Letting anger obstruct logical thinking would not help. And as her mind calculated her next move, she wearily descended the stairs to the road below.

Chapter 21

Tom was heading south-west towards New York City. From there, he would swing south-east and head into Long Island to meet Odin. He had just driven through New Haven, and so he still had a couple of hours left to drive but the roads were clear, and it was a pleasant, bright day with a clear blue sky. He arched his back, stretching his aching limbs and then slid himself back into a more comfortable position.

Tom had left the safe house two hours before, in a different car supplied by The Network. The Mazda he had used to escape the city had been taken overnight and would be disposed of. Every connection to the night before had to vanish.

It had been a busy night. After picking up Mikey, Tom had sped away from the industrial area, gradually slowing to a more relaxed pace when he thought they were out of danger. Once he got his bearings, he headed to the south of the city to pick up the 93 to Rhode Island and into Cranston.

As soon they had got clear of Boston, he found a quiet place to stop and made sure Mikey was OK. It had been very traumatic for him, so Tom got them coffee from a roadside diner. He then took the opportunity to call the support number. He reported that he had the portal and was on his way to the safe house. They advised that his contact was already there and waiting.

With a heavy heart, he had also reported Laura missing. They said they would run a GPS check and send an agent to try and locate her. Tom had wanted to plead with them to do it urgently but, as always with The Network, the call was quick and to the point and he was told not to call the number again unless advised to.

The safe house was due south in Cranston, and an hour later they drove through Providence and arrived around midnight – Three hours later than planned. It was an unassuming little house and the owner welcomed them and made them some pasta.

Due to their late arrival, plus exhaustion and the traumatic situation that Mikey had encountered, it had been decided not to have the discussion with him about what he was, who The Order were and how this will affect his life from now on. Tom was glad of this decision as, by that time, he had also had enough. His eyes stung, his body ached, he was exhausted, and he was worried about Laura.

He hadn't slept well. He was awoken three times by a recurring dream that involved him and Laura in a black void, sitting on chairs facing each other. With each passing moment she drifted closer to him until, eventually, when he reached out, the woman with the red hair came from behind her, grabbed her around the throat and dragged her away. He had heard Laura's screams in the darkness and when he had attempted to help her, he found that he was bound to the chair. Each time he woke it had taken him a while to get the screams out of his head and settle down again.

He had woken early, groggy from the broken sleep, made a coffee and worked out his timings. He had to be in Long Island at 2pm but wanted to eat on the way, so he needed to leave by 10am.

He also had to have a discussion with Mikey and would need to do that before he left. Mikey had woken soon after, and Tom had sat with him. He had explained it all as best he could but, as expected, Mikey never believed any of it. He had ended up getting distressed and Tom tried to muster as much energy as he could to quell Mikey's emotions, but knew he was failing.

Luckily for Tom, his contact at the house - a Network Agent called Ryan, stepped in. He was driving Mikey to Atlanta later in the day, so he had plenty of time to discuss it more with him then. Ryan also stated that the Internal Department were arranging for documents and information to be delivered to Mikey's new accommodation, which may help.

Tom had been glad of the intervention. The night before had drained him and, as bad as it made him feel, he was finding it difficult to give Mikey any more of his attention and energy. He felt like he just needed to get away from it all. He was keen to get going, so that he could be alone with his thoughts.

Before he had left, he had gone to Mikey's room and opened the door. Mikey had been sitting with Ryan. Tom had explained he was leaving soon and had wished Mikey good luck. He had assured him things would be better soon and that he just needed to be patient. Mikey appeared sad and his body language vulnerable, as he slumped in the chair. Tom felt sorry for him. As Tom had gone to leave, Mikey had smiled and just said, "Thank you."

It was unusual. A situation like the one they had gone through together the night before would, under normal circumstances, bond two people. But life in The Network was, at times, cold and unemotional. Things moved so quickly and there was little time for sentiment.

And, as Tom had set off, he had been angry with himself. Mikey had deserved more from him back at the house. He remembered how much time and support Odin had given him and how the things he had said gave Tom some hope. He realised that he had not had the same time to spend with Mikey and had hoped that Ryan would be able to offer him that. But, nevertheless, he had made a promise to himself to ensure that, next time, he finds more patience and energy to offer the portal.

Although, as Tom passed a sign for West Haven, he wondered if there would even be a next time. He recalled telling Laura about his thoughts on leaving The Network and living off grid in the northern wilderness. Last night had made that option more appealing. He had come so close to being killed again. Another few seconds and he would've been dead. Whoever the Japanese man was, Tom owed him his life. Tom imagined the man driving to the industrial site, running up the stairs and bursting through the door.

If, on the way from wherever he had come from, he had been held up by traffic or took a wrong turn, then Tom would now be dead. It sent a shiver down his spine. He shook his head at how lucky he had been. Tom believed the man wasn't from The Order. Although he wished he had concrete evidence. But if he was, why did he intervene? And if not from The Order then from where? Who was he working for?

And the woman. She flashed into his mind. He knew it was the woman from his visions. He had not seen her face in the visions, but he knew it was her. She had the same presence, movements and gave Tom that same fear. And when she had confronted him last night, he felt like he had known it was going to happen. He recalled the surroundings of his vision. In the storm, on the hill approaching the church. He wasn't sure if it was connected. Whatever it was, he hoped that she was now dead.

But, more than anything, the worry and pain of losing Laura weighed heavily on him. It was gut wrenching. He was desperate for some news of her whereabouts, but knew it wasn't normal practice for The Network to advise him. If, by some miracle, they had located her, and she was safe then she would be moved to her next accommodation and her life would go on. It wasn't a social group where members can ask for the contacts or locations of other members and call them up and go to visit. The contacting of other members of The Network was only when necessary and when authorised to.

He hoped she was safe. That somehow, someday, an assignment would bring them together again. He wished now that they had just left when they had the chance. He was annoyed for going ahead with the assignment. He knew how he felt and that he wanted to get away and he just wished he had driven north from the safe house in Beverly. If he had, right now Laura would be alive, and they would be setting up their new life together outside of The Network.

He looked down at her cap and phone on the passenger seat. He thumped the steering wheel. It felt good. He thumped it again and then again harder. He slammed his head back into the car seat and, as a tear rolled down his face, he drove on towards Long Island.

Chapter 22

A few miles past Greenwich, Tom stopped and checked his phone, which he had heard beep a few minutes before. He had received a text:

'Tom. I will be at East Islip Marina in 1 hour. Do not reply and delete this message. Odin.'

Tom checked the time and noted it was almost 1pm. He was on schedule. He knew the marina from past visits. It was a part of the world he loved and as a boy he had been here many times with his family.

He headed towards The Bronx, around Baychester and then cut back out crossing the East River onto Long Island. The unpredictable north-east weather had changed and, although it was still mild, a thick blanket of grey had blown in which covered the sky, and a stiff breeze had picked up.

He took the 495, through Brentwood and made his way into Islip and down to the marina. He parked, got out and looked all around. It appeared that there weren't many visitors. A few other cars parked and the odd person here and there. He walked across the car park and up onto a wooden bridge that crossed sand dunes and long grasses that were dancing wildly in the wind.

Scanning left and right along the beach, he noticed a few couples sat, wrapped in blankets. A jogger running towards him and an elderly couple walking a dog. Then, a few hundred yards away, a man stood, completely still, staring out to the Great South Bay. The man then turned. It was Odin.

Tom felt the wind blow through him and zipped up his jacket. He put his hands into his pockets and walked down to the sea. As Tom approached, Odin walked towards him. Soon after, they reached each other, but neither man spoke. They shook hands and then hugged. Tom was happy to be with him again. Odin pushed Tom back and held his arms.

"Look at you. You look good. A Network agent."

Tom smiled. "You too. Life must be treating you well."

Odin laughed and patted Tom on the shoulder.

"I suppose so. Shall we walk?"

They set off along the beach.

"How long has it been?" asked Odin.

"Not sure. Almost two years?"

Odin nodded. "Are you managing?" he asked.

"Pretty well. Christmas is a bit lonely though," he replied, with a grin, rolling his eyes. They walked on in silence. Neither man feeling a need to speak too much. Both comfortable with the silence.

"So, you were in Frisco?" Odin asked.

"Yeah, beautiful place. And my first assignment."

Tom then told Odin about his visit to New Jersey and that he had been able to visit his mum's headstone and also checked in on his sister and her family. Odin smiled and listened. Happy that Tom had found some solace in it. They walked on some more, the sound of the sea crashing as it rolled onto the beach close to them. The wind had picked up and up ahead two young guys dragged windsurfs down the beach to the sea, eager to take advantage of the conditions.

"As I was coming to see you, I got an update on your last assignment. Mikey is doing fine and is on his way to Atlanta."

Tom nodded in acknowledgement.

"Did it get rough?" Odin asked.

Tom explained to him what had happened after he and Mikey had left the bar. Losing Laura, the car chase and inside the factory. Then the woman and the Japanese man. Odin took it all in. Tom spoke for several minutes and gave as much detail as he could. They eventually reached a jetty with a seating area just off the beach and Odin pointed to the seats. They strolled off the beach and took a seat, both looking out to sea.

"It seems your training served you well," Odin commented.

Tom nodded in acknowledgement.

"You appear different, more focussed. Like you have grown into your role," Odin added.

"Well, I suppose the situation forced me to, as you know from your own experience."

"Yeah, it does that to a person."

A strong gust of wind blew in and they both felt spots of rain. The sky over the bay was now a solid dark grey as far as the eye could see and they both sat and stared out for a minute or so.

"Have you learnt anymore about you? What you are?" asked Odin.

"I have done lots of reading. Probably too much. Tried to understand the scientific and religious writings. It just gets blurred somewhere in the middle and..."

"You lose track?" interrupted Odin.

"Kind of. It's heavy stuff. But I suppose it's helped me understand it and live with it. Accept it? I'm not sure. I doubt I will ever accept it. I am learning to live with it though. What choice do I have?"

Odin shrugged. Intimating to Tom that he knew he had no choice. A group of seagulls squawked over-head and distracted them from their line of conversation. Tom took a deep breath.

"Has Laura checked in yet?" he asked, his gaze still scanning the horizon.

"No, not that I am aware of. I have asked for an immediate update if she does."

"I assume her GPS tracker has been checked?" Tom asked directly.

"Yeah. It showed a position just outside the city. A scout was sent and found the tracker but..." Odin cut short what he was going to say. He didn't need to tell Tom there was no sign of her. It was obvious.

"She's gone," Tom suggested.

"Well...You don't know for sure..."

"Oh, come on, Odin. You know as well as I do. She's gone."

Odin took a deep breath. "Well, yes…The chances are that they took her. It's common practice if they locate more than one Network agent. They always take one for questioning…"

"Questioning?!" interrupted Tom. "You mean torture…"

"Don't say that…" Odin advised.

"Why not? It's true. Why the hell was she even involved? I could've handled it on my own…"

"It was an ID decision, to help you. There was an amber alert on the city and so they deployed…"

"She shouldn't have been there! I could've handled it…"

"No! No, Tom, you couldn't. It would've been just as likely that you would be sat in that car dead or now captured…"

"Oh, I get it, she was used as bait, like a sacrifice. A pawn. Someone brought in to increase the odds of me surviving…"

Tom stood up as he spoke then walked towards the sea.

"It's not like that and you know it," Odin shouted over the wind, shaking his head as he watched Tom walk away from him.

Tom reached the surf. Staring out. Odin got up and walked down to him. He put his hand on his shoulder and moved around to stand next to him, staring out at the same horizon where the dark blue met the dark grey.

"Look, Tom. Don't over-react…"

Tom was confused. What was he going to say? Odin noticed this and prepared himself for a negative response.

"Did you say anything to her that may compromise The Network?"

Tom screwed his face in confusion, "Oh, fuck you! You know what? Fuck all of this. She is being tortured. Or already dead! And all you can talk about…"

"Tom, I have to ask. If an agent goes missing, we have to try and limit the potential fall-out…"

Tom shook his head and smiled sarcastically, "I know that. It still doesn't make the question less offensive."

"Tom, I have to ask. It's protocol."

Tom took a deep breath, "No, not that I am aware of. We discussed our own situations. Where we had been, what we had done…But, nothing of consequence."

"OK, what else? Think." Odin ordered assertively.

Tom turned to him, "Like what? We discussed what had happened to us since the training and then the assignment plan. What else are you referring to?"

Odin didn't respond, obviously satisfied with what Tom had told him. The fresh wind blew salty air into their faces and they both felt the rain get a little heavier. There was an awkward silence. Tom knew deep down he wasn't angry with Odin. He was just angry at losing Laura.

"You hungry?" asked Odin, breaking the silence. "I know a great seafood grill about a five-minute walk from here."

"Always. And I need a beer."

They headed off the beach and onto a track that ran adjacent to the beach behind the sand dunes. Now a little more protected from the wind it was quieter, and the sound of the tall grasses and rushes whispered in the breeze.

"Did you have feelings for her?" Odin asked calmly.

Tom didn't answer. He felt like he wanted to but there was no point. It was obvious to Odin that he did. He wasn't sure why Odin had even asked. After a few moments Odin spoke again.

"The Network advise against personal relationships within its members. You know the situation. People can be snuffed out in the blink of an eye. It's a dangerous life. It just makes it harder when..."

"I know why they advise against it," interrupted Tom, getting frustrated.

They walked on some more and reached some steps that led up to the road above. Odin pointed upwards guiding Tom. As they ascended, Tom spoke.

"I should've listened to her. She told me she didn't want any more pain in her life. And she was right to be cautious. Now look, that's me, I am struggling with losing someone again."

"Don't be too hard on yourself, Tom. Learn from it. It's a lonely and isolated life we live. But that's for a reason. It's to shut out the potential for more anguish and grief."

Tom nodded, "But I think I loved her."

They continued on in silence, then Odin Turned to Tom and put his arm on his shoulder, noticing a tear roll down his cheek.

Chapter 23

Both of them had ordered the special. Seafood bisque with freshly baked bread. They had eaten quietly, making small talk, but mostly commenting on how good the bisque was. Twice Tom was going to mention to Odin that he had been thinking about leaving The Network but as he had gone to speak, he stopped himself. He felt it may sound ungrateful to the man who had risked his life for him.

The waiter brought them their second beer and took their empty bowls and cutlery. The grill only had a few customers and there was a cosy, relaxed atmosphere. Tom sipped his beer.

"Oh, you said you needed to speak to me urgently?" he said.

Odin shifted in his seat to improve his posture then lent forward towards Tom.

"I know just meeting you out of the blue and then telling you this is probably...Well...It's going to be hard to take in, but..."

"You seem to make a habit of doing this to me." Tom smiled, although he was anxious about what he was going to hear.

"Yeah, sorry about that. Well, anyway...I have to warn you of a situation. Something major that is going to happen that will have huge consequences on the future. But it puts you in even more danger..."

"What? How?" asked Tom, frustrated that he could be in any more danger after what had happened to him the night before.

"This has been a long, long time coming. I'm talking for a generation at least. The brains within The Network have been working on something...It's to do with how The Order get their power. How they harness that power. Their ability to find out when and where angels are born."

Tom was surprised at the sudden directness of both the content of what Odin was saying and the tone of his voice.

Odin continued, "Remember when I told you we don't know how they do it? Well, we now know."

Tom sensed an eagerness in Odin's voice, so he sat back and got comfortable, interested in what he was about to hear.

"Every 44 years The Order take part in a ritual. A ritual that allows them to transmit a coded message. And in return they receive the power that gives them the ability to foresee the time, date and location of angels' births. It allows them to plan ahead, make contact and start the process of manipulating them and using them. It's how they knew when and where me and you were born…All portals."

Tom listened carefully, sensing that where Odin was going would lead to something of huge consequence.
"It's all transmitted via an ark. An ancient vessel that can hold the power of God. It's way beyond my understanding but not for some. The Network have people that have cracked the code. Deciphered the ancient and holy language…"

Odin stopped. Tom hesitated then lent forward to speak, Odin sensed this, held his finger up to stop him and continued. Tom slumped back into his seat.
"We know when and where the next ritual will take place…If we stop it then they lose the ability to locate angels. They become powerless. Meaningless."
"OK, so what does this have to do with me?" he asked.
Odin sat back. He took a deep breath and lent forward again, but this time he lowered his voice.
"It's you, Tom," Odin stated, smiling as if to emphasise to Tom how obvious it was.
"What?"
"It's you. Only you have the power to stop it. It all makes sense now…"
Tom shook his head, "No, it doesn't make sense to me…"
"Yes. Yes, it does. That's why I asked what else you had told Laura. If you told her that you feel special powers. If you knew. ID are worried that The Order know and will do everything they can to have you killed. If Laura tells them where you are…Or what you know…"
Tom interjected angrily, "She wouldn't have told them anything!"

They both stopped. Odin understood. He never pushed the matter. The insinuation that Laura would tell them what she knows upset Tom. He gulped his beer and peered out of the window. He was frustrated and angry. Just when he was getting his head around this life, Odin dropped this on him. Tom cleared his head and spoke calmly.

"She knew. She said you had told her before the training that I was special. That I would guide them. And that she fed off an energy from me during the training and when we..."

Tom paused. He flushed but then continued, "Well...When we were together. I mean, not just with each other but, y'know, together..."

"Exactly. I have known for some time and..."

Tom interrupted, "Why did you not tell me? I mean, before the training. Why did you not tell me that you were telling others I would guide them?"

Odin shook his head, "No, I couldn't tell you. It would've put too much pressure on you. If you had known they were looking up to you it would have been a burden. If you had all failed the training, then you would've felt like you had let everyone down. It is something you needed to find out on your own."

The drizzle outside had got heavier and rain clattered against the window. Odin ordered two coffee's.

"Have you noticed things? Like abilities? Powers?" asked Odin.

"Well, I suppose. I can read books in quick time, and several at once, within days. And it all goes in. I withhold information in such detail. I learn so fast. I read something once, a process or a technique, and I am an expert."

He paused. Then continued, a little hesitantly, unsure how Odin would respond.

"And I can sense danger..."

"Danger? How?" asked Odin excitedly.

"Like a sixth sense. It's difficult to explain..."

Odin's eyes widened, "Anything else?"

"I can meditate and control my surroundings. I can take myself to anywhere I create. And with who I want. It takes time to develop…"

"What places?"

"Just, beautiful places, with my family…"

Odin nodded, "I knew it was you from that night in the warehouse. When you lit up and elevated. Since then, the scientists have been working on timelines and theories. It all matches with the prophecy…"

"Prophecy?" interrupted Tom, with a confused look.

"Listen, in the city there is one of our guys, one of the lead scientists on this…Professor Lewis. He has all the information. All the research, documents, everything. He is ready for you. To meet you and to show you…"

"For what? Where are you going with this?"

There was a short silence.

"You are going to stop The Order. We both are but, well, it has to be you. I can help but…"

"How?" asked Tom

"Too much detail. Just wait. We will meet him and discuss the details then."

Odin cut himself short as the waiter brought their coffees. He smiled in thanks and then waited until the waiter had walked away.

"I just need to keep you safe…If The Order realise we know how to stop them then…"

"They know," confirmed Tom.

"What? How?" quizzed Odin.

"I have this feeling…"

"Explain. Tell me how?"

Tom took a sip of coffee and told Odin in detail about how he had developed his meditation and the visions that he had had. He then told him about the dark vision that had recently started to flash across it, the cold night, the storm and the church. The evil, unknown figure. The woman. With the red hair and the presence that he feared. He explained that he felt he knew her or, at least, would come face to face with her at some point.

159

"And she was the woman from last night. Who was a split second away from killing me."

"Holy shit," exclaimed Odin, mesmerised by Tom's account, "That might confirm The Order also know it's you. This changes things. We have to be much more vigilant."

There was a silence and anxiety crept its way into Tom's stomach. He took a sip of his coffee and then pushed the mug away.

"This woman? Did she die in the fall? Or did the Japanese guy kill her?" asked Odin.

"No. She's not dead. I sense her presence…"

"Are we in danger?"

Tom shook his head, "No, not right now. I feel a sense of calm now. But I know she is out there."

Odin took a deep breath, trying to analyse all of the information Tom had given him.

"OK, tonight we go to see Lewis, get the lowdown and then we have to fly out tomorrow…"

"Woah, fly out? Where the fuck are we going?"

"Tom, we have one shot at this…If we miss the window then it will be another 44 years and the chances of another Archangel coming along are almost zero. This could be our only chance…Ever."

Tom sighed and shook his head.

"What?" asked Odin, somewhat frustrated at Tom's response, "Tom?"

"It's nothing…Don't worry," concluded Tom.

"OK, let's just get going, get into the city, then we can talk. Meet the prof and take it from there."

Tom nodded. He was going to tell Odin about his thoughts on leaving The Network. But after the discussion they had, he knew it would sound stupid. Plus, he felt that he at least owned it to Odin to go along to see this professor.

He just hoped he wouldn't regret it.

Chapter 24

Agent 7 lay on her bed in the hotel room. She felt tired and uncomfortable. The pain from her injuries had kept her awake most of the night. The frustration of not finishing her assignment had also nagged at her and she had played it over and over in her mind.

She had been retrieved by another agent and taken back. Covered in blood, some of which was hers, but most of which was Ano Tora's, they had had to sneak her around the back and past the security guard who had already been paid to look the other way.

A doctor had been dispatched and had patched her up. Her worst injury was a cut on her head caused from the fall to the level below and it had required six staples to close. She had then been checked over and her other injuries were numerous but, to her, insignificant. Damaged ribs, dislocated finger and several cuts and bruises. The worst injury to her was the bruise around her left eye. She hated it. It showed that she had been injured. She detested injuries that were visible to others. They showed weakness.

But her physical injuries were nothing compared to the damage her ego and confidence had taken after the verbal attack she had received from Kane. He had been waiting for an update from her the night before. But after getting back to the hotel room, receiving medical treatment and assessing the situation, she had decided against calling him.

Although she had defeated the Japanese man, she hadn't terminated the portal. She knew that Kane would not be interested in how highly skilled her opponent was and the fact that she had faced her toughest battle. But her body had been in a lot of pain and she wasn't up for the conversation and the inevitable scalding from him.

The Order dealt with results, not details. She had failed. That was the bottom line.

So, she had woken and spent the morning relaxing and taking painkillers. She also took a long, hot bath to try and get some warmth into her sore limbs and bones. She wanted the repair of her body to get underway immediately, she needed to get back out there, locate the portal and finish her assignment. That was, of course, if Kane gave her a second chance.

By mid-afternoon, she felt able to make the call. It hadn't gone well. He had screamed down the phone, calling her incompetent, a failure and, most harmful to her, an amateur. She knew, of course, that she was the best, and that he knew it too. It was just rhetoric and him releasing his anger. Anger at her failure, but also because he would also be scalded when he updated Ganlar. Failure had a knock-on effect.

She had told him that she had the portal in her sights when a Japanese man intervened. He had reacted exactly how she had predicted and told her this was not his concern and that, regardless, she should have got the job done. But he had calmed down and had told her he needed to speak to Ganlar and seek consultation. He would then be back in touch.

She had taken another bath. Soaking in the almost unbearably hot water and steam. The heat seeping into her bones and the steam clearing her head, she lay there, eyes closed, hoping for another chance.

Around early evening, her phone rang. She recognised the number. It was Kane. She took a deep breath and answered the call.
"This is Agent 7."
"I have updated Ganlar and he has sought consultation from the Council," Kane advised.

There was a pause. Agent 7 held her breath. She knew that this could mean the end of her association with The Order and that, if it was, her future would be uncertain. She heard him breath and then he spoke.

"The Council are concerned with the involvement of the Japanese. However, they are content that it was not you that brought them into this situation."

The words came as a relief to her, but she did not intimate to him any indication of the relief, nor did she thank him. She waited, silently, expecting further instructions.

"But…You are to be deployed on another assignment for now."

She was confused. Why would they be moving her to a new assignment? Kane had told her about Ganlar stating how important the termination of the portal was. And whilst she was not being removed from duty for her failure, she was annoyed that she wouldn't get another chance to finish what she started.

"There is a sacred ritual, " Kane continued, breaking her from her thoughts, "It is very important and will soon be upon us. Everything relies on this ritual going to plan. You are to be assigned to ensure that the security of the ritual is not compromised. Get yourself prepared to leave in the next few days."

"Of course," she replied, not showing her anger.

There was a silence and she heard him breathing.

"More information will follow and arrangements for your travel will be made," Kane confirmed.

"And where is this assignment?" she asked, knowing this was outside of protocol and that, perhaps, the question had given him an indication of her frustration.

"All will be revealed," he replied, "but, more importantly, Lord Ganlar wishes to speak to you personally."

She shuddered. This was unexpected. A wave of nervous heat developed in her stomach and she waited anxiously. She heard breathing and then a dark, croaky voice spoke.

"Agent 7, you were adopted into The Order to complete important tasks. One of them was to stop portal 294574 from fulfilling the prophecy."

Her heart sank. She had not envisaged this happening. She wanted another chance and, although against her instinct, she spoke her mind.
"I will not fail you again, my Lord. Will you allow me another chance?"
"I have foreseen events. And there are plans afoot. A trap will be set. You will get another chance very soon. But, be warned, the portal is strong. He is a danger to The Order."

And with that, the phone clicked off. This was a very strange and unprecedented situation. She had only ever heard Ganlar's name mentioned before and he had, before now, only held mythical status in her mind. Now he had spoken to her directly.

But she was also aware that this was the second warning she had been given about the portal. Warnings that she failed to understand. Had it not been for the intervention of the Japanese man, she would have closed this assignment by now. Having him at her mercy the night before had been easy and straight forward. She had expected much more from him.

She had sent the two agents in as a decoy and they had flushed him out right into her path. It had been as easy as she could've imagined. She visualised him lying there, scared and panicking, fear in his eyes waiting to be snuffed out. What danger did the portal offer? He was weak and naïve. No match for her. However, she had now received two warnings, so she thought it might be best to at least take some heed.

Now it was just a waiting game. She laid back and lit a cigarette. Her bones and muscles ached, and her injuries were sore. She hated this feeling.

Chapter 25

Driving into New York City lifted Tom. As he approached from Long Island, the buildings in Manhattan rose up, the evening sun sparkling off them. They were like old friends. When they hit the city, the sounds, smells and atmosphere created a warm nostalgia inside Tom. The city was like no other. He was home.

They made their way through Flushing, along the East River and into Harlem. Odin took a few lefts and rights, criss-crossing and then parked in 132nd Street adjacent to a long row of Brownstone's. Odin pointed at one close to them that appeared to have not been renovated since it was built. Tom thought it looked derelict and vacated. The caged windows and doors added to its unwelcoming feel.

They went up the stairway to the front door and Odin banged the huge door knocker. After a short while, an old man opened the door and greeted them. Odin glanced at Tom and nodded his head towards the door. Tom went inside and Odin followed as the old man checked both ways along the street before closing the door and bolting it several times.

He had glasses that magnified his eyes to a huge size. His hair was long, thick and swept back into a messy, unkept style. As they stood in his dark hallway Tom noted that the house was old and a musty, stale smell filled the air.

Classical music blared from behind a door at the top of the stairway. The old man shuffled along towards the stairs, hunched over as he went, and Tom and Odin followed him up the stairs. As the old man opened the door the music got louder, almost to the point of being distracting. He went inside and they followed him, Odin closed the door.

The room was like a museum and an operations base. The walls plastered with various images, newspaper clippings, reports, data, charts and hundreds of post-it notes. Tom noticed a large map of the world with dates, various lines and crosses dotted across it. Astrology maps, religious images and copies of artist paintings from various periods. There were books everywhere, in tall piles and spread on the floor. And files, folders and written pages, in huge bundles tied together with string. Bookcases and small cabinets full of books and documents.

It was a mess. A table in the middle, had paperwork and documents spread across it. An opened bottle of whisky and a tumbler next to it. An ashtray with a burning cigarette, the smoke lingering in the air.

The old man walked across to the table and downed the whisky and took a huge drag of the cigarette. Tom watched the ash burn down, bright orange as the man sucked it. He breathed out smoke, whilst walking to a gramophone in the corner and lowered the volume, bringing with it some relief. Tom wondered how the man could even think with it being that loud.

The man turned to them and spoke in a high-pitched voice.
"Mozart's Requiem. My all-time favourite. Has to be loud so you can immerse yourself…It's thrilling."
Odin and Tom smiled politely as the man shuffled over to them.
"He wrote it while he was dying. It's his masterpiece…In my humble opinion, of course."
He approached Tom and stood close, facing him.
"So…This is the portal. The one of which the prophecy foretells…"
He glanced at Odin, "And you're sure?"
"Yes," replied Odin confidently, "it's guaranteed."
He peered into Tom's eyes and then checked him up and down, taking in every detail of Toms appearance.
"Amazing…Just amazing. I am honoured to be in your presence," he held his hand out to Tom.
Tom shook the man's hand, feeling awkward, hoping for some guidance from Odin, not sure what to say.

"I am Professor Lewis. And you are?"

"Tom. Tom Callaghan."

"Well, I have to say," said the professor, "you aren't what I expected…But, there you go…Anyway, we don't have much time."

The professor moved to the table and held his hand out towards it, "Take a seat."

They all sat down, the professor pushing documents onto the floor that were laying on the seat.

"So, what have you told him?" the professor asked Odin.

"Not much. A little about the ritual. The ark, how they get their power."

"And that he is the one?"

"Yes."

"And you are absolutely sure?"

"Yes, I told you…"

"We have to be sure…Otherwise this…"

"Look Prof, I am sure, OK," concluded Odin assertively.

The professor nodded, "OK, if you are sure. 44 years ago, I was a young man. We thought we had found the arch-angel then…But, as you know it wasn't."

"But that was then…" argued Odin.

"Yes, I appreciate that. But he doesn't seem to magnetise the correct energy…"

"I assure you. He is the one."

Tom felt like a spare part. Like some circus show freak that visitors gawped at and openly discussed.

"Hey," he interjected, "I am sitting right here!"

"Sorry, young man," offered Lewis, "you must understand the importance of this. It is vital we get it right."

"But Professor, we don't have much time," interrupted Odin, "they know where you are, and the ritual is in a few days…Let's just get this done."

Professor Lewis nodded. Odin was right. Time was not on their side. It was dangerous. The professor knew that The Order were in the city, hunting him, closing in. He knew it was just a matter of time. It was imperative that Tom and Odin spend this time with him so he can explain everything, and they can formulate the plan. They had one shot and the professor was determined to make it count. But the longer Tom and Odin were with him in the apartment, the more danger they were in. It was a huge gamble. A risky balancing act.

Then, with that in mind, the professor started talking.

Chapter 26

Professor Lewis had spoken for almost half an hour. Tom hadn't spoken and had just listened. Odin had asked several questions and got answers, although the professor wasn't good at hiding the fact that he found stopping to answer the questions annoying and obviously frustrating.

The table was strewn with images, timelines, charts and books of written research. Which, as he spoke, the professor flicked through, found a page, pointed to an extract that supported his theory and passed it to Tom and Odin. He introduced vast calculations and mathematical theories that led him to another series of books and documents showing more calculations related to a list of astrological occurrences taking place every 44 years stretching back thousands of years.

The professor highlighted a date on an astrological chart and advised them it was 1975. He then showed them a calculation which led him to another point.
"This is 1983. 16th June. 2.54am to be precise. The exact date and time you were born. Now, watch this, if I follow the calculated timelines..."
Tom and Odin watched as the professor moved two fingers across the separate lines. One of them dead straight, the other arching, way out into the solar system both eventually coming together at one point in the future.
"You can clearly see they meet at this point!"
The professor couldn't hide his excitement and became animated.
"The 11th of May 2019. 11.06pm to be precise!"

Much of what Tom had seen and heard didn't make much sense to him. However, from what Tom gathered, it appeared that Tom's date of birth coincided with the astrological occurrences every 44 years. The professor had calculated that Tom's birth was pre-destined to coincide with a specific date.

"So Tom," Lewis concluded, "I calculate that you were born at an exact point in time where your fate was already written. You are the one."

He picked up another book, flicked through the pages, stopped and then slid the book across to them.

"Here. Joshua crossing the River Jordan with the Ark of the Covenant."

Tom studied the image. A group of men in white robes carried a golden ark. Above them a cloud had split, and a bright light emanated from it connecting downwards to the ark.

"In simple terms the Ark is an ancient telephone. It allows the holder to receive power from God. The Order have the Ark and have held it for a thousand years. It's your job to stop them from receiving the transmitted message and the power. And to do that you would need to be there at the exact moment they open it…"

"How? How do I do that?" asked Tom, in obvious confusion.

"Odin?" replied Lewis, looking at him as if to prompt him to come in.

"Tom, remember in the warehouse…With Rutherford…When you used your power…"

"Woah, I don't have a clue how I did that…"

"Odin?" interrupted the professor, his voice a little angry and his face concerned.

"Wait, Prof, its fine…He can do it…"

Tom cut in, "It just happened…I don't know how…And it's not happened since…"

"Oh no, no, no!" shouted Lewis, "This is a disaster…"

He shuffled away from the table with his hands in the air, "This was supposed to be our glorious time…Our victory."

He glared at Odin, now angry.

"You promised us he was the one!" he shouted as loud as his voice would allow.

It startled Tom and he jumped. Odin lent forward with both hands on the table and looked downwards, shaking his head.

"He is the one. Your work proves that." He looked up at Lewis, "When the time comes, he will do it. I assure you. Have faith…"

Tom interrupted, "Hey, I don't want to rain on your parade, but how can you assure anyone. I don't know how I did it…"

"He's not ready!" shouted Lewis.

"He's fucking ready!" shouted Odin, standing up, this time startling all three of them. It was rare that he let anger get the better of him. "And what choice do we have!?" he continued, "Wrap this all up and wait another 44 Goddamn years, hoping he will be ready then!? Or hope another Archangel comes along and we go through this whole process again!? The Network are poised, ready…Everything is in place!"

Lewis knew Odin was right. They had to go with it. He had been working on this for almost thirty years. His head dropped to the table containing all of his work. Years of it surrounding him in the room. It was now or never. Odin lowered his voice.

"How the fuck can you just throw your life's work away based on you not being sure. I have seen him do it…"

Odin cut himself short. Angry. Knowing he had to hold his tongue. They all stood, silently. The professor and Tom, anxious and worried, Odin, angry and frustrated. It wasn't supposed to be like this. Odin took a deep breath, controlled his anger and spoke calmly.

"We don't have much time. Plus, we don't have any choice. He is the one. We know that. It's proven. I have seen it with my own eyes. And your work demonstrates that on the day he was born his life led to 11.06pm on the 11th of May 2019. Exactly as the prophecy states."

As Odin spoke Lewis had made his way back to the table.

"Agreed," he replied, pushing the negativity of the last few minutes away, "but can you assure that he can prevent them from transmitting the message?"

Odin felt their stares and took a deep breath.

"Yes," he said confidently, glancing at Tom, "He can do it."

Tom went to speak but Odin held up his finger and shook his head.

"Tom, just stop. We have a few days left. Relax. We will talk. When the time is right it will happen. I assure you."

Odin's words calmed Tom. He had that knack. But deep-down Tom was anxious and afraid. Afraid that, when it came to it, nothing would happen. There was huge pressure on him and all he could do was go along with Odin. A silence echoed around the room and then it was broken.

"And if it doesn't happen?" asked Lewis.

Odin didn't answer. He wasn't interested in arguing anymore and didn't want to go over the same ground. They didn't have time. After an awkward silence Odin spoke.

"Let's just get to the plan. We are running out of time."

Lewis stared at him unconvinced. Tom even wondered if Odin was convinced or if he was just saying it to assure Tom. Lewis bent down, grunting as he did, coming back up with a large map of the world. As he straightened, he grimaced in pain and put his hand around to his back.

"OK, let's get this finished."

He spread the map across the table and flattened it, ironing out the creases. The map had numerous circles at various points. Next to each circle was written a date. Lewis explained that these were the locations and the years that The Order had transmitted the message and received the power. Using historic data, a very complex calculation and some gut instinct, he had broken The Order's code and had been able to calculate exactly when and where this would next happen.

"So, as you can see, I have managed to go way back and create a calculated time and geographical line. I can take this back thousands of years…But obviously we will keep it as current as necessary…"

He pointed to a location on the map that was circled and, as he spoke, with calm assurance, he traversed his finger around the map from circle to circle detailing the dates and locations, very matter of fact and confident in his work.

"1799, Sousa, Brazil. 1843, Vasad, Hungary. 1887, Sekingchan, Malaysia. 1931, Zhanjiang, China. 1975, Stonewall, Canada…"

He stopped. He glanced up at them to ensure he had their attention. Then as he continued, he slowly moved his finger across to the final circle and banged his finger down hard directly in the centre of it.

"And…the 11th of May 2019. Ireland."

Lewis then went to a box behind him and rummaged through the files and documents inside. Tom got Odin's attention.

"Ireland?" he whispered.

Odin nodded, "Yeah. But, where exactly I don't know."

"Ah! Here it is," announced Lewis. "Clare Island in County Mayo. A point called Toremore. Just off the west coast. There is a church, centuries old…" Turning back to the table he placed a photo down and slid it across to Tom and Odin.

"This is it. The Church of the Sacred Heart."

Tom shuddered. A wave of fear ran through his body. He knew.

"No…It…It's the church…" he uttered slowly.

"What!?" asked Lewis frantically, "You've already been here?"

"Yes…Well, no, not exactly…But I have seen it."

"Where? How?" asked Lewis.

Tom studied the photograph. It was the same church. Old, decrepit and dark. At the top of the rocky hill, the huge doors at the end of a track. The same surroundings. And Tom sensed fear. The fear of the unknown secret hidden within the church that filled him with dread. Now he knew why.

"Tom! Where have you seen this place…" enquired Lewis.

"Visions. When I meditate…It flashes into my head…It's that place…"

"I told you he was the one," interrupted Odin.

"No! Odin, you don't understand…My visions…The ones I told you about. You can't go, it's too dangerous…"

"Tom, stop, just calm down…" assured Odin.

"No! If you go she will kill you…I know it…"

"Tom, stay calm…" Lewis intervened.

"Odin, it's too dangerous. Please…I will go…It's too risky for you…"

"Tom! Just calm down," Odin snapped, grabbing him by the shoulders.

"Listen to me. Everything is planned, our contact is waiting, local people ready to help, a support unit ready to go…"

"It doesn't matter! None of that matters…You cannot go!"

"I have to go…"

"She will kill you!"

There was a silence. Tom appeared solemn. Lewis looked at Odin, waiting for him to speak. Odin pointed to an old beat-up sofa in the corner.

"Sit down."

Tom and Odin walked over and sat. Tom felt anxious.

"Tom, you must understand, this is bigger than all of us. We must all make sacrifices. The prof has dedicated the last thirty years of his life to this. People have died getting information to The Network. Our people in Ireland are risking everything to help us. Every day there are people who risk everything. People who take us in, drive for us, deliver information…They all make sacrifices. We all do. Because we all have one thing in common. The Order have wronged us. Taken people from us. Taken our lives from us. And it is that which gives us our common goal. To bring The Order down."

Odin paused, ensuring Tom was taking it all in.

"Our fates are sealed. Yours, the prof's, mine. What will be will be, but it must not deviate us from our destined path. My life brought me to this point, as did yours. Your destiny is to stop The Order, and mine is to help you do that. And the consequences of that are meaningless. If we don't take this chance to stop The Order they will get stronger and stronger…Then, who knows what they will be capable of."

Tom nodded. Lewis noticed and felt relieved. Time had been wasted and they needed to finalise the plans.

"And anyway," continued Odin, "you don't even know for sure if she is still alive…"

"She's alive. I know."

Odin knew that the woman was still alive. If Tom felt that then he knew it was true. But he pushed that aside.

"Well, it's too late anyway," he replied, putting his hand inside his jacket, "I have already been given these."

He pulled out two small slips and handed one to Tom who immediately noticed it was a flight ticket.

"We are flying to London tomorrow morning."

Chapter 27

Father O'Dowd lay in bed, unable to sleep. He had gone upstairs around 11pm and it was now just after midnight. He had known he would just lay, staring at the ceiling, conversations and details going around in his mind.

Father Reilly had phoned him earlier that night and gone through the plan. It was simple. Two men would be arriving in two days. They were both agents for The Network but, more importantly, one of them was the one that held the power. The one that could stop The Order.

On the day of their arrival O'Dowd was to go to the old farmhouse up on the hill at Killary. He would meet them, and they would then direct him according to the plans. O'Dowd would then need to be ready to go with them and give them access to the old church up at Toremont on Clare Island. Nobody else could be trusted.

It would happen on May 11th at 11:06pm. They had to be there just before that time. If they got there too soon, they could be spotted. If they got their too late, Father Reilly had said the consequences would be 'the opportunity of a lifetime missed.' They couldn't be late. It was not an option.

O'Dowd felt anxious. The pressure was immense. So much rested on this and he wasn't sure if he could cope with it. He had asked Reilly if he could just give the men the key and leave them to it. The old priest had hesitated and there had been an awkward silence but eventually he told him that they needed guidance and direction.

It was a difficult walk to the church and at that late hour they would easily get lost. Plus, the old door was difficult to open, there was a knack. O'Dowd knew he was right. It had taken him months to find the way properly and, as for the door, he still found it difficult to open even now.

But it had been what Father Reilly had told him next that worried him. He had told him that what would be happening in that church was a 'devious and grotesque manipulation of Gods power' and that he would need to provide the Archangel with 'holy and sacred guidance and protection'.

More pressure. More responsibility. More anxiety.

He thought about the fall out. Reilly had said that the agents would have a support team. He pictured them rolling into the village in tanks or abseiling from helicopters. He knew this was a ridiculous notion but if The Order arrived too, would all hell break loose? It would be late, so he hoped it would all be covert and nobody who lived in the area would be none the wiser.

He also had to make sure that Maggie was out of the picture. He had mentioned to her that he would be taking some time off so he would be there alone. He didn't want her involved. Nowhere near any of this. She was too young and innocent and had to be kept well clear. Again, he knew it would be late and she would have, by then, gone home. But he didn't need her asking questions. Like why he was going up to the farmhouse, why he needed the key to the old church on the island and who the two strange men were. But, more likely, why he wouldn't be going to her mum's for dinner on that particular Friday. He would need to say that he wasn't well, or that he was tired. He would have to think of something.

Again, he cursed in his mind at the aggravation and worry of all of this. If only this had been due to happen in a few month's-time. He would already be in position at his new church. He was excited about his move to Cork and the fresh start. He loved it in Westport, but it had got too intense and too political. The village felt like a magnifying glass. His every move known throughout the village and by the locals. Not that they spied on him or gave him any reason to be paranoid. It was just the weight of it all.

He had become more than just their local priest. They relied on him for everything. Not just holy guidance and sermon but also for comfort, friendship, advice and guidance on daily matters. He chaired meetings, mediated disagreements, put on fetes, school shows and judged at farm shows. He even put some shelves up in the community hall the week before. And now, after four long years, he just wanted to do his job and then disappear away and enjoy time with his family.

One good thing was that Siobhan and Jimmy had gone on ahead to Cork a few weeks ago. He smiled as he thought of them. She had been decorating the old presbytery where they would live and was dealing with the move and the paperwork. Jimmy had already started his new primary school and was settling well.

They had also discovered the power of technology and caught up most nights on Skype. It had kept him going. Seeing her and hearing her excited voice when she would tell him about the decorating she had done. She had also given him a tour using her mobile phone, leading him from room to room. And seeing his beautiful Jimmy and hearing his excitement about joining different clubs and his new friends. The young boy was so happy.

Siobhan had asked him a few times in the last week if he was OK. It was obvious she had noticed his worry. He had created a story that as he was leaving soon, people were trying to get what they could out of him now, and that he was also busy tying up loose ends. She had told him he shouldn't be used like that and that he had to switch off. She had even got quite angry with him. It had confirmed to them that local life had closed in and was suppressing him and his family.

So, the move to Cork was the right decision. It had been a difficult decision to leave, one that they had toyed with for months. So, in reality, they were both glad of the confirmation that the decision had been the right one.

He wished he was already there with his family in the big city. Meeting his new staff, the congregation, new friends and associates. The new start would be like a wave of relief.

But, before all that, he had this one last thing to do and he had to see it through to the end.

Chapter 28

Professor Lewis was waiting. It was quiet, and all he heard was the muffled sound of the traffic, sirens and horns from the busy streets below his top floor window.

He was content. Although he was also sad that it had to end this way. But it was the inevitable conclusion of what he had been involved in. However, knowing that the work he had done in the last thirty years had finally come to something, gave him solace.

He was sad that he would never know if Tom succeeded. He imagined himself being informed that the Archangel, the one they had waited so long for, had dealt a blow to The Order and its religious fanatics. He smiled. He knew how happy he would be. Tom hadn't filled him with confidence, but he had something. The professor couldn't quite put his finger on it, but his instinct told him that Tom may just be OK.

However, the most important thing right now was that the apartment had been cleared of everything that linked him to The Network and the work he had been doing. All the documents, books, scriptures, charts, images. Everything. It had all gone. The two men that had arrived just an hour ago cleared the apartment quickly and efficiently.

Everything that had been cleared was now being burnt to remove any trace of its existence. The originals being kept safe in the secret archive, that only a handful of people within The Network knew the location of. For it may be that others have to continue his work once he is gone, so the originals may be needed. But he hoped not. He hoped the blow to The Order would be fatal and final.

He spotted his bottle of whisky and the tumbler next to it. He trudged painfully across and poured himself a large drink. "Enjoy this one, old man. You deserve it," he whispered to himself.

He lifted the tumbler, downed it and banged the tumbler back down onto the cabinet. He poured himself another large drink and wearily returned to his armchair. He put the drink on a small coffee table that had a picture frame on it. Close by, stood a chest of drawers. He leant over, opened the top drawer and pulled out a revolver. As he picked it up another pang of sadness rushed through him.

"Stop being silly," he told himself, shaking his head.

He had known for some time that this moment would arrive. It was the natural conclusion. He had gone through it in his mind many times and had come to terms with it long ago. He couldn't keep running. He was old and tired. His mind was still awash with grand ideas, mathematical theories and scientific innovation, but his body, was old and worn out. His back ached, his feet and knees throbbed, his hands and left shoulder, both riddled with arthritis, caused him sharp stabbing pain and pins and needles.

This was a young man's life. Running from The Order had taken its toll on him. But now his work was complete, he no longer had to run. But he had to take what he had learnt with him. The Order must never know. And if they got him alive, he daren't imagine what they would do to try and get it out of him.

He opened the barrel of the gun and checked it for ammunition. Six bullets. A full barrel. Good, he thought. No mistakes. He closed the barrel and cocked the hammer. Then lay the gun down on the coffee table next to his drink, which he picked up and sipped.

He then picked up the picture frame. He stared at the lady in the picture. She was beautiful. His dear Molly. The most amazing person that he had ever met. How she had fallen in love with him he had never known. His scientific work always came first. During their early relationship at university, through their engagement, and into their marriage, all the way up to her death. She had always come second to his first love. Science.

He had never been a good husband. They both knew that. He never had the time. Always working, researching and calculating. Constantly quenching his thirst for scientific progress. Always consumed by whichever project he was involved in. But she accepted it and loved him unconditionally. She had been a constant rock for him all his life.

Losing her in the way he did all those years ago was difficult. And he had never stopped loving her or thinking about her. She was so innocent, and it was all so unfair. The Order used her to get to him, but they failed. Although, taking Molly from him was the consequence. Now he hoped he would get his revenge.

He smiled at the picture. It had been taken in Austria on a summer vacation in 1979. The best time of his life. She looked amazing. A tear rolled down his face. He took another gulp of his drink and put the picture down, then eased himself out of the chair. He paced up and down for a few minutes, reminiscing about his life and remembering Molly.

Then, he heard a noise. A screech of tyres. He shuffled to the window and pulled the heavy, mustard curtains back. Down in the street below, two black vehicles had parked, and men were walking towards the main door.

It was time.

Awkwardly, he moved across the room, past the chair to his gramophone. He switched it on, and the vinyl started to spin. He turned the volume up full, grabbed the needle arm and carefully lowered it. There was a short crackle and then the eerie, sombre flutes and violins burst from the speakers.

He stood and closed his eyes, allowing the music to flow into his mind and through his veins. Filling him with passion. He smiled and then turned to the armchair, holding the head rest to help himself across to it and lowering himself down. He slumped, then moved his body from side to side to get comfortable.

He lent across, picked up the picture frame and the revolver and put them in his lap. He then grabbed his drink which he downed and dropped the tumbler onto the floor with a clunk. Over the violins, he heard a clatter of footsteps and a bang. Then another bang, but this time louder than the first. He picked up the gun. Ready. He took one last look at Molly and kissed the picture. Wishing he was back there, in Austria, on that balcony surrounded by the green, lush hills and mountains. The sun on his face. The smell of the crisp alpine air filling him with health and happiness.

Then he heard a loud crash and he knew that his time on this earth was over. And looking one last time at the picture he whispered, "Thank you, Molly."

In an instant, the door to the room burst open. Two men came rushing in. Tall, huge men in black. He looked into their hateful, nasty eyes filled with evil intent. The music suddenly burst to life. The full choir and orchestra joined the flutes and violins, engulfing the room in sound and immersing the occupants in its majesty.

Professor Lewis smiled and lifted the gun to his temple. "Good evening, gentlemen."

And with that, the sound of the gun shot rang out but was quickly enveloped by Mozart's Requiem exploding into a crescendo of sound that echoed around the room, along the hallway and out into the street below.

Chapter 29

Tom and Odin had holed up overnight in a bedsit close to Newark airport. Tom had spent most of the night lying awake. The sudden realisation that things had taken a dramatic turn were a lot to take in.

Since meeting Laura again and up to this point, everything had been a blur. And he was a little overwhelmed by how quickly it had all happened. One moment he had been in love, ready to slip away from The Network and live a quiet, peaceful life with her. The next, she was gone, and he was waiting to go to Ireland with Odin to try and prevent The Order from completing a sacred ritual. He was finding it all hard to believe and accept.

Several times he had got out of bed and walked to the window. Trying to quell his nerves and anxiety about the position he found himself in and the sadness of losing Laura. From his viewpoint at the window of the bedsit, the buildings in the distance twinkled in the night and he had recalled the good times from when he lived here.

He had remembered his old friends. Wondering what they were doing with their lives and if they ever thought of him. He was always very social and so it must have been a little strange for them that, from the moment when he transferred to Chicago, he had just vanished. Not one phone call, e-mail or visit. He felt upset that he probably won't ever get to tell them why. He wondered what his old work friends on the trading floor had been told. How he, Conway and Rutherford had all disappeared so suddenly.

It had then prompted him to remember Evanston. And the friends and connections they had made. Did anyone remember him? Or Jenna? Tom and Jenna had left so many people's lives in the blink of an eye, it wouldn't have been unusual if, from time to time, people recalled them and wondered what happened and why they suddenly lost contact.

And Sheridan Avenue. The old neighbours. He had thought about them and what they were doing. Pam Harrison, especially. He recalled her devastation at Frank's death and wondered if she had ever got over it. Did she ever remember him and Jenna?

He had then thought about Jenna. His mind raced back to the night he lost her. Poor Jenna. Their lives were manipulated and, no matter what happened and what she had done wrong, she didn't deserve to die the way she did. He realised that he still loved her in some way.

He wasn't sure why staring at the New York skyline had made him recall those things. He supposed that from the second he left Chicago to be in The Network, his life had been about him adjusting. About him coping with the losses he had experienced, getting over them and accepting what he was. It had been a process. And it had been a tough one to navigate. He hadn't had time to think about the past. It was all about the present. And coming back to New York city had obviously taken his mind back. Back to where this situation had started to unfold. Back to his old trading floor and that missing file. Back to when it had all started to go wrong.

Eventually he had got back in bed, tore himself away from his thoughts and managed to fall asleep. He only managed to get a few hours of broken sleep and when he woke, he felt anxious. A grey blanket covered the city skyline, and everything appeared dark to him. Not just in light but also in atmosphere. He didn't feel the usual buzz of the city. It was like it was in a slumber. Tom knew it was him and he did his best to hide it from Odin, who appeared in good spirits and raring to go.

He was also tired. Which didn't bother him too much as he would sleep on the plane. But he was surprised at how tired he was. He felt lethargic and that, if he had the choice, he would stay in bed all day. It wasn't like him. He had learnt to be positive and alert at all times. But he put it down to the night before and the city bringing back memories of his friends and the old life he once had that he had since forgotten. Plus, the thoughts about Laura and the new life that he had planned. As he got ready, he desperately hoped he would snap out of it.

But everything else had run smoothly. As always, the efficiency of The Network was obvious. A car arrived on the dot to take them to the airport and when they got out, the driver gave them two suitcases containing clothes and personal items. Odin was also given a folder containing fake meeting notes and data sheets which supported their cover story that they were from a packaging company attending a meeting in London.

Soon, the cloud across the city had lifted and revealed a bright, crisp morning. They had seats on the left side of the plane and as it took off, Tom looked across and saw Manhattan in all its glory. The docks, the bridges, and the skyscrapers with the early morning sun, breaking through the clouds, now glistening off them. He took the view in. Wondering if he would ever see the city again.

When they got into the air, Odin explained the reason they were flying to London first was to avoid any detection from The Order. Flying into a major airport in Ireland was too risky. London allowed them to get close enough to their final destination but not too close so as to get located. They were to be picked up from Heathrow airport and would hole up one night in London. Then they would be collected the next day, taken to a small private airport and flown to Ireland.

A base had been set up a few miles from Clare Island and their contact, a local priest, would meet them to discuss the plan in detail. He would guide them and help them get access to the church when the time was right, which, if all goes to plan, would be exactly 24 hours after arriving at the designated base.
Tom asked no questions. Odin, as always, had everything organised and under control. Although there was one huge question that Tom wanted to ask. But he didn't. It was about his contribution.

About what he was supposed to do in all of this. He was anxious and had butterflies because of it. What had happened back in that warehouse on that night seemed to him to be a one off. He had told Odin and Professor Lewis that he didn't know how he did it and that there had never been any indication that it would happen again. How on earth would he be able to do it again at the exact moment they wanted him to? It was crazy.

He still wasn't sure if Odin's confidence in him was mis-placed. Was it just a way of creating some confidence in Tom? If it was, then it hadn't worked. Tom was struggling and didn't feel like he had it in him. He was desperate to ask Odin if he truly believed in him or whether he was telling Tom that just to get him to Ireland. Tom knew if he had asked, Odin would respond with the same assurance as he had done at Professor Lewis' house. So, he never bothered. They were on their way anyway, so it changed nothing.

He sat and thought about the church. He knew from the visions that he feared it. But he hadn't known then what or where it was, or how it affected his life. So he had been able to brush it aside. But ever since he had seen the photo, a fog of anxiety had dropped down over him. He had to control it and focus.

One positive was the overnight stop in London. It would give Tom a chance to meditate. He was determined to take himself away to one of the beautiful places he had created in his head. It would be comforting to see his family, and, on this occasion, he hoped that it would be interrupted by the vision of the church.

It had occurred to him that with each passing mediation the vision of the church that flashed across his mind lasted a little longer and became more detailed. He was desperate to know what would happen to Odin. His last vision had taken him up to the point where the woman attacks. Would it go further? He hoped it did. He needed to know the outcome.

He was worried. Something told him it wasn't going to end well. The moment the woman traverses up the hill towards them left him with a feeling of dread. If the vision didn't end well, he was still hoping to talk Odin out of going. If the priest they were meeting got him to the church and inside, perhaps Odin could stay away and be safe. Tom knew what she was capable of and felt sure Odin was not taking his warnings seriously.

He and Odin were quiet for the majority of the flight. Tom slept for a few hours in between and felt better for it. Eventually they started their descent and, off in the distance, the skyline of London appeared. Tom had been to London on business twice before when he worked in New York. He enjoyed it.

This time he was afraid there would be little to enjoy.

Chapter 30

"I notice your accent. Where are you from?" asked Seamus.

Agent 7 wasn't interested in small talk. She peered out of the window at the bleak landscape beyond the farm. Green fields, low hills and grey skies. Very little else.

It didn't affect her. She was used to it. Where she lived as a child, before she was taken by The Order, was a cold, harsh and barren land that offered little in the way of beauty. The only thing that she could remember as being beautiful were the Ural Mountains in the distance which she would sit and stare at. Imagining herself climbing them and plotting routes up through the jagged, snowy network of rocks.

Her life after she was taken by The Order was isolated. In that dark, concrete building, security was tight, and she saw almost nothing of her surroundings apart from when she was taken out for physical training or manoeuvres. But then it was in dense woods and valleys surrounded by the snowy hills. She had no idea where it was.

It wasn't until she had become an assassin, training with Russian Special Forces and then afterwards working within The Order, did she see the outside world and more exotic places. But it was always limited and almost always ended with her killing people.

"I say," Seamus repeated, "Where are you from?"
She moved away from the window and picked up her bag.
"Where is my room?"
"Oh, sorry dear," he replied, a little offended.
He approached and attempted to pick up her bag, "Please, let me."
Agent 7 held the bag and just stared at him, "My room?" she asked again coldly. Seamus held his hands up to concede.
"Follow me."

He led her through towards the main hallway, ducking his head to avoid the old stone lintel. They passed the front door and walked through a small stone corridor to a door at the end. Seamus opened it and went inside, holding it open for Agent 7 to walk through.
"It's not much. But it's cosy…Oh, I will get some firewood for the hearth, get some heat in here…"
"No need," Agent 7 confirmed abruptly.
"But the nights get cold…It's May but the west coast of Ireland has its own rules with the weather and…"
"I said, no need."

Seamus conceded again. Knowing that it would be best to keep this woman at a distance. He stood and watched as she opened her bag and unloaded items onto the bed.
"Can I offer you some refreshments? Tea? Coffee? Or I have a nice bottle of brandy…"
"No thank you."
"Fine. So, will that be all?"
"Yes."

Seamus rolled his eyes, wondering what he had got himself into. The money he was being paid was too good to refuse. Almost three months' money that he would normally make from the Bed & Breakfast to put this woman up for just 3 nights to attend a religious meeting nearby. But she wasn't what he was expecting. She didn't strike him as the religious type. But, then again, the money had been deposited, so why should he care? He had visitors through the summer months, generally hikers or conservationists. He enjoyed having them around because normally they were engaging and happy and enjoyed his warm Irish charm and hospitality.

But if she wasn't interested in that then so be it. However, social and human interaction was in his nature and he found it difficult to be unsociable.
"So, a religious meeting? Sounds interesting."

Agent 7 continued with her business and never acknowledged that he had spoken. He realised that he was getting nowhere but, without thinking, he asked her another question.

"These people that you work for. The ones that contacted me to organise your stay. So, who are they?"

Agent 7 faced him.

"I am of the understanding that you were specifically notified not to ask any questions or, in fact, inform anyone of my arrival. Hence the reason why you have been paid so well."

Seamus was taken aback but knew he had gone too far. He had pushed it and cursed himself for doing so. He shook his head.

"Oh, my dear, no offence meant, I'm not prying, just trying to welcome you..."

Agent 7 stared at him and he looked into her eyes. They put a fear into him but somehow, he couldn't look away. He felt her peering into his soul. It was captivating, but also spooked him at the same time.

"Please leave now," she requested rudely.

Seamus didn't need a second request. He left the room closing the door behind him. As he made his way back to the kitchen, he continued to shake his head. He knew then to keep quiet. His Irish charm would not be needed.

Agent 7 looked around. He was right, it wasn't much. Stone floor and walls with one window out to the same view as before. Just a bed, table with a lamp and a wardrobe. But it was all she needed. She walked across to the window and glanced out again. She was frustrated. And the journey from Boston had been boring. Observing the fields and the grey sky, she knew there would be little chance of people watching here. All she wanted to do was finish this, get the assignment closed and leave.

Initially she had been more frustrated at being moved to a different assignment but had then been buoyed a little by Ganlar and the assurance he had given that she may get another chance. But how? She had been told her assignment was to provide security for a ritual taking place nearby in two days. How did this relate to terminating the portal? She hated not knowing. It was the not knowing that compromised her control, and she liked to be in control.

She tidied her personal items and put her bag away. Then she lay on the bed and closed her eyes, drifting to sleep. But she was soon startled by her phone ringing. It broke her from her slumber, and she leant across and grabbed it, composing herself before answering.

"This is Agent 7."

"Have you arrived?"

"Yes," she answered, recognising Kane's voice.

"Good. Listen carefully. Your initial presence was to ensure the security of our sacred ritual. The consequences of this ritual being compromised are catastrophic and will put our work back a generation. It is imperative it goes ahead unhindered. You must understand the importance of this."

"I understand." Agent 7 confirmed.

"To help you, a team has been deployed and will arrive within 24 hours. Your current position is close to the ritual site. The lead agent will make contact with you and has all the information you need."

There was a pause. Agent 7 waited. She wanted to ask about the portal but didn't want to appear desperate. Kane sensed this and gave her an opportunity to ask.

"Do you have any questions?"

"No," she replied, leaving the question that was burning in her mind, unanswered.

He stayed silent, toying with her emotions. He enjoyed having control over her. He knew how dangerous she was. That she could kill most humans in the blink of an eye. Since she had been reporting to him, he had enjoyed their brief communications. It made him feel strong. Like he was in control of a wild animal. "I have further news," he commented, then pausing, not immediately following up on this update.

Agent 7 restrained herself again. Not giving him the satisfaction of knowing she was hanging on his words.

"We have information from a double agent. A priest we have managed to get on side in the last few days. He informed us that portal 294574 will be arriving in two days with the intention to stop the ritual. He must be stopped at all costs. The trap has been set. Now that we know the portal is arriving, we can kill two birds with one stone. You can guarantee the security of the ritual and also eliminate the portal at the same time."

Agent 7 felt relieved. It was now obvious that Ganlar's recent assurance was based on this information and that he knew of the plans being made in the background. Her chance of redemption was coming.

"The priest has assured us that he will handle things his end. There are two keys to the church. We have one and he will ensure they don't get the other one. Without access, the portal cannot stop the ritual."

"But I can get the key. Who holds it?" asked Agent 7

"No. Do not get involved yet. The priest gave us his assurance. He doesn't want the keyholder harmed. We promised him. Plus, any intervention now might alert The Network to our presence and mean the portal may not show up…And then you lose your prize."

Agent 7 was frustrated. She felt the approach was sentimental. But she understood that moving too fast may spook the portal. She felt a little bound by the plan and just wanted to move. Her eagerness eating away at her.

"One more thing," Kane continued, "I appreciate you have high professional standards. And that your recent failure will have caused you distress."

Agent 7 tried to gauge where he was heading. She was confused. "But do not let your personal pride get in the way of your assignment," he concluded.

He paused again. Agent 7 felt offended but stayed silent. Her mind raced. How dare he? Who was he to question how she worked? Who was he to intimate she would allow her personal pride to compromise her ability to finish the job?

He was inferring she had weakness. She had to control her anger and hold her tongue. But she knew if she was next to him, she might have snapped his neck.

"This isn't personal, Agent 7. Do you understand?"

She didn't answer.

"Do you understand?" he repeated slowly and assertively.

With reluctance she answered, "Yes."

"Good. And use your team. They are there to assist. Don't try and do this alone. The portal and his colleague are strong. It's not about your success and honour. This is about The Order and our continual work to cleanse humanity. Do you understand?"

"Yes," she replied, more robustly than before. Kane knew then that he had riled her.

"And most importantly," he continued, "the ritual is the priority. It has to happen. If we achieve that and the portal gets away, then so be it. We can re-group and then organise his termination at a later date…"

"The ritual will go ahead unhindered and the portal will be terminated," Agent 7 interjected rudely.

She had had enough of his talking. She understood and, in her mind, there was no more to say. Kane knew. He sensed she was angry. He had played with her enough. It was time to end the call. "Be ready for when the support team arrive. The lead agent and our priest will then be in contact."

She never replied. She wanted to put the phone down but knew her insolence would be punished. She restrained herself. But Kane decided to play one last game.

194

"Do not fail us again, Agent 7."

With that, she heard the call click off. Her fists clenched and her body tightened. The anger that surged within her made her feel invincible. She wanted to punch the stone wall. But she controlled the anger. Assassins feed off anger. She had learnt a long time ago to use it positively. To put it deep down inside and lock it away. Ready for when she needed it.

Ready for the moment she would unleash it and deliver pain and a violent death to her target.

Chapter 31

Having arrived at Kings Cross, Tom and Odin had been taken around the back of a sex shop and up a flight of stairs into a hallway with several doors along it, all closed. The man that had showed them to their room was odd and made slight grunting noises as he walked. They heard the sound of a woman groaning in sexual pleasure, unsure from which room it was coming from.

The room was almost uninhabitable. Inside was a double bed and a table with a mirror leaning against the wall. There was a damp smell and mould on the ceiling. Tom walked over to the window and pulled back the stained net curtain.

A few hundred metres away was Kings Cross station and he noticed the diversity of people, all moving in their own directions. An obviously wealthy couple with suitcases walked across the road towards the station and were shouted at by a tramp. They glanced at him and rushed away. The tramp then shouted at the next person who walked past him. He stood in the road and soon cars were backing up waiting for him to cross. Horns beeped and he stuck his fingers up and shouted, shuffling out of the road. The traffic quickly moved again with horns and angry voices swearing as they passed.

Two homeless men sat below their window just in front of the shop window. They shared a green bottle of whatever fluid it contained and, from their manner, the drink seemed to be highly intoxicating. The area felt as rough as the room they were staying in. Tom turned to Odin and rolled his eyes.
"It's just for tonight," Odin responded.

After feeling a little more invigorated after his nap on the plane Tom felt tired again. And from studying their surroundings, he would be very surprised if, once the sun goes down, this was a place that quietened down suitably for a person to get a good sleep.

A police siren sounded, grew louder and then faded off into the distance. Tom felt uneasy. And he was concerned if he would be able to relax enough to have a successful meditation session.

"You hungry?" asked Odin.

"I suppose," replied Tom, not sure if he was or not.

"I am famished. Once it gets dark, we will slip out and grab some food."

Tom nodded. He then told Odin his plans around the meditation and that he hoped to do it later that evening after they had eaten. There was a silence and Tom hoped that Odin would ask him why, but he didn't, so Tom elaborated.

"I feel a little anxious. It will help me see my family."

"Yeah, makes sense," replied Odin, checking his mobile phone.

"I...Er...I may be able to go further with the vision of the church..."

"Look, Tom," interrupted Odin, "You don't need to..."

"I want to..."

"No," Odin cut in, "I don't want to know..."

"What? Why?"

"Why? Isn't it obvious? If your vision shows this woman killing me then why would I want to know?"

Tom was confused, "So you don't go..."

"I am going!"

"If you know, then why go?"

Odin shook his head, looked down at his feet and smiled.

"I am grateful for your concern. But you are missing the point. I am going because it's *my* destiny. Professor Lewis told you about yours but what about mine? My life has been driven along a path and it's come to this. Do you seriously think I am going to bail out now? It's fate. And my fate is to help you destroy The Order. And if by helping you I lose my life then so be it..."

"How can you be so relaxed about..."

"Relaxed about what? A vision? A daydream? So what if I die in your head? It doesn't mean it will happen for real."

"Oh, so you don't believe me?"

"I didn't say that…It's just…Even if I knew for sure. Even if it was guaranteed that I would lose my life, I would still go."

Tom knew Odin wasn't going to back out. His face must've appeared solemn. Odin noticed and walked over to him, put his hand on his shoulder and grinned.
"Hey buddy, I am your best man. It's my job to make sure you get to the church on time."

Chapter 32

It was around 9.30pm. Tom and Odin had slipped out an hour before and ended up getting food from a Turkish restaurant. They could've eaten inside but Odin decided that it was best to take the food away and eat back at the bedsit. The next few days were going to be vital. And, under normal circumstances, whilst members of The Network had to be vigilant, they could still live their life to some level of normality and go out and integrate into society. However, Odin needed to protect Tom now more than ever and he didn't want to take any unnecessary chances. They needed to avoid integration for a few days.

In the back of his mind, he knew there was a small chance that The Order knew of their plan. In this world of betrayal and deceit, where trust was rare, it was always going to be hard to keep it a secret. Odin just hoped that The Network's vail of secrecy and protocols would mean they could get into Ireland covertly, do what they need to do and get out.

The streets beyond their bedsit window were electric. People and vehicles passed on a continuous cycle. Police sirens, shouting, dogs barking, and all manner of noises could be heard. They also had no TV to drown out the outside world.

It had been difficult for Tom to settle and find his place. Three times Odin believed he was under and had gone into his vision but then, suddenly, Tom had opened his eyes and stood up, frustrated, shouting that the environment wasn't right. Normally Tom would do this in a familiar and calm place, a sanctuary, with the sound of birdsong coming through the window and the gentle aroma of fragrance hanging in the air.

But this place was anything but familiar, nor was it a calm sanctuary. It was unfamiliar, loud, brash and unclean. About as far from the ideal place for Tom to meditate.

Odin had noticed Tom's anger and assured him that it wasn't necessary. Tom had snapped. Furious that Odin kept trying to put him off. Odin had just held his hands up and sat back on the bed and had told him to do as he pleased.

But on the next attempt it appeared that Tom had managed it. He had sat with his eyes closed for almost twenty minutes and Odin had even stepped towards him and waved his hand directly in front of his face, just an inch away. Tom hadn't flinched. Odin also noticed his eyes flickering and, on the odd occasion, his head moving.

Tom's vision had been good. He had gone to the lake surrounded by mountains, swooping down to the pebble beach. As always, the time with his family had been comforting. But as his sister had waved the familiar interruption occurred.

A spike of lighting splintered above his head. He cowered. Feeling cold and frightened. The rain hit his face so hard it hurt. The dark building appeared in another flash. He now knew it was a church. Much clearer. Almost clear enough for him to walk towards it and touch the ancient, mossy stone. He felt a sense of dread. His body told him to run away. But he stayed put. Allowing its deadly secrets to penetrate into his psyche.

Either side of him were the two men. Clearer now. Two men that he felt loved and cared for him. He felt their support and guidance. It gave him strength. One man he had never seen before. The other was Odin. As clear as being next to him in real life. They ascended the hill together. Bonded by one goal. Stronger together. Helping each other with each difficult step into the wind and up the hill.

But then it came. A presence. A dark, angry presence with evil intent. Tom and Odin had stopped. The figure moved in. It was the woman with red hair. Clearer than ever. Odin stepped down the hill towards her and she diverted towards him.

"Odin, run!" shouted Tom.

But he stood motionless as the woman collided with Odin and they disappeared into a cloud of mist.

"No!" shouted Tom, desperate for Odin to appear again.

He was unable to see him. But then from the mist came movement. It wasn't Odin. It appeared to be multiple figures. Slowly staggering forward towards him. Tom tried to break himself from the vision. He realised that by now it should've flashed back to his family. But this time it was prolonged. He couldn't escape. The figures now closer. Shuffling, moaning, with unusual characteristics.

As they approached Tom, their obvious injuries became visible and although they were walking they looked dead. White, gaunt, bloodied, eyes wide in pain and anguish. Moans of anger, panic and hurt. Tom made out Jenna. Her face twisted, evil and almost unsure of what or where she was. Shuffling and limping.

Phil Carter, his face almost torn in half and his brain visible from an open wound. Angry, reaching out to Tom. Contorted and bony fingers. And Rutherford, blood oozing from his neck and his head slumped to one side, almost ripped from his neck. Eyes so wide almost bursting from their sockets.

The groans got louder as they closed in on him. Tom tried to move but, his feet submerged in mud, held firm with a squelch. He bent his knees, but his feet were stuck fast. He looked up and they were on him. Screaming and moaning. Their cold bony fingers and hands now touching, pressing and grabbing him.

He fell backwards onto the wet, boggy ground and suddenly they were over him. Grabbing, holding, gripping. Blood dripping from their mouths they held him down and Tom felt suddenly his insides being ripped as they began feasting on him. Each bite harder and more painful than the last.

Tom screamed under the night sky, rain lashing down onto his face, feeling like it was the end. Then he heard a loud voice.

"Tom! Tom!"

He opened his eyes and Odin was shaking him.

"Tom! Wake up!" Odin shouted.

Tom then recognised where he was. He sat up. Odin put his arm on his shoulder.

"You had me worried."

"What happened?" Tom asked tensely.

"You shouted my name…Then you were shaking, and you just fell back waving your arms."

Tom rubbed his head, "That was weird…It went on longer than normal and…"

Tom stopped. Unsure what to tell Odin. Odin sensed something was bothering Tom but never pressed him to explain.

Odin put his arm under Tom's.

"Come on, get up."

Tom walked over to the bed and sat on the edge. Odin noticed he appeared unsettled and wanted to ask him if he was OK but, again, held back. Giving Tom time to get himself together and decide when he wanted to tell Odin. That was even if he wanted to at all.

Tom rubbed his head again and then lent forward, putting his elbows on his thighs and connecting his hands. Head down. Odin approached and put his hand on his shoulder again.

"Take your time. Relax."

Odin walked to the window and pulled the curtain open. Not looking at anything in particular. A group of girls walked past the window below laughing and shouting.

"How long was I under?"

"About 35 minutes," Odin confirmed, turning from the window.

Tom was silent. Odin noticed him trying to assess something.

"Everything OK?" Odin asked.

"Yeah...I think so..."

Tom paused and then continued again, "Well, I don't know...I mean..."

"What did you see, Tom?" Odin asked, trying to prompt him and break him from the confusion.

"Huh? Oh, it was you and me. And one other. Someone friendly..."

Tom paused again, "And?" prompted Odin.

"And the woman...She came too. Attacked you. But...It was unclear..."

"So, there you go," assured Odin, "It's unclear..."

"But she attacks you..."

"I can look after myself...Don't worry."

"But I have seen her. Felt her presence. She isn't just a normal agent..."

"Tom, your vision was unclear. That's it. Just leave it."

Tom didn't respond. He knew that Odin wasn't going to change his mind. For a moment he had wished he had listened and not gone into meditation. Those people from his past had unsettled him. It had brought back feelings and images that he had locked away. But, then again, the vision had progressed, and he now knew that the woman will, at some point, attack Odin. And knowing that may allow Tom to at least try to avoid it. Even if Odin wasn't prepared to back down, Tom could try to prevent his vision from coming true.

"She attacked from behind. Up the hill towards a church. You turned to face her, and she attacked..."

Tom paused. Odin walked across and sat on the bed next to him.

"You came together and then both disappeared..." Tom continued.

"There you go. It's unclear. Just a vision."

"It's not just a vision," replied Tom frustrated, "it's much more. They are real. Vivid...Oh, you don't understand."

"No. I don't," snapped Odin, "I don't understand, Tom. But hey, so what? You have had visions that show a woman attack me and what happens is unclear. I mean, come on, do you expect me to run off with my tail between my legs based on that?"

Tom shook his head. Odin continued, "And, as I said to you before, if, in your vision, she kills me, I would still go. I don't understand why you are so bothered…"

"What?!" interrupted Tom now standing, "You don't understand? Odin, you did everything for me. Saved my life numerous times, explained everything to me, helped me. Everything. I owe you…"

"You owe me nothing. You are everything. You are the special one. It's my duty to make sure you succeed. Nothing is going to change that."

They stood. Staring at each other. Then Odin spoke and broke the silence.

"I appreciate your concern. And I know you are grateful. But this is bigger than that. This is bigger than us. Bigger than everything. Just relax and stop worrying. My part of this whole situation is to make sure you get into that church. Let me worry about the woman. You concentrate on your part. You need to just go with it and together we will get this done, OK? Trust me."

They stepped towards each other and hugged. Odin patting Tom on his back. Their bond becoming stronger than ever.

Later on, in the early hours, as Odin slept, Tom lay awake, thinking. He had not told Odin about the final part of his vision. About the people from his past. He hadn't had any bad dreams for such a long time, it surprised him. He had hoped he was over that. Obviously not.

Why had they appeared? Had he reached way down into the depths of his mind and pulled them out? Tom couldn't understand the connection. Maybe there wasn't even one.

He rolled over onto his side and closed his eyes. Still feeling lethargic, he knew it was important to get some sleep. But all he saw was Jenna's distorted and pained face. A face that was scary and vulnerable at the same time.

He hoped she was resting in peace.

Chapter 33

They had been picked up early from Kings Cross. Odin had been pacing up and down on the phone speaking and texting, then checking the window on a continuous loop. Tom sensed a slight edginess to him, which he found unusual. Tom hadn't asked if he was OK. He knew by now just to let Odin get on with things in his own way. Then, soon after, without any warning, Odin had turned to Tom.
"Five minutes."

Tom had gathered his items and personal matters into his bag and sat on the bed waiting. Soon after, Odin notified it was time to go with a nod of the head. Tom had been glad to get out of that place. It offered him no solace or comfort.

A car had been waiting in the rear forecourt to the building they had stayed in. They had worked their way through south London, with a lot of stopping and starting and crawling along in traffic, but soon after they were out of the city and heading through Croydon and then further south into Greater London. Almost within an instant the busy, crowded city was left behind, and they were cruising through the Kent commuter belt, eventually onto rural country roads surrounded by beautiful, green pastures.

They hadn't had much conversation except for Odin explaining that they were heading to a private airport to pick up a charter flight to Cork. And on arriving there had been no fanfare and no delay. The car had gained access and they had been driven to the plane at the side of the runway which was already running and ready to go. They had got out of the car, straight onto the plane and were up in the clouds within fifteen minutes.

The Cessna Twin Propeller bumped up and down as it took off, and Tom's stomach had turned. But it soon settled. It was exciting for him at first, seeing the fields, roads and houses below, never before having flown in a small plane. The pilot had informed them that the journey would take roughly ninety minutes. After crossing the West country, south Wales and the Irish Sea, they were soon on the final approach to their destination. As they zeroed in on Ireland the turbulence hit, and it got bumpy. Tom's stomach turned again. As the pilot slowly descended, he noted the rugged coastline and green hills, the landmarks and houses becoming more visible with each passing minute.

Again, like at the first airport, as soon as they landed there had been no delay. After a short taxi to a private hangar, they found a car waiting for them and very soon the lush green rolling hills, forest and farmland was passing them by quickly.

During the journey, Odin had asked Tom if he was OK a few times. Tom had informed him he was. But he wasn't. Odin also knew but never pushed. Tom was nervous. Nervous at what this had become and what his role was. Tom realised that Odin was just looking out for him. And had Tom told him he wasn't OK, there was nothing Odin could've done anyway. They both knew that this was the lead up to something that neither of them could control and that much of what was about to happen would be down to luck rather than judgement.

Tom felt, as detailed as the plan was, there was also still a lot they had to leave to chance. He had wondered if that was why Odin had been edgy. He knew how much Odin hated not being in full control and so this experience was also new to him. Due to lack of sleep the night before, the gentle movement along the country roads had rocked Tom to sleep. Soon he felt a hand on his shoulder, and he woke up to see Odin.
"We're here."

Tom looked around as the car slowly bumped and rocked across a muddy, pothole covered track into a farm. A gate house, various out-buildings, barns, and hay shelters to the right and fields as far as the eye could see to the left. The sea visible just beyond.

They bumped slowly along the track for a few minutes until they reached a large house, set back amidst a forecourt and surrounding gardens. Just beyond the house was a smaller cottage; the car approached and stopped. They got out and Tom stretched. Tired and hungry. He breathed in and the air was so fresh, it surprised him. It was a cool day but the wind that swept in from the open fields had a cold chill to it.

The door on the bungalow opened and a large man stepped out. He was wearing a flat cap, a thick navy jumper and hard-wearing trousers with wellington boots. His face was world-weary, and weather worn. He waved and stepped towards them.

They made his acquaintance and shook hands. His name was Patrick which he had confirmed in a deep, strong Irish accent. Tom noticed that his hands were large and as hard as concrete. Standing tall he dwarfed both of them. He led them into the bungalow as the car drove away down the track. Tom entered and the warmth engulfed him like a blanket. The bungalow was small and cosy. He led them to a lounge, which contained a large window looking out onto the fields and the sea beyond. A huge sofa, coffee table and TV. Also, a fire which was well ablaze.

Odin set his bag down.
"It's perfect."
"Good," confirmed Patrick who then stepped towards the lounge door and turned.
"OK," he continued, "I have set the fire and that will last till tonight. There's more wood at the back door if needed. In about an hour I will bring a stew across for ye."

Both Odin and Tom thanked him. Patrick was just about to leave but then hesitated, appearing concerned.
"Now, I appreciate ye have things to do. But I just want to state for the record I have no interest in it and I don't want any part of it. And I ask no questions, OK? Ye can stay here tonight and then late tomorrow night ye are gone, OK? That's the deal…"

"Absolutely," confirmed Odin, aware of the arrangement that The Network had made with the farmer.

"And I want a promise from you that, whatever ye are up to, nothing comes back to me…Ye never stayed here, OK?"

Odin nodded, "Tomorrow night we leave here around 10.30pm and you won't ever see us again. I promise."

"Good, I appreciate that. And I don't want any nonsense. I don't mind a few comings and goings, but no disruption. If it's like Dublin on New Year's Eve, then the deal is off…"

"Of course…" acknowledged Odin.

"I have a family and a livelihood here," Patrick continued, "a reputation to uphold. And I have no desire to be involved any more than has been agreed, OK?"

Odin stepped forward and held out his hand, "I promise," he said.

Patrick stepped forward and shook Odin's hand, "Thank ye."

As the farmer was about to leave the room Odin called him.

"Patrick?"

The door reopened and the man's head appeared, "Aye?"

"The gate house at the entrance. Is it available to use?"

Patrick paused and then nodded, "I will unlock it."

"Thank you," replied Odin and Patrick left closing the door behind him.

The afternoon had been comfortable. They had settled and put the TV on. It offered little in the way of entertainment but gave some background noise which created a sense of home comfort and familiarity. Around 5pm there had been a knock. Odin had checked the window before letting Patrick in who carried a huge casserole dish of lamb stew. Immediately the bungalow was filled with a savoury aroma which had both of them salivating. Patrick had also left a bottle of red wine on the side as he left.

They devoured the food and sat, uncomfortably full and watched more TV, whilst sipping wine. During eating Odin had informed Tom that their contact was arriving around 9pm. A local priest called Father O'Dowd. He would help them with getting to the

Church of the Sacred Heart and providing access to it. So, they would need to discuss the plan.

Around 6pm, Tom had gone to the rear door to collect more firewood for the now dwindling fire. He scanned the horizon and noticed a dark grey mass way off out to sea in the distance. It was huge and spanned for miles and miles. It was a storm and he felt it approaching. The wind suddenly picked up and nearby trees went from a whisper to a louder, more intense groan, as the wind snapped and caught in their leaves.

A crow cawed loudly above him. Tom glanced upwards, noting it circling ominously above the bungalow. It cawed again. And Tom felt that it was speaking to him. Warning him.

Nerves hit him. He took a deep breath and quickly went inside. Closing the door and locking it.

Chapter 34

Since just before 9pm, Odin had been stood at the front window in the lounge, gun at the ready in one hand and mobile phone in the other. He wasn't taking any chances. They had come so far, and he wasn't prepared to let his discipline slip now. Soon after, his phone beeped, and Tom noticed him check it.

"He's here," he said, not diverting his attention from the window.

Soon after, they noticed headlights heading up the track between the farm towards them, stopping close enough to flood the front of the property in light. The lights flashed three times and then went out. Odin never moved. He waited, looking at his phone. Thirty seconds later his phone beeped again.

"OK, his password checks out. Let's go. But remember, he's not clear yet. Get him in and sit him down," Odin ordered, walking to his bag in the corner of the room, "and make sure he doesn't move."

Odin passed him a handgun. They both went to door and Odin went outside.

"Stay here, I'll send him in." Tom noticed the wind had picked up and drizzle flickered in the air. Odin walked to the car pointing the gun at the driver. He opened the door.

"OK. Out. To the house. Move."

The driver got out with his hands up and, doing as he was told, jogged towards Tom at the door. As he approached, Tom stepped back and aimed the gun at him.

"Come on, let's go," Tom ordered, and the man ran into the house. Tom directed him to the lounge.

Outside Odin checked the car inside for unwanted passengers and then checked the boot. He switched the engine off, put the keys in his pocket and made his way inside. He closed the door on the blustery night and went through to the lounge where the man was sat down. Tom was stood at the far side of the room aiming the gun at their visitor. The man was nervous.

"Sorry about the welcome but we can't take any chances."

The man nodded. He was tense. Still unsure as to what to make of it all.

"Do you have your passport and driving licence?" asked Odin.

"Oh…Yes, of course," replied the man standing up, patting his jacket.

"Take it easy," said Odin assertively, emphasising the gun aimed at the man by extending it towards him.

The man put his hands up and then slowly reached inside his jacket pulling out his wallet and passport. Odin walked across and checked them. Tom noticed Odin's sudden relaxation and assumed it all checked out. Odin put his gun away and held out his hand.

"As I said, sorry about the welcome. I am Odin. We've spoke several times before. Nice to finally meet you, Father O'Dowd."

Father O'Dowd appeared a little taken aback but took Odin's hand none the less and they shook.

"This is Tom, the angel that you have been told about," Odin informed, pointing at Tom.

Tom stepped forward and extended his hand.

"Hi, Good to meet you, Father."

O'Dowd chuckled while shaking Tom's hand. Tom was surprised at how young he was. He put him in his mid-forty's but had been expecting an older man.

"Hi, Tom. Good to meet you at last. You know, for years I have been briefed and trained about this, but I never ever really believed it to be true…That it would ever reach this moment…"

"It's all true. I have seen it with my own eyes," Odin confirmed.

"I…I don't know what to say…"

"Neither did I when Odin first contacted me," interrupted Tom.

"No, I can well imagine."

Father O'Dowd stared at Tom and thought he was ordinary. Nice enough. But an Archangel? It didn't seem right. But was any of this right? The deeper O'Dowd got into this the more surreal it became. However, he suddenly felt a gentle wave of positivity and energy creep through his body.

They all stood facing each other. A silence descending on them as O'Dowd took it all in.

"So…A real angel," said O'Dowd with a nervous chuckle, "I mean, where do we start? I had always been told any rational argument of their existence should be taken with caution."

Tom smiled awkwardly as O'Dowd continued.

"The modern mind is sceptical of what cannot be proved. But I suppose in my position I have to be open to my beliefs."

"I still find it hard to believe, even now," said Tom.

Odin suddenly interrupted, "OK, first things first, let's discuss the plan and get the details in place."

O'Dowd nodded, taken aback at Odin's assertiveness, but also appreciative of him taking the lead in this unusual meeting. He took his jacket off and Tom noticed his white dog collar over his black shirt. They all sat. Odin did most of the talking. Tom and O'Dowd asked a few questions to clarify but, generally, the conversation was being led by Odin.

The plan was that at 10.30pm O'Dowd would collect Tom and Odin from the gatehouse close to the road at the farm entrance. He would bring with him the key to Sacred Heart church. They would then all go in his car to the jetty where they would meet the support team that were arriving first thing tomorrow.

A local guy called Rob, who runs conservation and tourist trips out to the island and around the coast, had been brought on side and he will be leaving four boats with outboard motors at the jetty. All fuelled and ready to go. Odin, Tom and O'Dowd in one and the support team of around eight men will follow. Two men will stay behind to watch for potential pursuers.

Once on the island O'Dowd will lead them up to the church, get them access and Tom can do what he needed to do. The support team will be on hand to deal with any armed protection the ritual group may have. But at this stage, that was unknown. Odin asked them if they had any questions to which they both confirmed they didn't. He then asked if they understood the plan. O'Dowd nodded in confirmation that he did.

Tom also acknowledged that he understood but, again, was still anxious about his part at the church. Odin had stated that he needed to 'do what he needed to do'. But it was still unclear. Tom realised it wasn't the right time to ask as it would just complicate matters. But he knew he must speak to Odin about it, maybe tomorrow.

There was a silence. All of them suddenly realising that this thing had thrown them together in such a random and unusual way.
"I have to say. I am still finding this all very strange," admitted O'Dowd.
"It doesn't get any easier," replied Tom, standing and stretching.
O'Dowd smiled, "So, what's your stories? How did you get involved?"

Odin got up and walked across to his bag. He pulled out a bottle of whisky, holding it up.
"Drink, Father?" he asked O'Dowd.
O'Dowd nodded, "Yes please, I think am going to need one."

Odin went to the kitchen to get some tumblers. O'Dowd stayed sat on the settee and Tom sat back down again. An awkward minute passed as they heard Odin banging about in the kitchen, he then returned with a tumbler, a straight glass and a teacup.
"You can have the tumbler, Father. Being our guest an' all. I will have the glass and you can have the teacup…"
"Hey," said Tom jokingly.
Odin smiled, "Don't worry…All tastes the same."

He poured them all a large drink, cursing the fact that they had no ice. Then they all settled down. The room was comfortable and warm as the wood from the fire glowed bright orange, cracking and spitting embers.

Odin told his story. Tom had been surprised. Odin had told him some details before but had kept it quite vague. He gave more detail this time. Was Odin cleansing himself? As he spoke about his childhood and the arrival of The Order, the fire in which his family died and other tragic incidents, he showed no emotion. Just stuck to the facts. He talked about how he became an agent, how he was trained, and his assignments. Eventually, he reached the point when he was assigned to Tom and when they first met.

O'Dowd listened intently. Sipping his whisky, shaking his head several times, expressing his disbelief at what he was hearing. Odin then told them in full detail about the night in the warehouse and the moments that led to Tom elevating in a bright light above Rutherford. As he spoke, O'Dowd glanced over at Tom, then back at Odin and then again, back at Tom. Tom knew how unbelievable it all sounded and that O'Dowd was obviously trying to work out how Tom, this normal, ordinary human being, was capable of this.

Tom sensed that O'Dowd might think they were mad. He tried to imagine himself in the priest's position and realised it must have been difficult. Even surreal.

Odin poured them all another large whisky and told them something that Tom wasn't aware of. That he had known about this for four years. The Network had also known. Even before Tom had even been part of The Network, they and Odin were aware that there was the possibility that they may find out when and where The Order were next going to have to undertake their ritual to maintain their power.

Professor Lewis had been close. He had been working on it for so long and they almost had the code broken. It was just a matter of time. And all they needed was for the Archangel to arise. To be uncovered. And then, soon after, Odin was assigned to Tom. The rest was history. Odin confirmed that, somehow, he knew straight away.

"Why did you not tell me?" asked Tom

"Well, I wasn't sure. I reported back to The Network and they asked me to monitor it. But, the night in the warehouse confirmed it."

"So, why didn't you tell me after that?"

"Really? After what you had already been through. No, the night you were kidnapped changed things. It had got out of control and it just needed to calm down. Besides, if I had told you then I might have lost you. You would have disappeared, scared to death. The Network advised me to re-settle you and just wait. Keep you under tabs, monitor, just to be sure. Then when the time comes to make contact and go from there."

Tom knew it made sense and nodded in acceptance.

"Interesting," interjected O'Dowd, "that you mention you have known for around four years, as that is similar to me."

"Yeah, Lewis had been working on it for many years, most of his later life, and had already pinpointed the location. The Church of the Sacred Heart. But he was unable break the code and get the right time and date. So, the Internal Department within The Network made moves back then to make sure we had someone in place that we can connect with at the right time. Someone local to be our guide. That was obviously you."

"Indeed," O'Dowd nodded, "and so that would be when Father Reilly introduced me to all this and prepared me."

"Who's Father Reilly?" asked Tom.

"He's my mentor. A Bishop. But also like a real father to me. Taught me all I know, got me up the ladder, nurtured me and supported me. I'd be nowhere without him. He told me of The Order. Their power and purpose. Told me what was going to happen and why. Prepared me, guided me. Kept reminding me of my significance in all this and how fate had delivered me to be the one to help you people."

216

O'Dowd sat back and made himself comfortable, sipping his whisky.

"I recall the night he told me. I thought he was going mad. I wondered what the hell was he talking about. But, over time, he educated me. It took time for me to properly understand and accept it. But, I did. All this time wondering if it was true. Hoping that I wouldn't be involved...With respect, I mean. This isn't something that ordinary people like me want to be involved in."

"I understand," confirmed Odin.

"And as for The Order. Father Reilly told me about them, called them a 'highly organised network of religious fanatics' but never much more than that. I mean, I know they are brutal and wield great power, but how do they exist? How are they funded?"

Odin answered, "Organised crime, arms and drug dealing, money laundering, human trafficking, real estate...You name it. Heavy connections within the mafia. It's a cobweb of all that's criminal. And you know that the church is also involved?"

"Father Reilly did tell me that it was known that members of the church were connected...But I don't know..."

"From the top," interjected Odin, "and with huge funds also being diverted. Vast amounts."

O'Dowd shook his head, "What can I say? I can't quite believe it."

"It's hard to get your head around."

"Indeed. And Father Reilly always warned me that if we were ever found out it would be the end. That's why I never wanted to be involved...I have a wife and child..."

O'Dowd stopped, almost too afraid to continue, thinking of the potential consequences. Odin stood and spoke.

"You are brave. And we appreciate your commitment and the risk you take. Both you and Father Reilly. Without you two The Network would not be in a position to strike."

"Thank you. Although one thing..." continued O'Dowd, "The Order purge the world of sinners. I cannot help playing devil's advocate here, but is that not a good thing?"

"That's the morality question," answered Odin, sitting back down.

"Technically yes, it is a good thing. And the people that I and Tom were brought close to did bad things. But can people not change? Be healed? Given mercy and a chance at redemption?"

"Of course," replied O'Dowd assertively.

Odin sat forward, "OK. But also, more importantly, it's the fallout, the heartbreak, children enslaved by The Order, families torn apart, threatened, blackmailed, paid off. Innocent people killed, snuffed out, their lives changed forever. Manipulated, altered. And the portals, or angels, suffering, falling apart, confused. Many of whom never recover, admitted to mental hospitals, spending their lives sedated. Or worse they take their own lives, unable to cope. And then, disposed of like rags once their work for The Order is done...It's just barbaric..."

"My son, I see your anger. I understand. Please believe me, I understand..."

A silence filled the room. Much had been discussed and for all three of them, thoughts traversed their minds. O'Dowd took a deep breath and smiled, trying his best to improve the sombre atmosphere that his comments had created.

"Anyway...I still can't quite believe I'm sitting here. With members of The Network. The resistance that Reilly told me all about. And with an angel...I mean, what in the name of God is happening?"

O'Dowd chuckled nervously again. It was surreal. Even Odin laughed at the situation.

"And so, what of you Tom? What about your story. I would be intrigued if you'd tell me how you ended up sitting in that wee armchair across from me."

Tom sighed. He had only told his story once before. He was about to speak when Odin stood up.

"Woah there. I have heard this story. I lived most of it. I have a few calls to make. And this whisky has gone to my head. I am going to pop out back, make a few calls and get some fresh air."

Before he left, he topped up both Tom and O'Dowd's drinks.

"This will keep you going, guys."

"Be careful out there," warned O'Dowd, "there's a big one blowing in and these coastal gusts will lift you off your feet."
Odin winked, "Thanks."

With that, Odin left out the back door leaving them alone.
"So where do I start, Father?" asked Tom.
"Right at the very beginning," confirmed O'Dowd.

Chapter 35

Tom had spoken for almost an hour. O'Dowd was captivated. He had not asked one question. He just listened, sipping on his whisky, taking it all in. He had shown emotion and reaction in his own way, shaking his head, widening his eyes, rubbing his forehead and blowing out air. As unbelievable as Tom's story was, O'Dowd also felt how genuine and sincere it was.

Odin had come back in halfway through and had sat down. He also listened intently. Even though he knew the story, he was captivated. Eventually the story was over.

"...and that, Father O'Dowd, is how I am now sitting here with you."

"I am just...speechless" O'Dowd confirmed, getting up from his chair. He walked over to Tom and put his hand on his shoulder. "God bless you child. How you coped with all that only God knows."

Tom nodded in appreciation. O'Dowd returned to the settee and sat back down.

"I am so sorry for your losses. Your mother and father. Even Jenna. It sounds like you loved her. And you wasn't to know, Tom. How could you? God rest her soul. And Davy, his family. May God have mercy on them all. And I am very sorry for Laura. I pray God is with her," O'Dowd crossed himself as he spoke.

O'Dowd continued, "Did you receive comfort from seeing your sister and her family recently?"

"Very much so. I just hope they never get involved."

O'Dowd nodded, "Well I will pray for them and ask God to allow them happy and safe passage through life."

Tom smiled, "Thank you."

Odin got up and attempted to pour the last of the whisky into O'Dowd's tumbler.

"Oh no! Please. I have to drive," he argued, pulling the tumbler to his chest. He checked his watch.

"Dear me, look at the time, it's past midnight…I must be going."
He smiled nervously, "There is one more thing though, Tom. The night in the warehouse. The burning sensation…And elevating, striking this Rutherford down…Was you afraid?"
"At first, yes. It burnt. And I was confused. But soon after, it felt perfect…Like ecstasy. Then power. Just pure unrelenting power."
"It was just stunning," added Odin.
"And this is the power he will use to break the transmission?" O'Dowd asked, turning to Odin.
"Absolutely."

O'Dowd sighed. Intrigued and amazed. But also very tired, and a little drunk.
"May I bless you?" he asked Tom, "In fact, I will bless all of us. I will ask for God to support us and be with us tomorrow night. Please, both of you, bow your heads and close your eyes."

Odin and Tom followed the request. Eager to show their co-operation and not wanting to offend the young priest.
"We bow our heads, and we pray for God's blessing. May the blessing of the mighty God, The Father, The Son and of The Holy Spirit, descend upon us and be with us in our moment of destiny tomorrow night and then forever and ever. Amen."

As O'Dowd had spoken, he had raised his hands and crossed himself.
"Amen," replied Tom and Odin, then opening their eyes.
"Thank you both so much," he replied, "I have to go. I want to try and get some sleep tonight. Hopefully the wee drink will help."

They all stood and approached each other. O'Dowd shook hands with Tom and Odin.
"It's been a pleasure."
He put on his jacket and made his way to the door, both of them following.
"Drive carefully," said Tom sincerely.
"I will, thank you."

"And you'll need these," said Odin, holding his car keys up. O'Dowd smiled and took the keys. As Odin opened the door, the wind howled into the doorway and the rain had got heavier.

"This one is going to hit the coast tomorrow afternoon," shouted O'Dowd, standing on the front step just out of the rain.

"Yeah, I saw the forecast," replied Odin, "We may have to take that into account and give ourselves some added time…"

"No problem," shouted O'Dowd back, "I know these roads and lanes very well, don't worry."

Odin gave him a thumbs up, "I will text you tomorrow with the final details."

"Good man," confirmed O'Dowd, "Oh, and Tom. I know you are nervous. I know you are unsure of what to do when we get to the church. But I feel the energy from you. Honestly, I do. I know when the time is right you will know what to do. Sleep well."

And with a wave, he jogged to his car and got in. The engine sounded, the lights switched on, glaring in their faces and soon the car had turned, and the red lights were bumping down the track.

Inside the warm bungalow Odin and Tom sat back down.

"He's a good man," Odin suggested, "He won't let us down."

Tom was glad to hear it. Soon after, Odin had declared he had had a long day and needed some sleep. Tom said he would soon follow. But as he sat, he felt more positive. More than he had since losing Laura.

It was Father O'Dowd. He had felt a connection to him. As soon as he walked in the room, Tom had felt it. Like he had known him before. He was familiar and comforting. He emanated warmth and gave off a feeling of support and guidance.

Tom went over to his bag and pulled out an envelope. It contained the photos of his family. He flicked through them. Talking of them earlier had made him desperate to be with them again. He smiled as he glanced at each photo. Soon after, he put them back. Hoping that, once this was all over, he would find a peaceful place to meditate and feel their love and presence again.

Then, as he was walking from the lounge, it suddenly came to him. He stopped. O'Dowd was the other man in the vision. Odin had confirmed that O'Dowd was to cross to the island with them and guide them to the church. It was the man he had seen. The one that Tom approached the church with. Knowing that he would be entering that place with him comforted Tom. O'Dowd wouldn't let them down. But now Tom was determined, more than ever, not to let O'Dowd down.

A surge of positivity flowed through him. Father O'Dowd had energised him. Before he lay down to go to sleep, he reached into his bag and took out Laura's Red Sox cap. He held it close to him. For the first time in weeks, as soon as his head hit the pillow, he fell asleep and stayed asleep.

Chapter 36

Overnight the storm had drawn in. The wind had picked up and was now constant, a continual cycle ranging from a low groan up to huge gusts and anything in between. The rain came in fits and starts, drizzly and cold.

Tom had noted that the grey blanket had got closer and now hung out to sea, slowly approaching land. Ominous. As dark a grey as he had ever seen. As the morning ticked by it came, edging ever closer. The only bright part of the morning was that farmer Patrick had knocked on their door around 10am carrying a basket and a flask of hot coffee. It contained six eggs, ham on the bone and a fresh loaf. Odin and Tom had been hungry and so it had been very welcome.

Patrick had told them he would be out in the fields most of the day and then planned to visit a friend later on. He would stay there overnight to avoid driving home in the approaching storm. He wished them good luck and walked away. Odin thanked him and, as he walked away, he raised his hand to acknowledge the comment.

Around lunchtime, Tom noticed Odin was edgy. He had asked him if he was OK and he had replied that he was just frustrated at being stuck without transport. He was also unable to contact the leader of the support team that should've checked in by now. He assured Tom all would be OK and that he would relax when all plans were in place.

Tom's job, right now, was to just sit and wait. He watched some TV, went out the back for fresh air, gathered firewood and sat and did some reading. From late morning to mid-afternoon, he did this on a loop. Although he was anxious and nervous about what was going to unfold later that night, he also hoped the clock would tick faster, so that it could just be done and over with. The tedium was becoming annoying.

During that time, Odin came and went from outside to inside and then back out again. Checking his phone and studying the coastline on the map he had brought with him.

But, by mid-afternoon Odin had become a lot more relaxed. The support team had checked in and were standing by. They had arrived by boat from the east coast, so they had been delayed by the weather. Hansen, the lead officer, had been unable to contact Odin as he had no network whilst out at sea. But he had now confirmed that they had all arrived and would be at the jetty at 10.30pm. Odin also received a text from Rob, the local man with the boats. Four outboard motorboats had been taken down to the jetty and were now moored up and ready to go.

Whilst sitting in the lounge watching TV, Odin's phone bleeped. Tom noticed him read it and then put his phone down. Odin informed Tom it was Father O'Dowd. He had the key to the church, he had no further appointments and he would pick them up from the gate house at 10.30pm.

Everything was in place and ready to go. With that Odin went to the kitchen and cooked the remaining eggs. They sat and ate the eggs with bread and drank hot coffee. And then, for the rest of the afternoon, they waited. By late afternoon Tom felt drowsy. He cursed this lethargy and tiredness. Odin advised him to go to bed for nap, which he did. He closed his eyes. The wind moaned monotonously at the rattling window and he was nervous; it prevented him from sleeping, but he was just glad that he was able to rest.

Several miles away Father O'Dowd looked at a photo of his wife Siobhan and Jimmy. Initially, he had believed his task was relatively simple. He was to meet the people from The Network, guide them to the church and let them in. But, as he found out more about The Order, he became more nervous. Wary of the consequences.

He hoped that Odin was correct. That he would cross with Odin and Tom, and they and the support team would go up to the church. He would let Tom in and that would be it. He could walk away, come back from the island, get through his last week or so and then go to Cork.

Things would be fine. Then he remembered Odin's words that it was unknown if The Order's ritual group would have armed support. He hoped they didn't. He hoped that violence was not part of the conclusion. Surely, The Order wouldn't know of the plan. How could they? Everything would be OK he reassured himself. But he didn't feel enough assurance. He picked up his mobile phone and selected Father Reilly's number. He would tell him of the meeting and get some words of support. Father Reilly was good at that.

He called him and the line at the other end rang several times. O'Dowd noted that the time was 5:40pm. Father Reilly should have completed his duties by now. But there was no answer. He would try again later.

He got up from his kitchen table, walked out into his hallway and unlocked the door beyond the joint access which led from his living quarters to the main church and the office. He stepped through the large oak door into the church. He felt a chill as he approached the main altar. He lit a candle and used it to light several more that lined the altar. A soft glow was created which allowed the face of the nearby statue of Mary to be seen clearly.

He knelt. He prayed for God's support and protection. For a clear and safe passage to be forged for him, Tom, Odin and other members of The Network. For the success of their goal and a calm, safe and peaceful life for them all.

He stood. Bowed and crossed his head and chest and sat at the front bench. He held his cross that hung around his neck. More than ever, he needed his faith to be strong.

It was an unusual situation. He had been told that The Order used God's power. But he hoped that God, himself, would not approve. He hoped that there hadn't been a strange, contorted manifestation of God's power and that he, himself, somehow approved. Would God approve of the way The Order operate?

The thought worried O'Dowd. Surely not? This was clearly a sick misuse of God's power. God allowed people forgiveness and a chance of repentance. That was clear. And how did The Order know if sinners had repented? He picked up a bible from the rack in front of him. He flicked through it, eventually reaching a page that he knew. He moved his finger downwards and then stopped, whispering the words as he read them.
"If we confess our sins, God is faithful and just, and will forgive us our sins and purify us from all righteousness…"

Had the people the dark angels had killed not confessed their sins? He flicked through some more pages, again, finding another that he knew. Moving his finger across, he whispered again.
"Whoever conceals their sins does not prosper, but the one who confesses and renounces them finds mercy…"

He sat up, realising something. It wasn't The Order that knew if sins had been confessed and repentance sought. It was God. A shiver went through him. He flicked through the bible one last time. Hoping for confirmation. He stopped. Moved his finger down the page and spoke the words louder.
"I tell you, no! But unless you repent, you too will perish…"

He looked up from the bible. Unsure what to do. Was this a manifestation? Or were The Order merely carrying out God's work exactly as the bible stated? He suddenly felt confused. Something jarred inside him. It unsettled him. But then he recalled the stories that Tom and Odin had told him. He realised that The Order may carry out God's work but the destruction they leave in their wake is evil and cannot continue.

His mind raced. Was he doing the right thing? A heavy weight descended upon him. Who should he believe? Father Reilly, Tom and Odin were on his side. He knew that. But were The Order righteous and working in line with God's will?

He stood. Panic came over him. He realised now that he was questioning God's involvement and his own faith. But, he must plough on, for Father Reilly's sake at least. He couldn't let his mentor down. He had to do what had been planned. He took a deep breath. His stomach full of butterflies and a ball of confusion in his head. The thoughts were nerve-wracking.

Suddenly he heard a thud from the back of the church. He turned. He saw nothing. His heart stopped. He heard the moaning of the wind outside. Then he felt a sudden chill descend upon him. He shivered. A presence enveloped him. He looked each side of him. Someone or something was close. His stomach turned.

A sudden wind whipped up and flashed across him. He felt its coldness touch his face. The pages of the bible he was holding fluttered, and all of the candles he had lit suddenly vanished and the plumes of smoke were carried away with the gust. Then it stopped. He held his breath. Unable to move. Silence and darkness surrounded him and injected fear into his body.
"Hello…Is anyone there?" he asked nervously.

No answer came. He turned and rushed to the door that led to his living quarters. Turning to check behind him as he went. He felt the presence move towards him from behind. He reached the door and opened it. He felt the warmth from inside enter the cold church. He walked through but looked back, something was there. He felt it. Although he saw nothing. He then quickly closed the door and locked it.

His mind told him to stop being silly. The church was old. But he had never known the wind gain access to the main church. Maybe a door was open on the outer buildings and caused a draft? He didn't know. Although, one thing he definitely knew, which this whole situation proved to him, was that his faith was not mis-guided. It was all true. There was a God.

And later tonight, at The Church of the Sacred Heart, he may actually see the proof of this. If he hadn't just done so already.

Chapter 37

The storm had started with real ferocity half an hour ago. O'Dowd needed to leave soon to make the pick-up time. He had his mobile phone, car keys and the key to the old church. The wind howled from outside and the rain clattered against the window. It reminded him that the local roads were hard enough to navigate at night under normal conditions, but in this weather they were treacherous.

It was just before 10:20pm. It gave him a few minutes buffer here and there at each stage of the drive to the safe house to meet Tom and Odin. Then onto the jetty to get the boat across to Clare Island and the hike up to the church. It would be tight, but if all goes according to plan, then they will have timed it perfectly.

Maggie had stayed late, just as he thought she would, and he almost forcibly removed her to get her to go home. They were entering a busy period for the church with some fundraisers and community events in a few weeks. Knowing that Father O'Dowd was due to leave for Cork soon, Maggie had taken on the role of chief organiser and there was a lot to do.

She had said goodnight and left to go home roughly fifteen minutes ago. There was now nothing else to delay him. He had to go. But suddenly there was a noise. A door closing. O'Dowd froze. "Maggie? Is that you?" he shouted.

There was no response. The only sound was the wind groaning at the window. He moved around his desk to the office door and opened it. He peered nervously along the dark hallway. A light from outside shone through the window and the trees blowing in the wind created a flickering effect with light dancing and twisting in the darkness.
"Maggie?" he shouted louder.

He was jittery and knew it could be his mind playing tricks on him. He went back inside, picked up his office key from the desk then patted himself down. He had everything he needed.

He left the office again, switched the light off and closed the door. As he locked it he heard a shuffle to his right. He jumped.
"Oh my God!" he exclaimed as he noticed a dark figure at the end of the hallway. His heart stopped.
"Who's there? Maggie? Is that you?" His voice breaking with fear on the last word.

The figure stepped forward. Moving out of the darkness and into a shaft of light. O'Dowd adjusted his eyes, frozen with fear, the flickering light confusing him but just giving him a chance to make out who it was.
"Father Reilly! You scared the hell out of me!"

Reilly took another step forward then stopped. Although O'Dowd felt a wave of relief, his instincts told him something wasn't right. Reilly was soaking wet from the rain. His face serious, which was unusual for him. O'Dowd realised the light could be playing tricks on him.
"What on earth are you doing here? I thought you was in Dublin?" he asked, hoping that everything was OK.
"No. I am back for a few days…You know, business…"
"Business?"
"Look, I am back, OK?" Reilly interjected, a little too assertively for O'Dowd, who instantly felt uncomfortable and isolated in the dark hallway.

O'Dowd unlocked the office and went back inside, switching the light on immediately. It gave him some relief. He rushed to his desk wondering what on earth was going on. What was Father Reilly doing here? And why now of all times? Reilly knew Tom had to go and meet The Network.

Reilly appeared at the office entrance and stepped inside from the gloom of the hallway. O'Dowd then noticed that Reilly's face was stern. It hadn't been his mind playing tricks. His body language was also awkward and completely out of character.

"I can't believe you are here. It's a surprise…"

"Yes. I realise it's out of the blue. But…Well…You know how it is when business calls."

O'Dowd sat down and gestured for his visitor to sit in the chair opposite, "Please, sit down."

"I'll stand, thanks," Reilly replied, leaning back onto the door.

O'Dowd sensed something was wrong, Reilly wasn't being himself. He had known him for years. He appeared bothered by something.

"Are you OK," O'Dowd asked.

"Why don't you go home?"

"Home?" O'Dowd laughed, out of genuine confusion, but mainly from nervous tension, "I am home."

Reilly never laughed.

"Your new home. In Cork. Go tonight, I will finish your tenure here…"

O'Dowd, confused, tried to maintain his composure, "No, I have things to do, people to see and…"

"You don't understand, Father O'Dowd. You need to go. Now."

"But…I am on my way to meet those people," O'Dowd stated under his breath, "it's all arranged…I need to go…"

"I will take it from here. Give me the key to the Church of the Sacred Heart."

O'Dowd glared into Reilly's eyes. They were negative. He was a warm, genuine and loving man. Had been like family to O'Dowd for the last four years but, tonight, there was an insincerity in his eyes. A coldness.

Neither of them spoke and O'Dowd realised that Reilly was assessing him. How should he respond? It could be the way out he had desired. He hadn't wanted to be any part of this anyway and there had been times when he would've accepted any excuse to

232

remove himself from it. It crossed his mind to give him the key, pack a bag and walk away. Forget it all and go and be with his family. It was what he really wanted. He had dreaded everything about this situation up to now and it had been the bane of his life. He now had the chance he wanted.

But something stopped him. This was all so unusual. What about the training that Reilly had given him? All of the information, guidance and preparation. For years Reilly had primed him for this moment. A moment which was now slipping away. This strange surprise meeting was now eating into his timings and the buffer he had given himself was being eroded.

Plus, in the short time he had been with Tom and Odin, he had become invested in them and their mission. They had made an impact on him. He had felt the goodness and positivity flowing from Tom. What he had been through to this point meant something. He was impressed by the calm and steely determination shown by Odin. O'Dowd felt part of that now. He didn't want to let them down.

"So where are you meeting them?" O'Dowd asked.

Reilly stared at him. O'Dowd felt the man's eyes piercing into his soul. It was a stare that felt like a test.

"Up at Sacred Heart church."

O'Dowd nodded in acknowledgement, "How are you getting across to the island?"

Reilly took a step forward, "Boat. Outboard motor."

"Oh, so you spoke to Rob? We couldn't get through to him and so we were unable to organise outboards. We're going to have to row across," O'Dowd lied, trying to maintain a sense of innocence.

"I spoke to him. It's organised. Now give me the key."

O'Dowd sensed Reilly trying to keep his cool. It was extremely uncomfortable.

"Do you know the names of the people you are meeting?" O'Dowd asked, feeling that it was a genuine question under the circumstances. Content that he had disguised the fact he was actually testing Reilly.

Reilly paused, then spoke, "No. I don't know their names," unable to hide his frustration, "It's been organised, and I am meeting them up at the church. That's it."

O'Dowd knew the answer was vague and lacked substance. He had been the one doing all the meeting and organising. It was what he had been here for. There was a silence. O'Dowd cursed himself in his mind for digging his heels in. Part of his mind told him to just give him the key and walk away but the other stopped him and told him not to. It wasn't right.

Reilly had taken all that time to take him under his wing, nurture him, train and educate him. To just appear now to take matters over was absurd. O'Dowd knew Reilly also knew it was absurd. But he had played his cards and had laid them on the table. Whatever was going on had forced Reilly to throw caution to the wind and do what he was doing.

O'Dowd knew that he had kept things civil enough for him to still get out and get away. His mind switched and danced from one option to the other, his mind instinctively re-directed, and he played his next hand. He spoke as he stood up from his chair. "OK, well, let's go…I will drive you. The roads are a wee bit nasty…"
"Sit down!" Reilly ordered, now agitated.

O'Dowd sat, a little shocked at the outburst. Reilly knew he had lost his nerve and openly calmed himself. He took a deep breath. "Please, Father O'Dowd. The key."

Reilly held out his hand. They stared at each other again. O'Dowd knew this was it. He had asked questions to try and gauge the situation without setting alarms off. But his offer of driving Reilly was almost certainly his final tactical play before he either gave him the key and walked away or took another option. The final play. But it was a play that would decide his fate. This was a play that if executed would be make or break. There would be no recovery from it. It was now all or nothing.

And at that split second, he made a decision. One that he believed was right, but one he may live to regret.

"No. You tasked me with this. For years I have had this burden. I am taking the key to them," and with that he walked around to the front of his desk.

It was an act of insolence and direct provocation. But he knew it was right. He thought of Siobhan and Jimmy, hoping to see them again, and then quickly put them out of his mind. He had openly declared war on Reilly, and he needed to be strong and get through it.

O'Dowd noticed Reilly's face change. He witnessed the split second the penny dropped, when the old man realised that the situation had taken a direction he wasn't navigating. It was the first time in his life that he never had O'Dowd in his control. Reilly cleared his throat then spoke.

"Father O'Dowd. There are things you don't understand. People that are involved. Things change… I was called and told to come down and do it myself…"

"No," interrupted O'Dowd, "I am taking the key and letting them in."

Reilly paused, knowing that to claw this back in his favour would now require drastic action.

"You have a family, a career. A life. Don't throw it all away. Just go, be with them, forget all of this. No questions asked. It's what you want. You said it yourself…"

"Get out of my way. I have to go," O'Dowd ordered assertively.

Reilly panicked. He had genuinely hoped it wouldn't come to this, but he now knew that O'Dowd had rumbled him. He had under-estimated the young priest.

"Please. You are making a mistake. You don't understand the people we are dealing with. Don't make this harder than it is. Now please, I will give you one more chance. The key."

Reilly held out his hand. It was a stand-off. O'Dowd felt the nerves and anxiety almost freeze him, but he had to fight it. He had to stay focussed.

"Father Reilly. I warn you. If you do not move, then I will be forced to…"

"Father O'Dowd! These people gave me a choice. Work with them or die…They wanted your name and I protected you! I told them not to harm you! I made a deal to keep you alive! I told them you would give me the key and leave… If it wasn't for me, you would be dead by now!"

"Shame on you, Father Reilly!" shouted O'Dowd. "After everything you taught me. How much are they paying you? I hope it's worth it!"

O'Dowd was angry. He wasn't going to let this happen.

"Now, for the last time. I warn you. If you do not move…"

"Shut up! Just shut up!" shouted Reilly, spitting in rage and moving his hand behind his back and pulling out a revolver.

"I fucking warned you, you little prick! Why are you doing this? I protect you from them and this is how you repay me!"

O'Dowd felt the fear instantly cripple him and he knew the situation had completely turned against him. The sudden silence was deafening. O'Dowd was too scared to speak. Reilly too angry to speak. Suddenly Reilly composed himself and took a deep breath.

"Now give me the fucking key or I swear I will kill you…" he spoke slowly through gritted teeth, obviously seething but trying to control himself. O'Dowd noticed the gun shaking.

"Please. Please no," he pleaded, putting his hands up and stepping back, "I will give you the key, no problem."

"Come on then!" Reilly shouted, "Stop fucking about!"

O'Dowd put his hand inside his jacket pocket and took hold of the key. He knew he had to hand it over. He didn't want to lose his life. He had done everything he could, hoping Reilly would back down, but with a gun pointing at him the game had taken a direction he was not prepared for. Talking and asking questions had gone. He needed to be the one to back down. For his own and his family's sake.

"Slide it to me," ordered Reilly, "Nice and easy."

O'Dowd took the key out of his pocket and noticed Reilly glance at it. He bent down, holding one hand in the air to show compliance. With the other hand he put the key on the wooden floor. Nervous, his hand trembling, he slid it across. It stopped in front of Reilly and O'Dowd slowly stood up.

"Step back!" barked Reilly. O'Dowd complied and as he did, Reilly slowly bent down to pick up the key. Watching O'Dowd and pointing the gun at him.

He put his hand on the key and as he did, to O'Dowd's surprise, the office door clicked and opened. He gasped not knowing what to expect. Maggie's head appeared around the door.

"Father O'Dowd, I saw Father Reilly…"

"Maggie! Run!" he shouted.

Reilly looked around. As he did, O'Dowd instinctively pounced and barrelled into him, reminiscent of his rugby days. They tumbled back onto the door and O'Dowd heard a gunshot and a scream from Maggie. His heart pounded. He hoped she had not been hit.

They grappled, Reilly, growling like a dog. O'Dowd was surprised at how strong he was for a man of his age. Then suddenly a wave of fear hit him as he felt Reilly gaining an advantage on him by twisting him over onto his front. He felt the old priest's weight on his back and forced himself from being pinned. All the while scared that he may hear another gunshot. The shot that would kill him.

Maggie screamed again and he knew he had to act. Forcing Reilly up and then manoeuvring his body around. Maggie jumped in, thumping, clawing and scratching at his Reilly's face and head. He slammed into him again and all three of them bundled unceremoniously across the office into a shelving cabinet. Items dropping and crashing to the floor.

Reilly hit out and caught O'Dowd square in the face, it knocked him backwards and stunned him for a second. He looked up to see Maggie pulling Reilly's hair and screaming like a banshee.
Reilly lashed out with a fist, "You little bitch!"
He caught her on the jaw and knocked her backwards. She smashed into a cabinet by the door and then slumped to the floor.

O'Dowd jumped up and slammed into Reilly again. Forcing him back into the shelving again causing him to grunt in pain. More items fell, smashing and crashing around them. He grabbed Reilly's hand with the gun. Desperate to force it away from himself and, if he could, onto Reilly. Both men, now breathing hard, twisted and spun forcibly across the office smashing into the drink's cabinet sending glass and cutlery flying with a smash and clatter.

O'Dowd suddenly sensed himself physically struggling, realising he didn't have much left in the tank. He charged into Reilly's mid-rift and pushed him back into the door with a thud. The glass of the door went through with a violent smash as it landed on the hallway outside. Reilly raised his arms and smashed them down onto O'Dowd's back sending electrifying pain through his body. Hurt, he went down onto one knee, then felt himself being grabbed and pulled upwards. In a flash Reilly had sent an uppercut to his face which knocked him backwards onto the floor a few feet away. Reilly stepped forward and aimed the gun at him.
"I fucking warned you!" Reilly shouted.

O'Dowd sensed it was the end. He closed his eyes and raised his arms to protect himself, waiting for the bullet to punch into his body. He heard a sickening thud. He grimaced. Was this it? Was he dead?

He breathed a huge gulp of air and opened his eyes. Reilly was on his knees, shock in his eyes. The gun clunked to the floor as he dropped it at his side. Behind him stood Maggie with a large, metal candlestick. Her face magnified a wild ferocity and fear. Her hair a tangled mess, clothes ripped and pulled.

She stood motionless for a few seconds. And then, to O'Dowd's surprise, she swung the candlestick high above her head and brought it down and round with amazing force. It smashed hard into Reilly's head and blood splattered across the room. Reilly's head buckled awkwardly, and his body was forced hard to the floor by the power of the contact. He lay in a heap on to the floor.

Maggie stood. Breathing heavily. Like a warrior in a muddy field after a day's fighting. Her whole body shaking. Blood spotted her face and body. O'Dowd stared, unsure what to say. He glanced down at Reilly who convulsed once and was then still. Blood pulsed from the wound and, in a few seconds had already pooled around his head and was populating the cracks in the wooden floor.

O'Dowd got to his feet. Breathing hard and struggling to compose himself. Maggie dropped the bloodied candle stick and it clunked to the wooden floor. He could see from her eyes that she needed help and support. Tom held her by the arms trying to comfort her. "Maggie. Stay calm...Don't panic."
"He...He drove past...I only wanted to say hello..." her voice breaking as she spoke. Her eyes trained on the lifeless body.
"Maggie. Listen to me..."
"What's happening? Why did he have a gun?"
"Listen!"
"I heard shouting and..."
"Maggie. Don't worry. I will explain later...I have to go!"
"No!" she panicked, "No, don't leave me..."

"Maggie!" O'Dowd shouted, shocking her and drawing her attention away from the grisly scene. He grabbed her face and forced her to look at him.

"Listen to me. Something is happening. I need to go. But I will be back soon, then we can get this all cleared up…"

"But…Why?" she asked and started to cry.

"Just stay calm. Everything will be OK. Father Reilly got involved with some bad people…I will explain later."

He led her out of the office, comforting her as she cried uncontrollably. This was not a good situation. He needed to calm and settle her and get her home. He shut the office door as the glass crunched beneath their feet.

"Now listen, Maggie. You need to stay calm. Get yourself together and drive home. Drive carefully. It's bad weather. Just go in, clean up and go to your room. Do not tell a soul about this…

"But, what about you? What about Father Reilly…"

"Maggie!" O'Dowd screamed. Instantly noticing her coming around, "You must do what I say! Or we will both be in trouble! Pull yourself together and go home. Do not speak of this to anyone. And I promise I will explain it all later and we will get this matter sorted."

Maggie nodded and wiped tears from her face.

"Am I in trouble?" she asked.

"Oh, my dear child," replied O'Dowd, "Oh no, no. You did the right thing. You're not in trouble."

He hugged her. Then leant back and held her shoulders.

"Be calm and go home. I have to go. Remember, not a word. And I will get it all sorted out, OK?"

O'Dowd noticed her calming down.

"Now go. Be careful,"

She nodded, walked backwards, then spun and rushed towards the exit door. As O'Dowd heard the door close, he darted back inside his office. He needed to retrieve the old key. He rushed over to the body and felt inside Reilly's hands. They were still warm. A strange feeling over-whelmed him. Reilly still had a human presence and O'Dowd felt like he was suddenly going to come back to life. But the key wasn't there. O'Dowd panicked. He scanned the office floor then lent down again and patted the body down and felt inside his pockets. He then realised that Reilly had not had time to deposit the key anywhere, Maggie had opened the door as he had it in his hand. O'Dowd had then tackled him, and they had slammed back into the office door. He quickly went to the door, but he couldn't see it.

"Jesus! No!" he shouted to himself.

Now desperate he turned again. Searching frantically around the office floor and it was then, to his relief, that in the pool of Reilly's blood he spotted something. He darted across and there, lying in the blood, was the key. His heart jumped. He bent down and picked it up. Blood now smearing his hands. But, that was the least of his worries. Several minutes had been wasted. Tom and Odin would now be wondering where he is. Everything now relied on him. He put the key in his pocket and ran to the door and out to the front drive not locking anything behind him.

As he got out, the wind and rain hit him and took his breath away. He was surprised at how fast the storm had come. He got into his car, turned the key and revved the engine, then skidded off the gravel drive as he headed off towards the farm. Driving way too fast for the conditions, knowing he had no choice. The wipers cranking back and forth, working hard to maintain his visibility.

What on earth had he done? It had got out of control. What was he going to tell Maggie? Would she tell anyone? He had a vision of her breaking down in front of her parents and telling them what had happened. The police arriving at his church while he was out with Tom and Odin. It would look like he was running. O'Dowd's stomach turned. If that happens he would have to come clean and just tell them everything.

Or should he just involve the police now? Tell them Reilly came to his office angry and attacked him and Maggie killed him. It wasn't far from the truth anyway. Just tell them that he had no idea why or what it was about. But then they would ask why he left the scene. "Damn! Damn it all!" he shouted at the top of his voice.

He cursed himself. Stop thinking! Stop analysing! But he couldn't help it. What was he going to do with Reilly's body? The whole floor was probably covered in blood by now. How would he clean it? He thought of Mable. Father Reilly's wife. Such a caring and loving woman. His stomach turned again. She would probably just be getting into bed now, completely unaware that she would never see her husband alive ever again.
"Oh no!" shouted O'Dowd, emotion and panic rising within him "No! No! What has happened?" he shouted, slamming his hands on the steering wheel, "What a mess!"

He took some deep breaths trying to calm himself. Suddenly a flash of lighting snapped above him, and he knew, for now, he had to put the incident to the back of his mind, concentrate on the road and get to Tom and Odin as fast as he possibly could.

Chapter 38

"We need to go. Now!" barked Agent 7 to her contact agent, Connor.

"We need to wait for the call," Connor replied, nervous of her.

"No, the call is late. We go now."

"It's only a few minutes after ten thirty. Father Reilly said he would call at ten thirty…"

"Listen. He hasn't called. Something has gone wrong. We go, now!"

Agent 7 was angry and frustrated. She had been holed up in the cottage all day like a caged animal and had not liked the plan from the start as she hated relying on others. Connor had contacted her that morning and informed her the armed support team had arrived and would be at the cottage at 10.20pm ready to go. The priest on the inside would be arriving later that evening and once he got the key from the key holder he would call and that would be the signal to get to the church. She could then kill the portal. Who would be flushed out and without access to the church, would be a sitting duck.

But during the day she reassessed the plan. She had wanted them to get the name of the keyholder from their priest and then she would go and get the key. Why were they relying on others? They didn't need to. She could've got the key and then tortured the holder to give up the portal's position. It made much more sense. She knew there was a chance it may spook the portal but if he was close, she would've found him. She was sure of it.

Why had The Order allowed the priest to dictate terms with them? She hated sentiment. She liked to do things her way and if she had been allowed to then she was sure things would've been under more control.

She knew they couldn't wait anymore. If Reilly had failed it would give the portal a free run to the church. She couldn't allow this. She needed to take back control.

"Stop being a fool. He hasn't called. If the portal prevents the ritual while we all sit here, then it won't just be me who will have to face the consequences."

Connor looked at his watch realising now that she may be right. It was 10.35pm. He looked back at her and then at his watch again. Agent 7 reacted.

"Imbecile! Get your men in the trucks. Now!"

Connor felt the fear rise and then pressure to act. He ran from the cottage, shouting to the rest of the men to board the trucks. In an instant the two trucks roared to life and the soldiers had boarded. Agent 7 left the cottage slamming the door behind her. She ran to the lead vehicle and got on board. They roared out of the cottage driveway and bumped onto the wet, slippery main road.

Agent 7 sat just behind the driver with her hand on his seat, watching his every move.

"Drive faster!" she commanded in his ear.

"I am going as fast as I can. Any faster and we lose grip."

"Agent 7, he is driving according to the conditions…" Connor interrupted hesitantly.

"Fuck the conditions! Drive faster!" she shouted at the driver again, ignoring Connor.

Lighting flashed across the sky and the torrential rain made driving at speed very dangerous. But nothing deterred her. She needed to be at the church site to stop the portal. Nothing else now mattered.

"Has Reilly called?" she asked Connor.

He looked at his phone, noticing that it was 10.37pm. He also noticed that Reilly had not called. He knew then that they had been right to go. He looked up at her and shook his head.

"I told you. He has failed us," she spat in disgust.

She looked ahead of her again, shaking her head. Connor didn't like her. She scared him.

"You better hope things go according to plan," she warned him.

Connor's phone suddenly rang. Agent 7 glared at him. He glanced at her as he answered.

"Yes?"

"Remember the plan. If she fails to get the portal, then take her out. If she does then even better, but she must still be eliminated. She knows too much and is no longer of use to us."

Connor's heart stopped. It was Kane. He had been waiting for this reminder. His stomach turned with anxiety. He glanced up at Agent 7 who he saw was watching him closely.

"Do you hear me?" Kane enquired.

Connor acted quickly to cover the intent of the call.

"Yes, understood. We will be there soon."

He terminated the call and looked straight ahead.

"Who was it?" Agent 7 asked.

He glanced at her, "The other support team. They are on their way."

This assignment was hard enough without Kane throwing this into the mix. It had surprised him a few days ago when Kane had called him to put her elimination in place. He had hoped that Kane would forget to remind him. He looked back at the road; aware she was still staring at him. He daren't look and held his nerve. Soon after, he felt her look away. He wasn't sure if she knew what his plan was.

He hoped for his sake that she didn't.

Chapter 39

Odin was anxious as he peered through the curtain out onto the lane alongside the gatehouse.

"Where is he?"

Tom sat by the door. His foot bouncing with nerves. He looked at his watch. It was 10.37pm. O'Dowd was due to be there at 10.30pm.

"He's late!" Odin shouted.

Tom never replied. He felt sick with anxiety. He was still waiting to get a sign that he would be able to do what was required of him. But he had not felt anything. He just sat and tried to compose himself.

"Fuck!" shouted Odin, moving away from the window, "We should've had a back-up...Why the fuck didn't we pick him up? Damn!"

Tom knew it was best not to answer. It would be the storm that had held O'Dowd up, or some other reasonable explanation. He could've suggested this, but Odin didn't need to know. He was just talking to himself and letting out his frustration. But Tom knew Odin was right, they should've had a back-up plan. Things had been difficult. They had arrived in this remote place just 24 hours before and were reliant on the plans already made. The people already involved. They had no choice but to rely on them. Tom felt sure that O'Dowd wouldn't let them down. He had seemed genuine and reliable. But a sudden realisation crossed Tom's mind that if O'Dowd bailed out then it would all be over. The whole mission was now utterly reliant on O'Dowd.

Then, to his astonishment, as his realisation loomed large in his mind, they heard a roar of an engine approach. Tom got up and went to the window. Odin pulled the curtain across and, as the roar got louder, lights appeared through the trees and over the brow that led to the house. A car appeared and skidded to a halt.

"It's him. It must be!" exclaimed Odin. Tom went to move but Odin grabbed his arm.

"Wait," he ordered.

The car sat for a few seconds, idle, the engine ticking over.

"Come on!" shouted Tom, desperate to get going.

Odin calmed him, "Wait…Just hold on."

Then suddenly the lights flashed three times and the horn sounded. It was the code Odin had given him.

"Come on, let's go," ordered Odin and they headed for the door.

The rain hit them as they opened the door. It was cold and unforgiving. They ran down the path to the car and, in that short time, their jackets were already soaked. Odin ran around to the front passenger seat and Tom got in the back.

"Where have you been?" asked Odin abruptly.

They slammed the doors and O'Dowd hit the accelerator. The revs screamed and the old engine did its best to power them off back onto the road. Tom looked ahead realising how bad the conditions were. He had also noted that O'Dowd had not answered Odin's question.

"Are you OK?" asked Odin, sensing O'Dowd's tension.

O'Dowd didn't answer again, concentrating on the road ahead trying to keep the car on the road.

"O'Dowd! What's wrong?" shouted Odin.

"Shit! Sorry!" O'Dowd answered, almost coming out of a trance.

"Look, I am sorry. I ran into trouble…"

"What? How?" asked Odin a little unsettled.

"Father Reilly. He came to my church…Came in the office. He…Well…He tried to stop me…"

"How? What the fuck happened?"

O'Dowd went to speak again but broke hard and they were all thrown forward. He got the car under control and steered around a hair pin corner, skidding on the wet road. As the car straightened up, he put the power down again and the car screamed into the night.

"Sorry…He gave me a chance to back out. To leave. No questions asked. When I refused, he pulled a gun on me…But Maggie came back…"

"Who is Maggie?" asked Odin

"My church assistant…A young lady from the village…Anyway, there was a scuffle and Reilly's dead. Maggie killed him. I mean she didn't mean to…He was going to shoot me…And, well, she's in a state…"

"They know…" exclaimed Odin talking over O'Dowd who never heard him and continued.

"I told her not to tell a soul and get home…She will be fine, but I need to explain to her…What do we do about the body?"

"They know!" shouted Odin, stopping O'Dowd's jabbering.

"Who?" asked Tom.

"The Order. They know we are coming. They got to Reilly. He was sent to stop O'Dowd…"

"But what about the body? There's blood…" interjected O'Dowd anxiously.

"What?" asked Odin.

"The body. In my office. What do we do…"

"Fuck the body!" shouted Odin surprising both of them, "We will get that cleaned up later."

He spun in his seat to look at Tom, "This could get interesting. If they sent Reilly, then they know something. Get yourself prepared and when we…"

Odin's voice was interrupted by the car almost taking off. It slammed down onto the road and all of their heads hit the roof. Tom ended up thrown back and then bounced forward almost ending up on Odin's lap. He gripped the seats in front to stop himself from toppling over and Odin pushed him back. Odin stared at O'Dowd.

"Jesus…Be careful…"

"How can I be bloody careful? We are late!"

Odin looked at his watch, it was 10.43pm.

248

"How far?

O'Dowd shook his head and shrugged concentrating on the road ahead.

"Five minutes if we take risks, ten minutes if I slow down…"

There was a pause then Odin spoke, "Take risks," he ordered.

Odin then turned to Tom again.

"Just be prepared and focussed. If they know we are coming they may have a surprise…"

"The woman," interrupted Tom.

"Don't worry about her. She's mine," Odin assured him with confidence, "just focus and prepare your mind. When we get there, we may not have time to discuss it. We get out and onto the boat then away…No delay."

Odin took out his phone and made a call.

"It's me. Are you there?…Good. Listen, we have info that they may be onto us. Be ready for a welcoming committee. Also, we have a clean-up, it needs doing tonight….send someone now…"

Odin glanced at O'Dowd, "What is the name of your church?"

"Er…St Mary's."

"Where?"

"Westport. The village isn't far…"

"It's St Mary's in Westport. One body."

He glanced at O'Dowd again.

"How was Reilly killed?"

O'Dowd glanced at him and then back to the road.

"What?"

"How was Reilly killed!?"

O'Dowd hesitated, confused, "Oh…Er, hit with a metal candle stick…"

"Head trauma. Heavy blunt object. Probably messy…Anyway, we are close. Assign the clean-up and they can take the car we are in."

Odin ended the call. Tom shook his head in disbelief. Even now amidst all the chaos and the uncertainty, Odin's mind worked like a machine. Covering bases, dealing with details, not leaving anything to chance. He amazed Tom. Even now after all this time.

The car whizzed frantically through the country lanes at dangerous speed. The wind and rain battered the old Fiat as it fought its way through the night. To make matters worse the rain outside and the humidity in the car was making the windscreen fog up. Odin had taken on the role of internal windscreen wiper and every thirty seconds or so he lent forward and wiped it clear.

They sat silently for a few minutes as the engine roared along the straight sections, then quietened as O'Dowd slowed to navigate a corner and then the revs increased as the car powered along another straight. O'Dowd felt sweat trickling down his forehead with the concentration. Suddenly Odin sparked to life.
"The key! Do you have the key?" he shouted at O'Dowd.
"Yes! Of course!" he replied, a little angrily as if to intimate he was concentrating.

Tom sat, putting his hands out to push against each side to prevent himself sliding from left to right. Suddenly, as they approached a corner, he felt the car slide.
"Shit!" shouted O'Dowd.

The car careered and suddenly there was a bang as the car collided hard with a rock. All three of them bounced up, hit the roof and then smashed back down again. O'Dowd slowed down as he fought to get control and gradually evened it out. As he pulled off again, he felt the car slithering.
"Jesus, we've got a puncture..."
"How far?" shouted Odin.
"Just up this hill and down to the jetty..."
"Put your foot down then..." Odin ordered.

The car screamed up the hill and in the head lights Odin spotted a white sign, 'Jetty – Ferry to Clare Island'. O'Dowd slowed and slid the car around the corner, they bumped down onto a rocky, gravel track and snaked their way down. The headlights bounced up and down and several times the image of two land rovers and several soldiers flashed into view. It was The Network's support team awaiting their arrival.

"There they are!" shouted Tom.

O'Dowd slid on the gravel and rocks at the bottom of the track and the car came to a stop.

"Let's go!" shouted Odin.

They rushed out and jogged towards the group of soldiers. The rain was still heavy, and they were already soaked again by the time they got to them. Two of the soldiers made their way forward. It was dark but as their eyes adjusted, they made out the men.

"Odin," one of the men shouted as they approached, and he held out his hand. Odin took the hand, and they shook.

"Hansen. Good to see you."

The second man stepped forward, "Keys?"

They all looked at O'Dowd.

"What?" he asked, confused.

"Car keys!" shouted Odin, "He is going to clear up your mess…"

"Oh, Jesus…" he patted himself down, then got them out of his pocket and handed them over.

The man took them and ran towards the car.

"It's got a flat tyre!" shouted O'Dowd.

Nobody acknowledged him and before he knew it the Fiat was barrelling its way up the gravel track and away. O'Dowd watched it go with a roar and then heard a shout from the jetty.

"Father! Come on."

He looked around and noticed Tom, Odin and the other soldier running onto the jetty.

"Shit!" he cursed and ran towards them, knowing he had to focus and keep up.

He ran past several other heavily armed soldiers all in black, across the sand and rocks and up onto the jetty. The roar of the sea crashing onto the beach close by. Odin had already jumped into the boat and Tom was ready to do the same. O'Dowd jogged along the jetty to the end and as he was getting in the boat, Hansen shouted. "Odin! We had eyes on them. The ritual group made their way across about ten minutes ago, but they didn't have any armed support…"

"Good. Hopefully any support got held up…"

The soldier turned, "Men! Two stay, the rest with me!" he shouted.

But just then, lights appeared from the direction of the gravel track leading from main road down to the jetty. Odin spotted them instantly.

"Hansen! We've got company!" he shouted.

The lights came over the brow and then bounced down so as to flash and shine directly at them.

"It's them!" Odin shouted, pulling the cord on the outboard motor, "Engage them, Hansen. Leave us. Hold them here!"

"OK! Good luck!" he shouted and ran from the jetty.

Odin tried again to pull the cord, then again without success. On the fourth pull the boat engine roared to life and the boat edged forward. Odin sat as the boat powered away from the jetty. Within a few seconds they heard the ferocious sound of automatic gun fire from the beach as the two enemy groups engaged. Odin hoped for their sake that their team could hold them off.

Agent 7's 4x4 that contained her team barrelled and bounced down towards the jetty under fire. Bullets thudding viciously into its side. But she was not interested. Her fight was not on the beach. She needed to avoid that and get a boat across to the island.

As lightning flashed across the sky, the 4x4 headlights bounced up and down the beach and the jetty lit up. She suddenly caught a glimpse of a boat powering away into the darkness. It was the portal. This was her chance.

A wave of anxiety rushed through her body, knowing that the mistakes earlier had cost her time. She realised suddenly that it may mean that the ritual is now interrupted or, worse, totally compromised. But, on the bright side, at least the portal would be somewhere on the island. And from there he was trapped with nowhere else to run to. Like a rabbit in a blocked warren.

The wolf was closing in on its prey.

Chapter 40

Agent 7's support team jumped out the 4x4 as it was moving. Shouts of "Go! Go!" and the hail of gunfire created an intimidating and disorientating environment, but Agent 7 was calm. The men that disembarked found positions behind rocks and in the long reeds then instantly engaged their enemy.

She, however, stayed put. Cowering as bullets smashed into the side of the vehicle. It bumped around and then skidded to a halt on the slippery sand. The driver made a move to get out, but a bullet smashed through the window. His head jolted back in a spray of red and he slumped in his seat.

Agent 7 waited for the enemy to divert their attention away from the vehicle, she made her move and slipped out of the door at the side away from the fire fight. She ducked down behind the vehicle; her senses instantly sent into over-drive. The sound of the sea crashing against the beach, the rain battering down, the flash of lighting and the sound of thunder and gunfire filled the air.

After several seconds, the rain had drenched her, but she didn't care. Her idea was to swim to the jetty and the moored boats away from the beach, avoiding the ensuing battle and any attention from The Network soldiers.

She took a look above the window through the vehicle. Sparks of bullet ricochets and tracers flashed in the dark as the gun fight quickly grew in intensity. Then she made her move. Flinging herself to the floor she pulled herself across the sand towards the sea, allowing it to submerge her quickly as she slipped into the surf. When in deep enough she started to swim hard and fast.

At first, she swum directly out but then turned and swam in an arc direction. Eventually she straightened up and, with the beach to her right, she was now heading to the jetty roughly fifty metres away.

The fact that it was the Atlantic coast did not lessen any surprise she had for how strong the tide was and she knew immediately she had drifted out too far. She cursed her situation. It was unprofessional. She knew she should not be in this position. Had she worked alone; things would have been different. She would've had the portals head in a bag by now.

But she had no time for regrets. She fought hard against the current, trying to keep her position steady and her breathing under control. Now, just 25 metres away, she surged and pushed herself harder towards the jetty. Her heart beating hard, but this was what she was trained for. The unexpected and the physically demanding.

For a few strokes she felt herself stay in the same position and had to dig deeper. Her breathing now harder and more strained. But she did not lose focus and found energy from her deepest reserves. Soon she was close to the jetty.

To the right of her, she heard shouting and gun shots. She glanced at the beach and noticed several men lying motionless on the beach but wasn't sure from what side they were from. But she now knew she needed to be careful. The Network were encamped at that end and she knew that when she started one of the boats it could get their attention.

Several more, hard and desperate strokes later she reached one of the boats, bobbing awkwardly in the sea. She grabbed the rope hanging off its side and took several deep breaths through her nose and out of her mouth. Her muscles needed oxygenating again and she wanted to get her heart rate down. She then focussed, knowing that her next movement would leave her open and defenceless.

Then, after a count to three, she hoisted herself up using the rope and grabbed the side of the boat. With all her strength she pulled her drenched body from the sea and clambered into the boat with a thud. She never moved. Waiting to hear if bullets hit her position.

They didn't. She peered over the edge of the boat and was confident that she had not been spotted.

She stood, walked to the other end and pulled the engine cord. The engine growled but it didn't start. Then she pulled again, and it came to life. She then knelt down next to the engine, twisted the throttle and the boat bumped forward and surged away.

Close to the jetty, under fire, Hansen heard the boat and looked around. He jumped up from his position and made a dash for the jetty. He slipped on the wet sand, then found some grip and made good headway. Two bullets zipped by him sending sand flying into the air.

Agent 7 noted her position. She was about to pass the end of the jetty. In her mind she believed she was just a few minutes behind the portal, so she could get to him before he reached the church. It was then she spotted the shadowy figure, moving fast along the jetty. At first, she was confused but then realised what was happening. She twisted the throttle, but it was already at full speed. Then she noticed that the figure had bound onto the jetty and was approaching fast. Hansen knew he was now all in. He had made his move instinctively and there was no going back. He realised then, that with a final effort and a solid jump, he would reach the boat.

Agent 7 put her hand around her back into her holster. She pulled the gun and aimed it at the figure and fired. Hansen felt the bullet whizz past his head and knew he had one more step. He hit the end of the jetty and, like a long jumper, leapt forward towards the boat through the air, but as he was about to land on the woman, she fired again.

He hit her with all his force. Smashing them both to the deck at the front end of the boat. The engine went into idle. Hansen, on top, grabbed her throat and, with all his energy, tried to squeeze the life out of her. In a flash, she had fed her arms through his and smashed them from their grasp and sent a sickening headbutt to his nose and he grunted in pain.

She then bent her legs and lifted his weight off her, launching him to the back of the boat. He grimaced, as the engine and seat smashed into his spine. He focussed and got to his feet, the waves making them both stagger side to side.

He glanced and spotted her gun in the boat well. She dived to grab it and he did the same. She got their first, but he grabbed her arm. She spun and elbowed the back of his head sending him stumbling to his knees. He spun and grabbed the gun and pointed it away from him. The gun fired into the darkness. He grabbed her hair and slammed her down to the deck, she dropped the gun and it hit the side of the boat and bounced into the rolling sea.

Hansen turned and she stood, facing him. Staring at him. Her anger building at yet another obstacle that stood in her way. He smiled. Tempting her to him.
"Come on you bitch…."

He laughed, but then suddenly felt a burning in his stomach. He looked down and noticed that his body was red. He put his hand on it. The pain made him wince. He knew it was a bad injury, almost certainly fatal.

He looked up at her. She gave him an insincere, predatory, smile. Then, in a flash she surged forward. He threw a punch which she dodged underneath, then grabbed the bullet wound with one hand, and, with the other hand, grabbed him around his collar and lifted. He felt his feet lift up onto his toes and the pain burnt him like nothing he had ever experienced. His scream could be heard from the beach.

The pain froze him, and he felt the last of his energy drain from his body. He knew it was the end. He was helpless. But he hoped he had done enough to delay her.

257

Then Agent 7 leant forward and sunk her teeth into his nose biting down as hard as she could, then ripping the feature from his face in one sickening, bloody movement. She spat the morsel into the sea and dropped him to his knees. He screamed in pain and cried out like a child.

He felt the pulse of blood from his injury but, in an instant, she grabbed his hair and hoisted him overboard into the cold, black depths. His last vision was her standing on the boat staring down at him as he sunk.

Agent 7 growled and let out her anger. Blood dripping from her mouth. Like a wild animal. Then she stopped, breathed and focussed. She had her hunting knife. Still enough to claim her prize. She darted to the end of the boat and grabbed the throttle and twisted. In a few seconds, the engine was roaring again. She kept the throttle on full, smashing through the waves sending the front of the boat up and down in a brutal motion.

Soon the light from the headlights and the sound of shouts and gunfire on the beach were fading into the distance and, before long, with the aid of the moon that pierced through a small break in the cloud, up ahead she made out the island.

Despite the night's obstacles, she believed the portal still wasn't too far ahead. And so, she continued as fast and as hard into the waves as the boat could manage. Her heart racing, her lungs burning and her body freezing. But her mind totally focussed.

Nothing was going to stop her now.

Chapter 41

Halfway across, O'Dowd had shouted to Odin to adjust their direction to a more north-westerly position. He did this several times until he was confident they were headed in the right direction. Odin complied each time until O'Dowd confirmed it was the correct course with a thumb in the air.

Without O'Dowd they would've been lost, as the darkness, solid and heavy, surrounded them and, to Tom, it appeared that they were just sailing into a black hole. But after what seemed like an eternity, in the darkness ahead of them, they made out a small light. "There!" shouted O'Dowd.

Odin, sped up, now able to make out a destination to head for. Tom gripped the side as the rain lashed into his face, just trying to remain inside the boat as it lurched left, right, up and down across the rolling waves. His hands stung with the cold and his body shivered as the freezing night air, the wind and rain penetrated his body.

As they rounded a rock and approached, they made out a jetty which Odin headed for. The light, on a buoy, anchored close to the end of the jetty, rocked back and forth violently. Odin zeroed in but then passed the jetty heading to the beach. Soon after, the scraping on the underside of the boat grew louder and the boat skidded to a standstill on the beach with a thud. Their bodies lurched forward with the momentum. Odin stood, switched the engine off and jumped out the side of the boat into the shallow sea. "Let's go!" he shouted.

Tom and O'Dowd sprang to life. Tom found it difficult as his cold muscles felt stiff, and suddenly his back ached from the position he had sat in on the journey across. He had to remember his training and dig deep to find that energy and focus from somewhere. That intense place inside him that the training had created.

They stood together on the beach. A roll of thunder cascaded across the sky and rain continued to pound them.

"Which way?!" shouted Odin to O'Dowd, who realised it was now his time to lead.

"Follow me. Up that way," he shouted, pointing above a large rock in front of them.

With that O'Dowd leapt into a sprint and ran across the beach towards the rocks. Tom and Odin followed right behind him. The wind picking up and slamming into them, slowing them down. He led them across a rocky area to some steps and, as Tom approached, he noticed that they got higher and higher, meandering all the way up the side of the high rocks. Heading one way across then turning sharply and heading back across.

They started up the first level and Tom noticed how slippery the rocks were. They all had to move fast but also try to keep their footing. Tom slipped and fell. Scraping his hand on the jagged rock. He jumped up and continued on. They got to the second level when suddenly Odin stopped.

"Wait! Listen" he shouted.

They stood. Waiting to hear what Odin had heard. It was difficult to hear anything over the rain and whistling wind. But, suddenly, above the noise of the storm, a boat engine could be heard.

"I hope that's our boys!" shouted Odin.

"No," replied Tom, not loud enough for the others to hear properly.

"What?" shouted Odin.

"No!" replied Tom, now shouting.

"What do you mean, no?" screamed O'Dowd.

"No! It's not our boys. It's her!"

Odin looked down but couldn't spot their pursuer.

"OK! Keep going!" and headed off with O'Dowd closely following.

Tom looked down at the bobbing light at the end of the jetty and a black shape flashed past it. He felt the dark presence. He knew it was her. It energised him. He picked up his speed, catching up with O'Dowd and pushing him from behind.

"Come on, Father! Faster!" he shouted.

Odin noticed this and used Tom's sudden energy to push himself and soon all three of them were bursting up the various levels of steps across the span of the rocky terrain.

O'Dowd was next to trip and he went down hard. Scraping his hands and face on the rocks and stones. But he had no time to dwell on the sudden pain. Tom grabbed one of his arms and Odin the other. He didn't want to let them down, and so he powered on using all his energy.

Soon they came to the end of the steps. The waves crashing into the beach, now well below them. Up ahead, they noticed some lights coming from what looked like windows. It was the church. It stood way above them at the top of a hill, up ahead of them.

A sudden crack of thunder crashed above them. Scaring them so much they all cowered and bent down. They looked at each other and went to move on again. Then, out of nowhere, ahead of them a robed, hooded figure attacked. Swinging a large blade that flickered as the lighting flashed. The blade swung forcibly towards Odin, but he reacted quickly. Ducking below, it missed him by inches, with a deep swoosh.

The figure attacked again, this time thrusting the blade towards him. Odin evaded to the left and grabbed the figure's arm that was holding the sword. He pulled it into him and delivered an elbow which struck with sickening force.

The robed swordsmen was knocked back, but quickly came at him again. This time with the blade high, ready to chop down on its target. Odin leapt forward and grabbed the figures hands, stopping the downwards motion. Now both caught in a test of strength. Odin lost his grip and was now being pushed down the hill. Tom reacted and dived at his opponent, hitting him side on, knocking both him and the attacker down the hill into the darkness.

Out of the darkness another robed figure stepped into the fray and ran at O'Dowd. O'Dowd glanced, his heart pounding with instant fear, but Odin moved in to supress the new assailant.

The blade swung in and O'Dowd ducked and surged at the attacker, grabbing around the waist and powering them both back up the hill. The figure held the weapon in the air and spun it around, so the blade was facing downwards above O'Dowd's unprotected back. However, Odin had already taken the initiative and, before it was thrust downwards, he had jumped over O'Dowd's back, hitting the figure hard around the chest area sending them both sprawling onto the wet, slippery grass.

They landed in a heap and Odin barrel rolled and spun. The attacker quickly jumped up, but Odin was too quick and had already removed his gun from its shoulder strap. As the robed figure spun and charged at him, he fired three shots into the head and chest area, the power of them knocking the figure back through the air onto the grass, motionless.

At the same time Tom found himself slipping down the hill. His attacker not in sight. He grabbed his gun from the shoulder strap and aimed at different directions in the darkness. The storm made hearing the attacker impossible, the darkness made it hard to see.

Suddenly to the left he felt a presence and a blade flashing towards him. He evaded, stepping back, the blade passing close to his face and chest down to his feet. But before Tom could react a punch had followed which knocked him back onto the ground. He focussed, aimed the gun and fired three shots into the darkness.

He jumped up but the blade flashed again. Tom side stepped but was too slow and it caught his shoulder sending a burst of sharp pain through his body.

Again, another attack came at him, this time the blade being thrust towards his stomach. He evaded to the right. The attacker then tried to strike him from the side and as the blade swung at him again, he moved around the robed figures back and stuck his gun deep into their back and fired two shots.

Blood exploded out of the front of the swordsmen who dropped to his knees and fell forward.
"Odin!" Tom shouted, catching his breath.
"Over here!" he heard above the rain.
He ran towards the voice and after several seconds Odin and O'Dowd appeared in the darkness.
"You OK?" asked Odin
"Just about," replied Tom, breathing frantically.
"You are injured!" shouted O'Dowd, moving forward to assess Tom, noticing blood seeping through his clothing.
"Don't worry. It's not deep...We need to go."
"Yeah! We've lost time," Odin said looking at his watch, "Shit! It's just after 11. Move!"

With that, O'Dowd led the way and they ascended the hill to the church. It was tough. All three of them, already exhausted, dug deep and headed upwards. The wind hitting them head on, making progress hard and slow.

The rain and cold sapped their energy, but they marched on. Every step upwards burning their thighs and calves. Tom groaned as he slipped and hit the saturated surface, but he felt an arm pull him up and he carried on. O'Dowd then slipped and Tom bent down and helped him up. Lightning flashed and splintered the night sky. The smell of electricity hung in the air, metallic and deadly.

The church then appeared closer, up ahead in the darkness. Odin beckoned them on with a shout, pulling Tom's arm to keep him going and Tom doing the same to O'Dowd, who was now struggling to keep stepping upwards, being battered by the storm and the wind.

Tom now felt the fear for real. In his visions the church had spooked him and created a sense of anxiety. At the time, he hadn't known why. But now he knew. As it appeared in front of them it loomed high and Tom sensed its secrets were soon to be known to him. His destiny had arrived.

They reached a gravel path. All three of them stood just a short distance from its wooden doors. They looked at each other. O'Dowd reached inside his jacket and pulled out the black key. "It's time, Tom! Good luck!" shouted Odin over the wind. Then they all walked together towards the church.

Agent 7 surged up the hillside. Anxious that she was too late. Everything had gone against her, but she never gave up. Determined to fulfil her assignment. She knew she may now be too late. But she would wait. The portal would be inside the church. He had to come out at some point. If he did achieve his goal of stopping the ritual, then so be it.

Now, she just wanted him. Further down the hill she had found evidence of their progress in the form of two dead ritual guards. She had taken one of their swords which she would use to take off the portals head.

The wind and rain slammed into her, but she moved up the hill with speed and efficiency. Her legs burnt and her body ached. Suddenly the whole sky lit up. As sheet lighting flashed above her the church lit up. To her relief, three figures stood in front of it. She realised that she may have made it just in time and prepared to attack.

Odin heard her first and turned. Tom and O'Dowd stopped. Tom felt the danger surge through him. It was her. The moment he had known was coming had arrived. He moved to Odin and stood behind him as she surged towards them.

"Go! You know what to do!" shouted Odin as he raised his gun and aimed ahead of him.

Tom noticed O'Dowd react and run towards the church. Tom's vision came to him again in a flash. He knew he had to go. As much as he wanted to stay and help Odin. He knew what he was there for. Fate had played its part and his destiny was inside the church.

"I said go! You have to get inside!" shouted Odin.

Tom turned and ran.

Ahead of him O'Dowd had opened the heavy doors. As Tom ran towards them a wave of fear and anxiety crashed into him. The rain and wind also hit him at the same time. Everything was telling him to stop. Pushing him back. Trying to prevent him from entering. But he pushed on harder against his natural instincts.

As he got to the door, from behind him he heard Odin roar a battle cry and the sound of gunshots. He then stumbled, fell and smashed onto the stone floor inside the church. As he lay on the cold stone, he looked up as O'Dowd slammed the doors shut and locked them both inside.

Chapter 42

Agent 7 had suddenly disappeared from Odin's vision. His gun clicked informing him that he was out of bullets. He threw the gun down and pulled the hunting knife from his leg strap. Thunder boomed. He spun one way and then another. Then full circle, trying to pre-empt her attack. He stepped forward and got onto his front foot. The rain preventing him from hearing her movement. Unsure if one of his bullets had found its target.

Lightning strobed above and all around him. Then he spotted her. A few metres ahead of him. Her eyes menacing, staring into his soul. Her body still. Almost robotic. He tensed and stood firm, holding the knife up, ready for her to pounce.
"You're too late, bitch!" he shouted, smiling at her, hiding his fear.

She never responded, nor reacted to his comment. Her face remained as still as stone. Rain cascading down, dripping from her hard features. Slowly, she pulled up the sword that she was holding from behind her leg, holding it in two hands and pointing its tip towards him. Through gritted teeth Odin spoke.
"Come on, you whore. I have been waiting for this!"

He felt the anger, tension and sudden thirst for a fight surge through his body. He felt himself shiver, but not with the cold and wet, but with the tenacity and adrenalin that now flowed through him. He was ready.

She then pointed at him with her left hand and moved the sword with the other hand in an arc motion, so it was now above her head, the tip pointing downwards, directly at him.

Lightning cracked and Odin saw it flash on the sword. She took a deep breath and prepared herself. Then she attacked.

And in an instant, was upon him.

Chapter 43

Tom instantly noticed the change in atmosphere inside the church. Its eerie darkness and cold air enveloped him. He felt supressed and enclosed.

O'Dowd grabbed his arm and pulled him up. Their eyes adjusted, noticing they were inside a domed foyer area. Up ahead a large arch lead to another room with a set of huge wooden doors illuminated by the wall mounted braziers on either side. Tom looked at his watch, the fluorescent hands showing him that the time was 11.03pm. They were almost out of time.

They stepped forward, wary of the area beyond the arch and what might be lurking inside. O'Dowd's heart pounded and he felt threatened by the dark space that he left behind him as he walked. Tom now realised that whoever or whatever was beyond the doors may now know of his presence. But it was irrelevant. Whatever was about to unfold was going to happen in the next two minutes. So being covert was no longer a requirement.

They reached the door. Tom took a deep breath. This was it. A low, eerie chanting emanated from beyond creating an ominous and creepy environment. He lifted the wooden beam that held the door closed and both he and O'Dowd looked at each other before pushing the giant oak doors open.

As the doors slowly lurched open, a huge expansive chamber with a large domed roof was revealed. Tom noticed several robed figures stood in the middle of the floor, in a circle, hands raised towards the ceiling. The domed ceiling's central point revealed a hole, the meagre illuminations allowing the rainwater falling through to flash and flicker. Inside the circle was what appeared to be the ark. Even in this gloomy environment its warm, golden finish was clearly visible.

Suddenly Tom and O'Dowd felt movement. The sound of scuffing and stepping on the stone floor, then a presence around them. Several robed figures with large swords now stood in front and around them. Tom reached down and pulled his knife from his leg strap. Holding it in front of him and aiming his gun, moving it from side to side at the numerous targets.

O'Dowd reached out and supressed his arms, lowering them. "Tom, please. No weapons here. Not in God's house."

Tom looked at O'Dowd, understanding his meaning. He lowered his weapons, breathing hard.
"What is the meaning of this?!" shouted a voice from the central part of the church.

One of the figures stepped out of the circle and pulled his hood down, but his face was still hidden by the shadows. It was Kane. "You believe you can stop the power of The Order?"

Tom and O'Dowd stood. Motionless. Surrounded by the armed men and unable to answer the question. Neither sure what to do. "Fools. If only you knew what you are dealing with."

Kane laughed, and it echoed around the chamber. Then, in a flash above them, a light cascaded through the hole in the roof. A blue, silver light. A colour of which Tom or O'Dowd had never seen before. It grew in ferocity and suddenly the whole church was illuminated. The light pierced through like a laser, down to the floor, moving slowly towards the ark. As it crept closer a golden light emanated from inside the ark, glowing brightly, creating more illumination. Almost too bright to look at with the naked eye. "Kill them!" shouted Kane, who put his hood back up and walked back to the circle.

The robed figures surrounding Tom and O'Dowd moved forward into attack mode. Swords now inching towards them from all sides.

Tom, instinctively raised his gun and knife again, knowing that one bullet and a knife against several swords was a futile gesture.

But then he two lights connected. And from the golden orange light of the ark and the blue silver light piercing the ceiling, a beautiful orb of white light was created that floated just above the ark. A gust of wind suddenly swirled around the church and all within felt a surge of energy like no other. The noise grew, a thunderous roll, like a train, the power of which was felt surging and pushing into every person present.

O'Dowd noticed two of the robed figures stop and look around. The church shook, the noise got louder, the chanting got louder and the light from the orb hurt Tom and O'Dowd's eyes. O'Dowd grabbed Tom by the arm.
"Whatever it is you have to do, I think now is the time!"

But, as he spoke, Tom had already felt power rising from below him, into his feet. O'Dowd felt a burning sensation from Tom which surprised him, and he stepped back, bewildered. He noticed Tom looking dead ahead, trance like. His knife and gun dropped to the floor. The robed figures noticed too, and they also stepped back, unsure, even frightened of the situation.

The power and energy ascended through Tom's body and then he felt it. The energising warmth flowed through his veins. O'Dowd stepped back further, mesmerised. A glow emanated from Tom, orange and yellow, slowly becoming stronger and brighter.

He then felt hot, almost burning. But he wasn't fearful. He felt joyous, ecstatic and powerful. A burst of energy shot from him, pushing O'Dowd and the robed figures backwards. O'Dowd was knocked off his feet, sliding backwards towards the main door. The robed figures were sent flying backwards, falling and sliding away. They scrambled, one of them crawling on all fours away from Tom. O'Dowd then looked beyond Tom, back to the ark. The orb above it had grown brighter and more powerful. The wind swirling around the church, had now also increased and resembled a mini hurricane within the chamber. He became fearful, the unknown power within the church, unrelenting and unpredictable.

Then, in a flash, the glow from Tom became a ball of light. Bright yellow and orange, fire-like, powerful and all absorbing. O'Dowd held his arm up to shield his eyes from the glare but daren't look away. The light then rose up with Tom inside. Gradually at first, a few feet, then some more. Then higher and higher until Tom hovered way above everything and everyone. Like a star. Way above the church floor. Light piercing and shooting from him.

O'Dowd crossed his head and chest, aware that he was witnessing something that he would never be able to understand or believe.

Chapter 44

The fight had been ferocious.

Both competitors had dis-armed each other of their weapons early
on and Agent 7 had been surprised at how skilled the man had
been with his blade. In the ensuing fight she had also been shocked
at how strong he was and the fighting ability he had. Agent 7 had
been reminded of her battle with the Japanese man and had cursed
the fact that she had now faced two of her hardest opponents to
get to the portal.

The fight had seen each of them gain the upper hand several times.
Both of them thinking at that time that they had won. Only for
their opponent to fight back and turn the table once more. Moving
in different directions across the hillside, up and down. Not only
struggling with the power and skill of their opponent but also the
conditions and how slippery and muddy it was.

They had ended up at the back of the church. Both suddenly being
distracted by silvery blue lights coming down from the sky and into
the roof. And the following glow that suddenly emanated from all
of the windows and openings in the old building.

But, with the amazing lights in the background, the fight continued,
and eventually Agent 7 had worn her enemy down. A successful
flurry of undefended punches and kicks had sent the man
sprawling down the hill through the wet and mud. She had
followed downwards into the darkness and came upon him lying
on his back, covered in mud, soaking wet, face bloodied and
beaten.

Odin tried with all his might to stay alert. Fading in and out of
consciousness. He felt sick and his head was spinning. He looked
up. In the background, off in the distance, he made out the church
and the lights. Then he saw her silhouette approach.

She stood over him. Her own face bloodied. He tried to get up, but
his body failed him. He lifted his head hoping that his body would

follow but the exertion was too much. His head dropped. He knew now that he had been defeated. This was the end.

She knelt down on his chest and he exhaled with the pressure. She raised her fist and punched his face. It felt like he had been hit with a rock. She raised her other fist and pummelled his face again. Then again and again and again. His head twisting left to right with each impact. The punches continued, each blow knocking him into unconsciousness.

Suddenly Odin saw his parents. They came towards him. Their faces, that he had not seen since he was a child and had long since gone from his memory, now clear as ever. Their beautiful, loving faces. He held out his hand and they came to him. They stood before him, then they all embraced. Love flowed through him like never before and a feeling of happiness and contentment washed over him.

A light appeared. Warm and glowing. Odin stood between them and they held hands and walked towards it. A calm serenity engulfed him, the touch of his parents and the lure of the light enticed them in. The cold, tiredness and pain left him, and a floating sensation took hold as they all gently moved towards the light.

Then, just before entering, everything went back. Odin suddenly felt cold, wet and the pain hit him like a freight train. Confused, he wondered why his parents had gone. Why did he feel this horrible feeling? Was he dead or alive?

He gasped for air and felt his lungs fill with oxygen. It gave him another surge of energy. But only enough for him to open his eyes. With his right eye socket smashed and swollen he only viewed through his left eye. He saw her again. Stood over him, looking up at the church.

She turned and looked down at him. Apparent disgust written on her face, annoyed that he was not yet dead. She spun and put both feet on either side of his shoulders. She lifted her knee high, bringing her foot directly above his head. Odin held his breath. The final blow soon to descend upon him. A brutal end now inevitable.

Then a shot rang out. It startled him. He gasped and lifted his head. With one last effort he opened his eye and saw the woman lying on the ground next to him. His head fell back to the mud and his consciousness left him and everything went black.

Vast, expansive black. No sound or vision. No feeling or thought.

Chapter 45

Tom suddenly felt the burning sensation increase in temperature and ferocity. But he embraced and controlled it. The he dug deep and used it.

As he rose, he soon found himself looking down on all within the church. In slow motion, he saw the robed figures fleeing, the ritual members, standing, staring, aghast at what they were witnessing. The one who had shouted at them, now had his hood down and was shouting and pointing, gesturing to the guards to attack. Tom barely heard him shouting, and it was inaudible due to the thunderous roar of the power within him.

Some of the ritual members backed away, much to the dismay of the leader. Tom saw and sensed the anger and frustration in him. Then Kane walked in front of the ark and held his hands up.

In this time, Tom had floated towards the ark. Not purposely, it had happened naturally. Soon, without realising, he was hovering above the ark and the glowing orb. He looked down and noticed the ritual leader's face, contorted with rage, shouting, screaming, spittle flicking from his mouth in slow motion. Tom felt in complete control. He looked beyond them at the orb. Concentrating on its light, glowing brightly. Electrical currents flowing around it, shooting from it.

The heat inside him increased. The surge surprised him, but he knew he was in no harm. Now, almost too hot. It burnt. But he knew if he stayed calm and allowed the power to flow, he would be OK.

Suddenly his arms raised, and he felt a surge of energy hit him. At first, he felt like he was going to burst. But he stayed firm. Using the power, allowing it to build up within him. Then an anger, like a tight ball inside him, released and the fire within now flowed to his hands. Naturally, without his own control, his hand pointed at the orb of light. His body shook, his hand trembling. He felt the power coming, ready to be released.

Then he stiffened. His hand solid. His fingers opened and he felt the fire flowing through him and beyond, out into the chamber. The noise of thunder came, the fire and light flashed from his hand, power and heat transmitting from his body outwards, towards the orb. The wind increased. All below ran for their lives as the light and power created an unimaginable ferocity.

As the light hit the orb there was a shockwave which sent everyone flying and rolling towards the outer walls. Kane, desperate to prevent the connection, initially prepared to put himself in the line of fire, but he found himself being flung across the stone floor like a ragdoll. O'Dowd, who sat on the floor near the entrance, some way from Tom, felt himself being lifted and thrown back towards the door, which he hit with force.

Tom then felt pain. He knew he had to fight it. A resistance hit him, pressing and pulling him from all angles. He tried to stay solid, balanced and in control. He dug deep, trying to force more energy from within him, towards the orb. The heat, pain and stress on his body was taking its toll. His face now contorted with the immense forces he was experiencing.

Then, to his relief, the silver blue light from the ceiling faded, losing its power and ferocity. Tom then felt more power. It hit him and then burst out, through his hand. A shot of fire and lightning struck the orb, and everything began to shake. Tom unable to control himself, trembled and felt himself falling from his axis. He tried to hold on. The orb shook and the currents around it increased. The noise increased.

O'Dowd instinctively held his hands to his ears. The noise now too loud to bear. He looked one last time and the light burnt his eyes and, sensing the explosion coming, he pulled himself into a foetal position, covered his ears and hoped he would survive.

Tom felt his body stretch and then tighten. A crushing force bearing down onto him. His bones cracking and his muscles tearing. He held on, for a few more seconds, as the power surge came. Then with one last flash of light and fire from his hand, the orb exploded.

A light flashed. All within the church suddenly saw their own bones and skeletons. Then for three seconds after there was silence and darkness. The sound of nothing. Then a sonic boom hit, a split second of sound as loud as a fighter jet engine, another flash and then the following wind.

O'Dowd felt himself being pushed hard into the door again. He adjusted his body position as he was lifted upwards. Soon he found himself a few feet from the floor, stuck to the door like glue, the wind holding him in position as it roared into him. Then, as quickly as it had started, the wind eased, and O'Dowd fell to the floor with a thud.

Tom then went cold, and dropped, slowly at first and then, as the gravity was no longer defied, he fell the last ten feet, hard and fast, hitting the stone floor, the impact crunching his body, pushing the wind out of him and knocking him unconscious.

O'Dowd turned. At first, he saw nothing but black. Then moonlight drifted through the hole in the ceiling and illuminated the chamber inside. Just enough for him to make out Tom's body lying on the floor next to the ark. He got up. Pain hitting him at various points in his body. The pain in his shoulder was the worst. He circled his arm and rubbed his shoulder and made his way into the main chamber. He heard groaning, then voices. Fear, shock and disbelief. Figures darted past him, desperate to get out, now oblivious to their duty after what they had just witnessed.

Then, above O'Dowd, there was a crack and the sound of breaking concrete and timber. He looked up. Rubble and timber fell. He cowered. It smashed close to him and dust suddenly filled the air. Then he heard it again. The hole in the ceiling had grown larger with splintered joists hanging down. Beyond that the night sky, with drizzle falling inside the church.

To his right, a large chunk of rubble hit the floor with a crash. He needed to move fast. He ran to Tom who was slumped and motionless. O'Dowd, himself, tired and in pain, suddenly taken over by instinct, rolled Tom onto his back and knelt on one knee next to him. He grabbed his arm and put it over his shoulder, bent his body and grabbed Tom's legs with his other arm. Then, with all his might, he lifted Tom up to his waist. Then, using what energy he had left, he swung him up and over his shoulder into a fireman's carry.

The weight made him stumble backwards and almost topple. He moved forward to balance himself but fell to his knees, almost falling flat. But he held firm and stayed up. He took a deep breath, pulled one leg from under him, pushed hard and straightened up.

He wobbled, trying to gain his balance. Knowing that he only had enough energy to get Tom closer to the exit. He set off, surprised by the weight and unable to lift his feet high enough for proper steps, so he shuffled as he went. He heard a clatter and smash of more rubble and wood behind him which made him wince and cower.

His back began to ache, and his legs burnt but he got to the door and went through, his legs now shaking uncontrollably. From behind he heard an almighty crash. The whole roof had fallen in and engulfed the whole chamber in rubble, timber, iron and dust. Small flames now jumping and dancing amongst the rubble. He fell forward and both he and Tom sprawled across the floor as a burst of dust filled the small foyer they were in.

He lay there and tried to focus. He looked across at Tom laying on the floor. He knew he wouldn't be able to pick him up again. So, in desperation to get out, he grabbed Tom by the arm and dragged him across the floor towards the main door. It was physically draining, and he groaned with every heave of Tom's body. But he summoned every last ounce of energy to drag his stricken colleague towards the exit.

As he got closer, he heard banging and shouting.
"Help! Let us out!"

He looked up and two figures in robes stood at the door. A few minutes ago, mortal enemies, but now just fearful and desperate human beings. O'Dowd ignored them and dragged Tom up towards the door. No longer concerned with them. It was a surreal situation. As O'Dowd neared the door, they stepped back allowing him access. He dropped Tom's arm and looked them in the eye. They looked scared. He took the key from inside his jacket, put it in the lock and spoke as he opened it.

"If you choose the right path you will both be forgiven," he told them, "Now go!"

They looked at each other and darted through the door to the outside.

"Thank you," one of them uttered as they rushed past.

O'Dowd turned and looked down at Tom. He knew he couldn't drag him across the gravel track outside of the church. So he bent down on one knee beside him and got his arms underneath him. Again, with back breaking pain and effort he lifted Tom up, held him at his waist and walked outside.

He noticed the storm had passed and heard the sound of thunder rolling away into the distance. As he walked along the track the drizzle fell, and there was a flash of lightning way off in the night sky. Each step harder and harder. But he wanted to get Tom as far away from the church as possible.

As he staggered with Tom's weight. O'Dowd observed lights, bobbing up and down, coming towards him up the hill. He was confused. Then he heard a voice.

"Father O'Dowd! Stay calm. We are from The Network!"

Then a group of three men in combat gear ran towards him. Knowing that he and Tom now had help, his muscles gave in and he collapsed onto the sodden grass, dropping Tom as he fell.

Chapter 46

Tom suddenly became aware of his environment and the warm softness that surrounded him. A gentle, quiet voice close by. His instinct told him to open his eyes but the comfort he felt stopped him from doing so. He relaxed and slipped further into the deep, calm place. Drifting away. Then he heard the voice again.
"Tom?"

It pulled him from his slumber, and he woke up. Grimacing a little from the gentle light at the side of him.
"Thank God," came the voice.

His eyes adjusted and he noticed he was in a small bedroom and sat beside him was Father O'Dowd. Tom went to speak but nothing came out except for a deep croak. His mouth was dry and sore. O'Dowd got up, grabbed a jug of water and a glass from a nearby stand and poured a glass. He lent into Tom and put the glass to his mouth. Tom at first sipped and then gulped the water. It was so refreshing.
"I've been praying for you," O'Dowd confirmed as he sat down again.

Tom sat up but felt some pain and aches. He grimaced again.
"Take it easy. Here, let me," offered O'Dowd. He helped Tom to sit up and plumped the pillows behind him. Eventually Tom felt comfortable enough to sit.
"Where am I?" he asked.
O'Dowd sniggered, "In my bed, you cheeky sod."
"How?"
"Do you not remember?" asked O'Dowd. Tom put his hand to his head.
"I...I can recall going into the church. And then the light...The heat...Elevating."
He paused, thinking, "Then...That's it. That's all really."
"A lot more happened. Believe me..." confirmed O'Dowd.

O'Dowd then proceeded to tell Tom, in detail, exactly what had happened and what he had witnessed. Explaining what Tom had done, the light, the power, the wind and the fire. Escaping the collapsing church, right up to the moment they fell down outside. The story then triggered Tom's mind.

"Odin! Where's Odin!" he shouted.

His face became ashen and fearful. He tried to sit up. O'Dowd lent forward and held him.

"No, listen, there's nothing you can do now…"

"What? No! Where is he?"

"Calm down. Please…"

"I have to go…"

Tom pulled the covers aside and tried to adjust his body to get out of the bed and stand up. As he did, he felt light-headed and nauseous.

"No!" exclaimed O'Dowd, rushing around to the other side, holding Tom in a seated position.

"You need to get back into bed. You took a bad fall…"

"But where is he?" Tom asked desperately.

"Look, get back in and I will get one of your men. Just stay calm."

Tom did as he was told. Hoping to hold down the sick that he now felt. Once O'Dowd was satisfied that he was staying put, he left the room. He returned soon after with one of The Network soldiers who had brought them back. They both entered and sat down on either side of Tom.

Tom noticed the man looked battle weary and had blood and black stains on his face, hands and uniform.

"How do you feel?" the man asked.

"Where's Odin?" asked Tom, ignoring the question.

"We supressed The Order on the beach and I sent a team across by boat to help out. As they approached, they saw lights from the church…"

"Where's Odin?" interrupted Tom.

The man paused, "They reported that as they got to the top of the hill, they saw you two outside. But no sign of Odin."

"I explained to the gentleman that Odin was there when we went into the church but…" added O'Dowd shrugging.

"But the woman attacked him…" interjected Tom.

There was a brief silence, "I have a crew searching for him now…" continued the man.

"So, he's not dead?" asked Tom.

"Just missing at this stage."

"He will be alive. I feel it. Please don't give up," pleaded Tom.

The man nodded and stood.

"I am glad you are OK. Arrangements are being made to ship you out first thing tomorrow."

The man walked to the door, opened it but then turned and spoke.

"Look, Tom. We lost a few good men tonight. And have a few others missing. But we have limited time. You know the protocol. We clear up what we can and get out. I have ordered the search crew to return in thirty minutes. I am sorry. But it's all the time I can spare."

"But…We can't leave him…"

"Too much went down tonight. You know the rules. The team and I are departing at 1.30am."

And with that he left the room.

Tom sighed, anxious. He lay back, relaxing his body.

"He'll turn up. Don't you worry," assured O'Dowd. Tom smiled but he wasn't feeling the same positivity.

"Do you know what happened to her?" Tom asked.

"That woman?"

Tom nodded.

"Never saw her. Neither have the other agents."

The answer unsettled Tom. What could've happened? If she had killed Odin, then surely she would've attacked them afterwards. Although, the fact that she didn't, could be a good sign. Odin might have killed her? But where was he?

O'Dowd poured them both another glass of water. He handed one to Tom who drained it then lay his head back and closed his eyes. O'Dowd sipped his water then spoke.

"Tom, can I say something?"

"Of course," replied Tom, opening his eyes.

"As I lay there in the church. After being thrown back by the power. I just watched. I felt like I had been transported to heaven. It was like nothing I had ever felt or seen. The energy flowing from you into me...Well...I felt like I was touching God. It was beautiful. Like paradise."

Tom smiled, feeling the genuine sincerity from O'Dowd.

"Tom, I owe you everything. From the second I met you I felt your energy. I am a believer but, by God, I have had my moments, I tell you. Times when I have been so low, I have sometimes wondered what on God's earth I was doing in this job. I've witnessed things that have tested my faith to breaking point. But, you...My dear, Tom, you are the embodiment of my faith. You have shown me the light. Given me hope. The power to carry on spreading the word of the Lord. What I witnessed tonight was the pinnacle. You have taken my dwindling light and set it aflame..."

O'Dowd's voice broke. He tried to speak again but nothing came. His emotions overwhelmed him. The years of anxiety and worry, the stress and pressure of the last few weeks, culminating in the night's events. It was too much. He started to cry. Then got down on one knee and held Tom's hand and cried more.

Eventually O'Dowd composed himself. He looked up at Tom. "Tonight, I saw and felt the presence of God. I witnessed his divine power. I barely believe it was real. But I know it was. My brain tells me it wasn't true, but my heart tells me it was. All that I live for and believe in was there... My view into the Almighty. I... I just don't know what to say..."

Tom held his hand. Knowing his energy was flowing into O'Dowd. Calming and healing his weary and battered body and mind.

Soon after, O'Dowd got up and stood over Tom, laughing in embarrassment.

"Look at me. I'm a wreck. It's just been so hard. The build up to this has…well…It's been a test. And now the relief that it's all over…"

"I know," assured Tom.

O'Dowd leant forward and hugged Tom.

"Thank you, my son. Thank you for everything," he said.

"It's you I should be thanking. I wouldn't be here if it wasn't for you."

"It's my pleasure," confirmed O'Dowd, "It was my holy duty."

Chapter 47

Three weeks later

Father O'Dowd lent on his kitchen counter looking out into his garden. Siobhan and Jimmy were sat on the grass, Jimmy was organising a make-believe picnic. O'Dowd smiled as he handed her a tray of Play-Doh lumps which, in his young mind, were sandwiches and delicious cakes.

The church house was perfect. Siobhan had worked so hard in the lead up to the move to Cork and had made their new home comfortable, but with her own splash of individual design flair. It was a fine June day, the sun that shone into the garden was filtered by the over-hanging trees, creating a warm, hazy and shaded environment. O'Dowd wanted to join them, so he made his way to the back door leading out to the garden.

The fall-out from the night at The Church of the Sacred Heart, those few weeks ago, had been substantial, although, to O'Dowd's relief, nothing was too damaging or unmanageable.

When he and Tom and had been taken back to his living quarters at the church on the mainland, it had been a hive of activity for an hour or so. The Network had used it as a return point to de-brief, assess, gather themselves and depart. People were coming and going, bringing weapons back and changing out of their military gear.

O'Dowd had helped get Tom settled in his bed, then his other immediate concern was Father Reilly's body. To his astonishment, as he had rushed to his office, the door had opened and a man in black emerged. The man nodded and walked past him. He had entered his office and it had been clear. Cleaner and tidier than it had ever been. All that remained was a black refuse bag which contained the broken items that were damaged during the fight. O'Dowd had put the black bag in the bin and said no more.

But it had then triggered his mind about Maggie. The poor girl. He had called her mobile phone and she had answered quietly and, although she sounded anxious, she had been calm enough for him to feel that she would be OK. They had met the following day and he had comforted and assured her as best he could. She had then promised him that she had not told a soul. He believed her. She would never have lied to him.

He also gave her his own assurances that she had done the right thing. She had saved his life. He had told her that Reilly had got himself involved with some dangerous people and had made some bad decisions. He has been forced down the wrong path. He wasn't a bad person. Those people made him do what he did. He also briefed her about the potential questions the police could ask and told her that she just had to say she had not seen Father Reilly for months.

He had known it was risky. If the police did speak to her, she could break. But that was a chance he had to take. He had been hard on her and told her that if she told the police that she had seen Reilly that night, and they force the truth from her, she would very likely spend a long time in prison. It wasn't something he had wanted to say as it frightened her but he had needed to be clear. It was a cold, hard fact.

Saying goodbye to Tom the day after had been hard. Hard because he just hadn't had time to say goodbye properly and the way he had wanted to. But he knew the reasons why and how The Network operated. There was no room for sentiment. O'Dowd had been asleep on his settee when he felt a nudge. He had looked up and a huge man in combat gear was looking down at him. He had thanked O'Dowd for his help and told him they had to go.

O'Dowd had sat up and noticed Tom standing at the far side of the room. Tom had walked towards him and hugged him, turned and left quickly. They drove away out onto the main road just as the sun was coming up. O'Dowd was upset that he never got a contact,

285

forwarding address or some way of getting in touch. But he knew this was impossible. It would almost certainly be the last time he ever saw Tom.

Also, the day after, there had been a news report on the damage to Sacred Heart church which was reported to have been caused by the storm. There had been four bodies found in the rubble. All male and wearing robe and gowns. The story made national news a few days later. It had been reported that the victims were members of a 'religious cult' who had been there for a 'storm ritual'. A spokesperson from the Local Council had been on TV advising that the church had been in bad condition and there had been signs up warning people not to visit it. Especially in a storm of that magnitude.

On a positive note, the story had highlighted the need for restoration work to be completed. And so, an unknown trustee had donated a huge amount of money and the work to repair the church was being planned.

Another local story that emerged was based on reports from locals of a high level of activity around the village and surrounding area during the night of the storm. Some of the locals were interviewed and reported to have witnessed, 'several vehicles travelling at speed' and, 'seeing unusual men in combat gear'.

An assumption had been made that they were 'storm chasers.' A spokesperson from the Local Authority was given a brief moment on TV to remind any visitors to the area that this activity is very dangerous, and that they should not be visiting to chase or watch storms at it causes 'unnecessary inconvenience and unrest to locals'.

Again, it went national, but given little airtime. In fact, both stories didn't linger around too long and disappeared quickly when different and fresher news came to the fore. Resigned to history and out of people's minds.

The stories had been the talk of the village for a week or so and everyone had their own views and opinions but, after its fifteen minutes of fame, the village returned to its normal, slow and sedate way of life.

However, a week or so later the inevitable happened and O'Dowd had received a phone call from a Detective Harper from Dublin. It was not unexpected. Harper had explained to O'Dowd that Father Reilly had been reported missing by his wife. O'Dowd had done his best to sound shocked and distressed.

The detective had explained that, after some initial investigation, they had picked up Reilly's car on CCTV leaving Dublin on the 11th of May around 5pm. Using ANPR cameras and other CCTV they had managed to locate its journey towards Westport, but at roughly twenty miles from the village they had lost track and had no more to go on. So, after some basic detective work, O'Dowd, being a friend and close colleague of Reilly's, had been the obvious link.

O'Dowd had stated that he had not seen Father Reilly for roughly two months. It had been at a charity event in Dublin. The detective had accepted this but had told him that they had to come to Westport to continue their investigation. They would speak in more detail then.

He had warned Maggie that the police were coming to the village but assured her that she would not be a in trouble, and it was doubtful that they would even speak to her. To help O'Dowd cover himself and Maggie, he had, immediately after the call, taken a deep breath and phoned Father Reilly's wife, Mable. It had been the hardest conversation of his life. She had sobbed down the phone as the guilt racked O'Dowd's body. All he could do was assure her that he would be praying for her husband's safe return, knowing deep down she would never see him ever again.

Two days later, Detective Harper and a colleague arrived at the village. They visited O'Dowd at the church office. Harper appeared nice enough, but his colleague was cold and unengaging. And they were direct, but he realised that they just had a job to do. It wasn't a social visit.

They asked him some very basic questions. When did he last see Father Reilly? Did he know of his whereabouts? Why was he heading in this direction? Was there anyone else nearby he may have visited? O'Dowd answered them innocently and unknowingly. Dropping in comments that he had tried Reilly's phone several times since he heard.

They also asked him if he had noticed any unusual behaviour from Reilly prior to him going missing. Tom said he hadn't and asked why. It was then that they told him that Reilly's wife had reported him acting a little unusual a few weeks prior to him going missing. That Reilly had been stressed, anxious and distracted. She had also reported him being in the garden on his mobile phone in the early hours of the morning. And that, when they were together, often his phone would ring, and he would look concerned then rush out to answer it no matter what they were doing.

O'Dowd knew exactly what this was. It was the period when The Order had got to him. Tapping him up. Negotiating with him or threatening him. It was obviously when Reilly was pulled under their control and turned against The Network. But he told them he had no clue why he would act like that.

O'Dowd acted in a helpful manner but gave them nothing. He never felt that they suspected him at all. He hid any pangs of guilt or suspicion and he never showed that he knew more than he was saying.

They then informed him that they had traced many calls from Reilly's landline to O'Dowd's. A total of five in the last three weeks. Two of which were after midnight. O'Dowd noticed them watching him absorb this information. They wanted to see how he would react. He stayed calm and reacted innocently, confirming that the two of them spoke regularly. Especially in the last few weeks as Reilly was overseeing O'Dowd's transfer from the village church to Cork. He had notified them that the transfer was imminent and could easily be verified. They appeared to accept this but then Harper's colleague, who O'Dowd didn't get the name of and didn't particularly like, asked him why discussions of this nature would take place at such unsociable hours.

O'Dowd's answer was simple. Reilly was a workaholic. He had no set hours, and he was always on duty. He often spoke to O'Dowd later in the evening before they went to bed as it was often the only spare time they had. He embellished this by telling them that he had told Reilly that he was nervous about the transfer and the step up to a larger area and bigger communion. He was worried about the new responsibilities he would have. Reilly had merely been offering him support and guidance.

It was all scribbled down in their notepads. They asked if they could look around and O'Dowd had obliged. He surprised himself at how well he handled it, but he was mightily relieved when they left the church. However, they had remained in the village for a day or two, knocking on doors, asking locals, showing a photo of Reilly to people. Reilly was known within the village by a handful of people and O'Dowd soon started receiving phone calls from those people asking if he knew Reilly was missing. He merely confirmed he knew and had helped the police with their enquiries.

Maggie came to work the next day and informed O'Dowd that they had come to her house and spoke to her parents and her at the door. Her parents had never met Reilly, but she had told them she had met him only once before but had never seen him since. They had finally asked her if she was working on the night of the storm and she had confirmed that she was but had gone home at around 10pm.

Later that day O'Dowd and Maggie both solemnly promised never to speak of it again. No further questions were asked of O'Dowd, Maggie or anyone else. Soon, Harper and his colleague were gone from the village and nothing else was heard about it.

A week or so had then passed and O'Dowd's imminent departure was now in full flow. He had packed and any of their belongings still left were boxed up and taken. With a few days to go, a leaving party was organised at the Cross Keys pub. All the locals turned out and it had been quite an emotional night. O'Dowd had wanted to get away so much, but the party made him realise how much he still loved the village and its inhabitants. He would miss them all dearly. He was surprised by the emotion shown by a lot of them towards him and a few tears were shed.

At the end of the night, he had found himself outside, just him and a whisky, when Maggie came out and sat with him. They hadn't spoken for a few minutes. They had no need to. Their bond strengthened by the unfortunate events and the things that they knew. The promise they had made standing strong.

The next day, he had left the village for good.

As O'Dowd stepped out into his new garden, the warmth caressed him. Things had worked out well. Despite the dark and difficult period he had gone through, and the sickening secret he and Maggie now held within them.

He had thought of The Order. What their response would be to that night. His darkest thoughts concerned if they would ever catch up with him or come seeking revenge for his involvement and the fact that he had helped The Network. He had assured himself that he was just a pawn and that the magnitude of what had occurred was way above him. He knew he was right and that he and shouldn't worry. But, on occasion, those dark thoughts returned and flashed through his mind, and he realised that he never truly knew if he and his family were totally safe or not.

He would never forget Tom and Odin and had prayed for them since that night. He would probably never find out if Odin was safe, or how Tom's life would pan out. What had happened and what he had been involved in still amazed and surprised him. He had been so close to a living angel. He had experienced the Lord Almighty's power.

He had wondered if he would ever speak of it but had resigned himself to just accepting it and putting it to the back of his mind. Nobody would believe him anyway and so it was best left stored in his head.

He sat down on the grass and Jimmy rushed over and flung himself into his arms. He smiled at Siobhan and she returned a loving gaze. He winked at her. For now, he was happy and content, their life was moving in the right direction. For that he was thankful, and he knew he had been blessed.

His prayers had come true.

Chapter 48

Eight Months later

4:50pm, January 19, 2020

The fire danced and flickered. Time stopped for a few fleeting moments and even the sounds around Tom dissipated. Images flashed through his mind as he stared into the orange glow, hypnotised into seeing people, places and events, that were now long gone and resigned to his memories.

He broke from his daydream and his vision re-focussed. Making out the fire again, that was cracking and spitting. The deer carcass was rotating on the spit above it, crispy and brown, dripping with fat that popped in the heat as it fell. Potatoes were boiling in a large saucepan that had been nestled onto the firewood.

The warmth from the fire and the smell of the cooking re-engulfed him as he swiftly returned to reality and the present. His counterparts sat around the fire, close to him, an orange glow on their faces. The calm sound of gentle small talk and conversation could be heard.

The early evening brought its usual chill. He zipped his coat up and rubbed his hands together. He was hungry and looking forward to the meal. He had worked hard during the day, harder than normal. The settlement had needed firewood, fresh water and repairs to the boundary fencing. All members of the community were responsible for the upkeep and smooth running of the settlement and Tom was no exception. He enjoyed it. It kept him and his mind busy and stopped him from remembering events. Remembering the people he loved, who he now missed.
"You hungry, Tom?" came a voice from his left.

Tom looked up and Arnold, an old, grizzled Patriot and the settlements creator, was stood by the fire, holding up a bowl.

"Famished," Tom replied.

"Good. Plenty to go around."

Arnold carved a few huge chunks of meat from the deer carcass and fished out some large potatoes. He added gravy from a smaller saucepan and handed the bowl to Tom. It looked delicious.

Tom smiled, gratefully.

"Thank you."

"You're welcome, son."

Tom ate his meal. It tasted so good. Luckily, it was a pretty common meal at the settlement. They ate well. Using the land as their larder and their outdoor skills to thrive.

Little had he known, but his journey to Montana had begun the day he left Ireland. And it had been pure chance that Tom had made it there, to the extreme northern wilderness.

His goodbye with Father O'Dowd had been too quick and he had regretted it. There was no chance he could stay in touch or go to visit him. It was too dangerous for O'Dowd. But Tom owed him everything and he had not been able to thank him the way he had wanted to. Tom and another Network agent had taken the same journey back the way he had originally come with Odin. In a haze he had left Ireland in a private plane back to England. He found himself winding his way through the countryside, through Greater London and back to that horrible, dirty apartment in Kings Cross.

It had been the last place he had wanted to be. It was dirty, damp and brought back memories of Odin. To make matters worse the agent he had been with had left the next day and told Tom that he had to stay for another three nights, until he would be provided with more information about his next move. He had given Tom a mobile phone and £100 then left.

Tom hadn't been able to stay in the apartment. The smell and noises made him uneasy. He hated it and its surroundings. So, in the evening, he would go out. Just walk the streets. Get on the tube and go to different places. Embankment, Soho, Covent Garden, Camden. The exploring kept his mind busy.

He came into contact with lots of homeless people and night dwellers. He gave them money, food and drink. Conversed with them. He felt an affinity to them. Like him they were the underbelly. Unable to operate and function in normal everyday life. Part of society's secret community outside of normal rules and laws. Just trying to get through each day and night.

After two nights, his phone had bleeped. He had received a text from the Internal Department. Telling him a package was to be delivered to his apartment at 10pm that night. He made sure he was there, and a man had knocked, handed him an envelope and walked away. Inside had been £100 and a plane ticket from Heathrow to San Antonio International. Tom had flown out of Heathrow at 11.06am the next morning.

During that flight he had had a lot of time to think. Laura and Odin going missing had devastated him. He had hoped that, when he returned to the States, he would get news of their safety. But he knew the chances of that were slim at best.

As he had stared at the clouds below him, he realised the magnitude of the last five to six years. His losses were immeasurable. Losing Jenna, his mother and his good friend Davy. Unable to contact his sister and her family. And now, more recently, losing Laura and Odin.

As the madness of the last few weeks had hit home, he had gone to the toilet and cried. Letting out all of his emotion. And after doing so, he made a decision. He no longer wanted to be part of The Network. He had told Laura this before. He knew it was right. The world of violence, secrecy, paranoia and loss was never something he had wanted anyway. His mind had been made up at that exact moment.

His resettlement in San Antonio had then got underway. Taking refuge in a modest house in the suburbs owned by a plump, cheerful lady named Irene. She looked after him and was a good parent. A few days after his arrival, she had given him a credit card, some cash, a car to drive and a mobile phone. Soon after turning the phone on, it bleeped and there was a text message:

'Tom. We thank you. Your assignment was a success. The Order have been critically damaged. Settle and then we will be in touch about the future. Please do not reply and delete this message. ID'

He had been glad it was a success. But it left a bitter taste in his mouth. And much frustration. Going against their advice he responded:

'ID. Can you please provide an update on Odin and Laura. They are network Agents currently MIA. Tom'

He never received a reply.

A few weeks later Irene had slipped a note under his door which notified him that at 9pm that night, he was going to be visited by someone from The Network who would 'provide an update'. Later that night, at 9pm on the dot, Irene had informed him that a man had arrived. He had felt an excitement and a sense of relief, hoping that it would be Odin. Expectantly, he waited but, to his disappointment, it had been a young man by the name of Earl. He had seemed very excited to meet Tom.

He had told Tom he couldn't stay long, so had to be brief. He passed on thanks from the Internal Department. Intelligence had told them that Tom had been successful in cutting off their ability to communicate with the higher power. They were, as it stands, unable to operate in the normal way and now had no way of knowing when and where angels were born.

Intelligence also reported that The Order had moved into a phase called 'Code X' which is a protocol that pushes the organisation into hiding in a dormant state. All activities with angels were suspended. However, ID did know that they were preparing for something else. The hope was that they would not rise again for another 44 years.

As it stood, The Network continued. In fact, Earl had reported eagerly, that ID were planning a new operation called 'The Purge' which would take advantage of The Order losing much of its power. All agents will be updated and will be used in an assignment to hunt down The Order and remove any possibility of a second coming.
"Kick them when they are down!" Earl had said.

Tom had listened intently but had not spoken. Several questions had come to him as Earl had spoken but he didn't ask them. Earl finished by saying that ID have identified Tom as the leader of the purge. Playing the key role in the hunt and elimination of all dormant Order agents and anyone in the hierarchy.
"The next few years are to be our busiest and most important," Earl had confirmed with an eagerness that Tom was unable to match.

He had handed Tom a thick envelope and told him that all the plans were inside, and that he was to read it. The ID would be in touch. Tom had put the envelope on the side and asked Earl if he had any news of Odin and Laura. Earl's face had dropped.
"Oh, yeah. Sorry. They remain logged as MIA. But no further searches will take place."

And with that, Tom had known that his decision had been the right one. He picked the envelope up and handed it back to Earl. He asked him to pass on his sincere thanks to The Network for all they had done; but his time with them was finished. Earl's face had been one of utter shock. Tom had known that Earl was privileged to have been selected to make this visit and that he had been a little upset that he had not able to reciprocate Earl's eager attitude.

Earl had not responded at first. Obviously not knowing what to say in the midst of the unexpected situation that had arisen. Tom had apologised and told him it was nothing personal and that, for his own reasons, he no longer wished to be part of it. Earl had asked Tom to keep the envelope at least. Not only was it dangerous for him to be carrying it but he had been tasked with delivering it, so he had completed his task. Tom had obliged. But told Earl to report back to ID that he would not be reading it and that they would no longer hear from him.

Earl had been unable to hide his disappointment which had left Tom ashamed. He didn't know Earl's story and how he had got involved. He might have been an angel himself, pulled to safety by another agent. Or just on the payroll, keen and eager to take the fight to The Order. And now, here he was, being let down by The Network's new hope. Their talisman.

As he had got up to leave, his final words had resonated with Tom. "I am disappointed. They told us you were our saviour. That you would lead us to the final victory."

Earl had then put a small card on the table and slipped it towards Tom. After he had left, Tom looked at the card. It had 'Earl' written on it with a mobile phone number. Obviously in the hope that Tom would change his mind and call him.

Tom had sat for hours pondering. And he came to the conclusion that he had made the right choice. Why did he want to be a part of this war? Leading people in the hunt for The Order. It would just lead to more bloodshed. More than he could ever imagine. When did it stop? He had had enough of the killing, the violence and the loss. Too many people he loved had been lost.

He had imagined undertaking 'The Purge' with Odin and Laura. It felt much more of something he would want to do if they were still here and part of it. He even realised that it would have been quite exciting. He thought of himself getting his final revenge on The

Order. Revenge for Jenna, his father's murder, Davy and his family; and leading The Network to deliver the fatal blow to The Order. He almost had second thoughts.

But without those two it all seemed so uninspiring. He struggled to find the focus and commitment to it. Losing them, on top of everything else, had taken something from him. He had not wanted any of this. But once he was in, he had found a fire inside him. A focus. But the loss of Odin and Laura extinguished that fire. The losses had been too great. He had been damaged.

Moreover, he had had enough of being a nomad. Being moved from place to place. He wanted to settle. If he did lead the purge for The Network then it would take him from place to place, never settling, hunting, chasing and moving. He was tired. So very tired. He had had enough.

But where would he go? Where would he settle? How would he survive? It had left him confused. Later in the day, Irene had brought him a coffee. They started talking and it led to families and their histories. She had told him she had a son. He had always been in trouble with the law, unable to hold a job down, achieved nothing. But that he had been brainwashed on the internet by a group of 'Preppers'. Tom had enquired about them, she had said they were, "A load of wacko's who believe the world is ending. They live outside of society, off grid, armed to the teeth and waiting for some so-called war…Just a crackpot theory."

But it had got Tom thinking. And he had started his research. Lots and lots of research. He found that the true name for them was 'Survivalists' and his research over the next few weeks was intense and he read every website, article and book he found. It soon dawned on him that he had found his path. All he needed to do now was try to make contact with a group in the far north where he had always wanted to settle.

Using social media, the internet and private messaging he eventually found and made contact with a particular group and began conversing with a person that went by the name of 'A'. Over the next week or so communication became more frequent and 'A' had asked questions about Tom's beliefs, morals and skills. Tom knew he had made progress and was being considered. His only issue was the distance. He knew he had to get closer.

One day soon after Irene had come to him. She had told him she had received a message from The Network Internal Department that he would soon be moving to Dallas. He was going to be visited in three days by a member of The Network who wished to talk to him and then the member would drive him to Dallas. Later that night Tom had received a text:

'Tom. You are our future and our hope. Someone is coming to see you soon. An important event is due to begin. Please wait. ID'

His reply had been simple and to the point:

'ID. Thank you for everything. My time with you has come to an end. I will make no further contact. Goodbye. Tom'

He had then switched the phone off.

An hour or so later Irene had come to his room to tell him someone from The Network was coming that night. She had fostered many people from The Network before but had never known ID to act in such a way. She had wondered what all the fuss was about. She had knocked but Tom hadn't answered. When she had opened the door, Tom and his bag of personal stuff had gone. All that was left on the bed was the thick envelope Earl had given him and a small note.

She picked up the note and it read:

Dear Irene,

Thank you for all your hospitality. You are very kind.

I will miss you.

Good luck.

Tom x

p.s. Sorry I didn't say goodbye

Over the following weeks he had continued his contact with 'A'. Gradually moving further north in stages. After a month or so he made it to a town called Whitefish in Montana. It was the USA's most northerly major town, at the foot of the mountain range bearing the same name that shadowed the rugged, harsh wilderness beyond, stretching all the way to the Canadian border.

He was directed to take the bus along the Kootenay Highway and to disembark at Grasmere General Store. After an hour, he was picked up in a beat-up old truck. Six hours later, after being driven further and further into the wilderness, and then embarking on a slow and arduous hike, he arrived at the settlement. Reminiscent of his journey, all that time ago, to complete his training for The Network.

After a process of interviews, background checks, ability tests and a variety of other protocols he was eventually allowed into the settlement on a trial period.

It was perfect. It was so far from civilisation that it was barely believable. It was about as off grid as a human could get in this part of the world. It was remote and Tom was completely uncontactable by anyone other than the people in the settlement itself. It was also very secure, and the inhabitants had enough firearms and ammo to start a small war. If ever The Order did locate him and came for him, he was confident they would never get in and, almost certainly, not get away with their lives.

His cabin was small and simple but cosy, and he had everything he needed. A bed, storage, sink and basic cooking facilities.

'A' had turned out to be Arnold. Arnold was the settlement Governor and made sure everyone lived and worked together in harmony. He made final decisions, mediated, set tasks, chaired meetings and made sure the running of the settlement was efficient and productive. He had taken Tom in and was responsible for him.

Tom had a month to prove his value to the settlement and demonstrate that he had what it takes to live the life of a 'prepper'. That he could live and function in a civil, efficient and positive manner. Arnold set high standards of work ethic and social conduct.

Tom breezed through it. And within two weeks, he had earned the respect of Arnold and all of the other members of their tiny community. Tom kept to himself but, when working with others, socialising or at meetings, always made sure he made a good impression. The other members grew to like him and he slotted into the life almost immediately.

During that first month Arnold had said to him, "There's not a cat's chance in hell I am letting you leave us now, son." It was exactly what Tom had wanted to hear.

The other members were made up of a variety of people from all different walks of life. They all had their own reasons for being there. One night, Tom had been asked to say a few words on how he had ended up there. He had told a simple story. As an investment banker, he made more money than he had ever needed or, in fact, wanted. It hadn't brought him happiness and, after his wife left him and his mother died, he felt society no longer offered him what he wanted. It was as simple as that.

The other members were there for a variety of reasons. Some genuinely believed that the collapse of human society was imminent, and that the world was soon to be taken over by a crazed fascist regime. A few others had even more apocalyptic ideas. Some were 'true patriots' who just felt they had been forgotten by a succession of modern governments that had allowed America's foundation to be eroded. Others had more extreme nationalist views.

But Tom didn't judge. It wasn't his place to judge anyone. And Arnold kept things under control and made sure that nobody forced their view or opinion on anyone else. Despite the varying views, opinions and reasons for people being there; they all had one thing in common. They didn't want to be part of modern society. They felt they had a better chance in the settlement. And they all lived by that common goal and, for the most part, kept their views and opinions to themselves.

He had made acquaintances, but nobody he would call a 'friend'. But that was what he wanted. He was more than happy with being friendly and helpful but at arms-length. He wasn't interested in getting to know people on a personal level, nor allowing anybody to get to know him too well.

All the members had jobs, tasks and duties. From one day to the next Tom would find himself hunting, farming, making general repairs, helping with renovations, or going on patrols around the perimeter of the settlement. All members were also asked to attend a communal meeting once a week where tasks, concerns and any other issues were openly discussed. Nothing went off record and Arnold ran a very open and fair system.

Tom enjoyed his life and the part he played in making the settlement a success. But aside from that Tom also found that he had plenty of time to himself and took advantage of the calm and ordered society he found himself in. The environment that surrounded him was rugged and harsh, so it was good for his training. He had worked his way up to runs of four, five and even six hours. Way, way out to the most extreme wilderness where he would sleep outdoors overnight and then run back the next day. Arnold and the other members said he was mad, but he told them it was something he needed to do. Just to be alone with his mind and body in the harshest environment, testing himself. Whenever he returned from one of his long treks, he felt great and so alive.

One of the other members had weights and a bench which they donated to Tom and he used regularly. His mind and body craving to be tested and as each week passed his fitness and body shape improved, and he reached a point of peak physical fitness. His body shaped and chiselled to match the environment he lived within.

There was also a small library that had been built up over the years. He devoured every book in months. Books of all different varieties - Religion, travel, survival and sport. He read and absorbed information faster than ever. And when it was his turn to travel down to the nearest outpost and reconnect with civilisation in order to take pick up welfare items and food that couldn't be garnered or harvested from the land, he made sure he got new books. Anything he could get his hands on.

He had started to sketch and found enjoyment in new crafts, hobbies and past times. He had also found a beautiful spot, higher up than the settlement on a ridge which overlooked the forest and mountains. He was halfway through a sketch that he was going to colour with oil paints.

The view reminded him of a place that he had dreamed up for his meditations. A place where he would like to spend time with his family. And the serene, calm environment had allowed him to find solace in his meditation again, which over the months he had reintroduced back into his routine. The quiet nights had allowed him to improve his technique and his positive state of physical and mental wellbeing. His mindfulness allowed him to take himself to beautiful places where he spent more time with his family.

He was still very sad that no news had come about Odin and Laura. Some nights he got upset at their fates. But he removed it from his mind and thought of the happier times he had with them. Albeit those happier times were brief and even fleeting.

Tom finished his meal. It was sumptuous but filling, so he politely declined Arnold's offer of seconds. A chill had fallen onto the camp, but all around the fire were in good spirits. A few songs were being sung and the atmosphere had taken a happy, joyful direction.

But Tom had other plans. He had recently started to meditate using Odin and Laura as the people he spent time with. He had created a place, very much like the one that surrounded him, and they had been there. Sitting at rocks down by a pool deep in the forest. He just had to delve deeper into his mind to allow him to get down to them. All in good time. He had plenty of it. And nothing to distract him in this perfect wilderness.

With a full belly and a mind open to exploration he made his way back to his cabin. As he walked, he looked up at the stars. So clear and bright. Thousands and thousands of them. Somewhere up there was a power. The power that he had connected to. An almighty power that no human on earth could ever comprehend.

He had touched God.

Chapter 49

It was the early hours of the morning in downtown Tampa. The door of the apartment had been kicked in and the lock now hung from the door, broken and smashed.

The apartment had been trashed as the two agents from The Order frantically searched. It was small and basic, with just one bedroom, a lounge and a kitchenette. So, the search didn't take them long.

They had known as soon as they had arrived that they were too late. One of their targets, a young woman by the name of Laura, a Network agent, was still there. She had escaped them once but now they had found her. Although she would be of no use to them. Her body, cold and rigid, was sprawled across the bed. A single trickle of blood from her nose had now dried and encrusted.

Various bottles lay on the floor next to the bed. All empty. A vodka bottle and three other small pill bottles that had contained strong sleeping tablets. A lethal cocktail had been created and the men calculated that she had only been dead for an hour, maybe a little more. They had been close, but not close enough.

Their other target wasn't there. A new-born baby. However, the cot, baby clothes, diapers and a few toys suggested that it had been there at some point. They had hoped, at first, that the baby was still there, hidden away. But the search had not borne any results. She had moved the baby before taking her own life. She obviously knew they were coming.

Whilst one of the agents continued the search the other made a phone call. After a few rings, the other end clicked.
"Yes," came a voice.
"Sorry, boss. The girl is here but she's dead. Suicide. Must've been tipped off."
"And the baby?"
"Not here."

"And you've searched everywhere?"

"Yeah. It's a modest apartment. Small. Not many places to hide."

"Look for anything that can lead us to it. A note. An address... Anything."

"Yes, boss. I will update you soon."

A short while later a phone rang in a Berlin office situated above a renovated industrial warehouse. The office was stark. The floor and walls were concrete, metal air-conditioning ducts were visible and there was a huge window looking out onto the Kreuzberg district. The deep bass from the techno music below throbbed through the floor and walls.

Kane limped across to the phone to take the call he had been waiting for. He sat down in a leather armchair, grimacing with the pain and exertion. Next to it was a small stand and on top was an old, dark green rotary style telephone. He picked up the receiver, put it to his ear and spoke.

"Update me on Agent 7."

"No trace. Still missing. Assumed dead."

"I need confirmation."

"Yes, sir."

"And what of portal 294574?"

"Again, no trace. The Network have hidden him well."

"I don't care. I want his head. Find him."

"Yes, sir."

"And what of the baby?"

There was a pause, "I confirm it exists."

Kane processed the implications of the news.

"And?"

"No trace yet. It had been moved before our men arrived. I think the mother was tipped off..."

"I don't give a fuck what you think! Find the baby!"

"Yes, sir."

"Use all your resources and agents. Code X is upon us. Our holy activities are subdued for now. But we must prepare for the second coming. The slate must be clean for the next generation. The portal must be wiped from existence and the baby found."

"Yes, sir,"

Kane calmed himself and took a deep breath.

"I will now lay low under Code X. Now go, there is much to do."

Chapter 50

Sister Rose adored baby Thomas. In the last two weeks, since he had been left at the convent entrance swaddled in a basket, she had grown very fond of him. He had been in good health. A little under nourished and in need of a bath but, generally, he was fighting fit and alert.

The note left in an envelope with him was simple but poignant:

Dear Sisters of St Elizabeth Convent.

This is Thomas.
He was born 5 weeks premature on the 5th of January.
I am in trouble. Keeping him will put him in danger.
He is very special, just like his father. I wish things were different, but they aren't. I was dealt a cruel hand, but Thomas has a chance.
Please give him the best start possible and when he is old enough please tell him that I love him.
I have departed to the safest place I can think of.
Pray for me.

Laura

It had been wrongly assumed that his mother was either a prostitute or a drug addict. That she might have tried to free herself from the control of a pimp or had unmanageable debts due to drugs. It had also been suggested that the father may have got into trouble and involved the mother and baby. Nobody knew for sure. And nobody could've ever imagined the truth.

But the nuns didn't judge. Life for many women in these situations was hard and the nun's understood that, often, a baby simply compounded the difficult situations people found themselves in. It wasn't safe for babies to be brought up in bad environments which, sadly, were too common.

From the moment Sister Rose had picked him up, she felt the warmth that emanated from Thomas. And, although she told herself she was being silly, she thought that he always appeared more relaxed and content when in her arms.

Many of the nuns had taken a shine to him. They all adored him. But Sister Rose, the one who found him, had been tasked by the Mother Superior, with ensuring he was fed, clothed, bathed and loved whilst his case was assessed by the CPS.

Sister Rose had felt an energy from him. It made her feel alive and gave her focus. A surge of happiness and contentment from the day he was found. Each day and night she was with him, she felt a great joy in being able to share time with him. Many of her duties had been delegated to others because her main responsibility was Thomas. It was a duty that she relished.

The mild January weather in Florida had been warmer than usual. Warm enough for Sister Rose to be sat in the flower garden with Thomas. He had just finished his bottle and had been winded. She lay him down on the soft picnic blanket as a gentle, mild breeze flowed through the garden, carrying the soft scent from a variety of flowers.

She dangled his favourite toy above him. Knitted butterflies on string made and donated lovingly by Sister Francesca. She noted his eyes, so focussed and alert, looking at the brightly coloured moving objects above him. Too young to stretch up and hold them but she knew he wanted to. She felt his eagerness and boundless energy. She chuckled to herself, sure that she witnessed his frustration at not being able to grab the butterflies.
"Feisty little boy," she whispered as she caressed his head.
He whimpered and broke into a cry.
"Oh no," whispered Sister Rose.

Thomas cried again. This time louder. Sister Rose lent down and picked him up, holding him to her chest and calmly assured him, "There, there. Do you want your butterflies?"

Thomas responded positively. His cries becoming a whimper and then Sister Rose heard his calm, gentle breathing that she found so addictive. She gently rocked him and his breathing became calmer and he closed his eyes.
"Sister Rose?" came a voice from the other side of the garden.

She adjusted her body and moved around to see the Mother Superior walking across the grass smiling. She smiled back. They were very close. As the Mother Superior approached, she spoke.
"I have some news from the CPS."
"Oh?" replied Sister Rose.

She hid her sudden anxiety. It had been a long time since a baby had been abandoned at the convent. Someone had checked and it had been roughly five years, so it wasn't a common thing. Nevertheless, the protocol was, generally, a few weeks was as long as they stayed. Sometimes less, sometimes a little longer.

She felt a pang of sadness hit her chest and had to quell the emotion that suddenly flowed through her. Mother Superior sat down next to her and gently caressed Thomas' rosy cheek and smiled.
"You are so beautiful."
After a few seconds, she diverted her attention to Sister Rose.
"They have called. They have a huge backlog at the moment and are struggling to assign an officer to assess the case. They have to try and trace the mother first to make sure she has made the right decision. But...As you know, it's assumed she is sadly no longer with us...If they can't trace her, then they have to start looking at potential foster parents. All the paperwork needs to be done. It all takes time."
"Yes," replied Sister Rose, anxious for the news she wanted.
"Well, they asked if we could prolong his stay."

"Oh…OK, well that's fine," replied Sister Rose, trying not to sound too excited and maintaining her professional conduct.

"Yes, they may not be able to do anything for at least four to six months. I told them I would discuss this with…"

"That's fine. It's no problem," interjected Sister Rose.

Mother Superior chuckled, "I thought you would say that."

"Well, it's my duty. We can't allow this little one to have a bad start, can we?"

"Of course not," replied Mother Superior. Knowing full well of the love Sister Rose had for the baby.

"Well, OK, that's settled. I will ring them back."

Mother Superior stood up and smiled affectionately back down at Sister Rose and Thomas.

"You are doing a grand job," she said, as she walked away.

Sister Rose smiled. She was determined to give Thomas the most love and care as was possible. And now she knew that she had more time with him, she planned to enjoy it. She held him tighter. As she did, she felt a loving energy flow from him into her. A tear ran down her face. A tear of joy. She had found her goal. Her calling. He made her so happy and joyful. She knew each moment with him was a blessing.

And from then on, each night as she put him in his cot, she prayed for the mother and father, and that whatever path they had followed or been forced down, the Lord would protect and shield them, wherever they are, in this life or in the next.

She also prayed that the Lord would look down on Thomas. Protect, guide and love him. That he would grow to be happy and healthy and that one day he would make a life for himself and achieve something.

That he would be someone special.

Author message:

Dear Reader,

I would just like to thank you for reading my book. I hope you enjoyed the story as much as I did in creating it. Please look out for the third part of the Dark Angel series which will be published in the future.

I published this book independently through Amazon and so I would be hugely grateful if you could spare a few minutes to submit a review or visit the Dark Angel Facebook page and leave some comments.

This would mean a lot to me.

Thank you for your support!

Happy reading.

Russell Panter

Acknowledgments and thanks:

Ben Hurren
Amanda Hill
Peter Butler
Natasha Wyatt
Paul Sargent
Rayne Hall
Chris Hilleard
U Walleed
Janiel Ascueta
Fiverr.com
Amazon.com
Kindle Direct Publishing